"I was a good friend!" Billy said.

"Exactly," Grace replied quietly. "You were a great *friend*."

Billy was silent, his expression softening.

"A fantastic buddy," she went on. "And I was just as silly as those other women who were groveling after you, or maybe more so. I had a good thing with you, but I wanted more..."

"You..." The word came out in a breath, and he stared at her, dark eyes moving over her face inch by inch as if looking for a chink in her armor. A smile flickered as if he thought she were joking, then it dropped away.

"Was there a guy I didn't know about...?" he started.

Tracy had said what she wanted plainly, and Grace had always held back... Maybe it was time to stop that.

"I wanted more *with you*." The words were so quiet, as if she almost wished he wouldn't hear them. But he froze, and she couldn't read his expression anymore.

Dear Reader,

I went to high school in a picturesque mountain town in the Canadian Rockies, so it's a special treat for me to revisit the mountains in my Home to Eagle's Rest miniseries. Life is slower in the mountains, and you gauge the seasons by the tourists and the snow line on the mountainside. When I created this little town, it felt like coming home in a lot of ways, and I settled right in. I hope you do, too!

If you'd like to see more of my books, you can find me online at patriciajohnsromance.com. I'm also on Facebook and Twitter and love to hear from my readers.

Patricia Johns

HEARTWARMING

Falling for the Cowboy Dad

—

Patricia Johns

Recycling programs
for this product may
not exist in your area.

ISBN-13: 978-1-335-51057-0

Falling for the Cowboy Dad

Copyright © 2019 by Patricia Johns

HARLEQUIN®
www.Harlequin.com

Printed in U.S.A.

Patricia Johns writes from Alberta, Canada. She has her Hon. BA in English literature and currently writes for Harlequin's Love Inspired and Heartwarming lines. You can find her at patriciajohnsromance.com.

Books by Patricia Johns

Harlequin Heartwarming

A Baxter's Redemption
The Runaway Bride
A Boy's Christmas Wish
Her Lawman Protector

Love Inspired

Montana Twins

Her Cowboy's Twin Blessings

Comfort Creek Lawmen

Deputy Daddy
The Lawman's Runaway Bride
The Deputy's Unexpected Family

His Unexpected Family
The Rancher's City Girl
A Firefighter's Promise
The Lawman's Surprise Family

Visit the Author Profile page at Harlequin.com for more titles.

To my husband, who lies in bed with me at night, listening to me talk about fictional characters. I love you.

CHAPTER ONE

GRACE BEVERLY TACKED the last finger painting to the corkboard, then stepped down off the footstool. She smoothed her hands over her hips and surveyed her work. This classroom wasn't hers—not officially. She was only covering for the full-time preschool teacher's maternity leave, and she had a little over two weeks left here. But she'd gotten attached to this classroom with the sand table, the reading carpet in the middle, the puppet theater in the corner…and the twenty-three little live wires she was teaching every day.

Grace had grown up in Eagle's Rest, Colorado, and she'd come back for this temporary job. Teaching positions were hard to come by lately, and she hoped some experience on her résumé would help with that. In three weeks, she'd be covering another maternity leave in Denver, and she'd applied for multiple full-time positions for September, but there would be hundreds of applicants. She needed a full-time teaching position if she was going to have any kind of financial stability, but her chances were slim. Fingers crossed.

Grace picked up an errant hand puppet and returned it to the proper box. Then she pulled her fingers through her long chestnut waves. By the end of a day with twenty-three preschoolers, her feet ached in her high heels, but her heart was full.

A tap on the door drew her attention, and she turned as the school principal came into the room. Mrs. Mackel was middle-aged and had a kind smile. The principal had a little blonde girl at her side—a wisp of a thing with big blue eyes and small hands clutched in front of her.

"Hello, Miss Beverly," Mrs. Mackel said with a smile. "We have a new student starting tomorrow, and she and her dad wanted to say hello."

"Hi there," Grace said with a smile. "I'm Miss Beverly, and it looks like I'm the lucky teacher, doesn't it?"

A small smile tickled the corners of the little girl's mouth. But those round blue eyes remained solemn and cautious.

"What's your name?" Grace asked softly.

There was silence from the child, but a deep voice behind the principal said, "Poppy Austin."

Grace froze, her heart skipping a beat, then hammering to catch up. Her gaze whipped up as a familiar man stepped into the room. "Billy?"

"Hey." He smiled, that same lopsided grin of his that had always made her melt. He was tall and lanky, with broad shoulders and dark brown eyes... He pulled his cowboy hat off, revealing close-cropped hair, and tucked the hat under one arm. "When they said Grace Beverly was teaching preschool, I couldn't believe my luck."

"Yes, well..." Grace looked toward the principal, who was watching them with a mildly curious expression. "Billy and I were friends," she explained.

"Well, I'll let you catch up, then," Mrs. Mackel said with a nod. "Poppy here is starting in your class tomorrow, and she's had a lot of change lately. So we'll have to take that into account." To Billy, she said, "But I think she'll have a wonderful time in Miss Beverly's room." Then Mrs. Mackel bent down to

Poppy's level. "And you can come say hello to me any time you like."

"Okay," Poppy whispered.

Mrs. Mackel straightened herself and shook Billy's hand. "Feel free to stop by if you have any more questions, Mr. Austin."

Billy thanked her, and Mrs. Mackel left the classroom. Silence closed around them, and Grace regarded her old friend. It had only been three years since she'd seen him last, but he'd aged. There was a sprinkling of premature gray at his temples, and some lines around his eyes that hadn't been there before.

"What do you mean, we *were* friends," Billy said. "You're talking like that friendship is in the past."

It *was* in the past, but maybe Billy was the last to figure that out. When Billy left town with Grace's best friend, Tracy, three years ago, Grace had made the painful choice to cut contact with both of them. It wasn't the easiest decision, but it was probably the healthiest. She'd been in love with Billy from afar for too long, and watching him build a life with the vivacious Tracy—that was too much. Grace doubted that either of them had noticed when she stopped talking to them.

"Sorry, I'm just surprised to see you," Grace replied.

"So, you're teaching here now?" Billy asked.

"I'm covering a maternity leave. The regular teacher will be back in two weeks," Grace said. "Mrs. Mackel mentioned a lot of change for Poppy, so I'm afraid there will be a little more…" Grace looked down at the girl, who was looking around the classroom, her thoughts spinning to catch up. A daughter…? Where had she come from? "Billy, I had no idea—"

Billy cleared his throat and glanced down at Poppy. "Neither did I, but I think Poppy and I are going to be okay. Don't you think, kiddo?"

The little girl looked up mutely at her father, and he shot her a reassuring grin.

Now was not the time to ask more questions, so Grace turned her attention to Poppy. "Would you like to see some of the fun things we have in our classroom? Come on. I'll show you." Grace held out a hand, and Poppy tentatively took it. "This is our sand table. It's fun to play in, and when you feel anxious, you can use this rake to make nice lines. It feels good. Do you want to try?"

Poppy took the rake and made some slow strokes across the sand. "Will I learn things?"

"All sorts of things!" Grace said. "We're learning our colors, and our animals—"

"Daddy said I can learn calculus," she said softly.

"Your daddy is a funny guy." Grace chuckled, but when she looked up, Billy hadn't cracked a smile.

"That's the thing…" Billy nodded toward the other side of the room. "Can we talk over there?"

Grace glanced between Billy and Poppy. Billy as a dad—it was hard to imagine. Besides, Billy had gotten together with Tracy three years ago, and this child would be at least four… Grace followed Billy to the other side of the room. "What's going on, exactly?" she asked quietly.

"She's…" Billy shrugged. "She's smart."

"They all are, Billy," Grace replied with a small smile. "Way smarter than adults give them credit for."

"No, I mean, like…crazy smart," Billy said, locking her down with his dark gaze. "Here's the thing. Her mother announced

I had a daughter and dumped her on my doorstep on the same day. Carol-Ann and I only dated for a summer, five years ago—remember when I went to work that ranch in South Colorado? Anyway, I had no idea she'd gotten pregnant. She tracked me down in Denver, said she had this modeling gig she couldn't pass up and told me it was my turn with Poppy. Carol-Ann is in Germany right now."

"Modeling, apparently," Grace said dryly.

"Apparently."

They exchanged a look, and for a split second, it felt like the old days, when she and Billy were best friends and could finish each other's sentences. Before he fell in love with Tracy. She tore her gaze away from him.

"Wow…" Grace cleared her throat. "So, where is Tracy, then?"

"Tracy left me when she found out about all of this," Billy replied. "That's why I'm back in Eagle's Rest. I need help. I can't raise a daughter alone, so I came home. And it turns out that Poppy is strangely brilliant. She's only four, and she reads anything she can get her hands on. You know me—I never was the intellectual sort. I have no idea what else I can teach her, and I've only had her for two weeks! She's desperate to learn and she misses her mom something fierce." Billy heaved a sigh. "I was joking about the calculus, but she wasn't. I don't know what to say."

"Tracy left you?" Grace's emotions were still stuck on that part of his story. Her best friend had known about her feelings for Billy, but when Billy showed interest in Tracy, all bets were off. She'd sopped him up like gravy with a dinner roll, and the couple had moved to Denver. It all happened so fast, Grace's head had spun.

"I'm not saying Tracy and I were on great terms before Carol-Ann showed up, and I guess it was the last straw. She said she hadn't signed on to be a stepmom." He shrugged weakly, and when he looked across the room toward his daughter, Grace saw the tenderness in his eyes. His chiseled features softened into a look of protective pride.

"You're smitten," Grace said.

"Yeah..." Billy smiled, then glanced back toward Grace. "I'm a dad. Can you believe that? It's pretty huge."

"It really is," she agreed. "And she's adorable."

He nodded. "Honestly, I'm here to give Poppy a stable life. Social services is going to check in on me to make sure everything is running smoothly, and I guess they'll be judging my parenting abilities, too."

"You'll be fine," she said.

"I have no idea what I'm doing," he retorted. "None. First of all, she's a little girl! I hardly know how to deal with women, let alone the pint-size version. And she's just so smart…"

"You'll do what everyone else does," she replied with a shrug. "You'll figure it out."

They exchanged another look, one that made Grace's heart squeeze in her chest. He'd always been able to make her feel that way. There was something about those dark eyes, his playful smile, his cheeky banter… But no matter how he made her heart flutter, she'd just been "good old faithful Grace" to him. She'd been there for him through thick and thin, and he'd never once seen her as more than a friend. She'd never told him how she felt.

"I'm just really glad to see you, Gracie," Billy said with a smile. "I missed you."

It wasn't fair, because when he said he missed her, he meant it in a casual sense. He missed having that loyal friend always ready to hang out with him, help him out when he was in a bind and watch movies with him on a weekend. He missed the friendship, but she missed something much deeper than a pal—she missed him, his heart. His way of seeing things, the way he'd lean close and nudge her with his elbow when he was making a joke...

She pulled her mind out of the past and forced a smile. "I've got two weeks here, and then I'm heading back to the city."

It was a reminder for herself as much as for him, because she was going to keep him firmly at arm's length. Billy Austin was her weakness, and she wasn't willing to lose her heart to him all over again. She's spent too many years in love with the man, only to watch him fall for the more beautiful, funnier, more spirited Tracy Ellison. Grace had learned a lot through that process—the most important lesson being that she was tired of being the best friend. She was tired of being seen as a buddy instead of as a woman. And she wasn't going to apologize for her figure, her looks, her personality or anything else about her that shuffled her off to the friend zone over and over again with Billy Austin.

It was a painful lesson, but a necessary one. Grace was a different woman now, and if Billy thought they could just pick up where they'd left off, he'd better think again.

"Daddy, come see!" Poppy called from the sand table.

Daddy. It still felt weird to be called that, but Billy liked it more than he ever imagined he would. He was this little girl's dad—the muscle-bound bodyguard who stood between her and an unfair world.

Billy glanced over at Grace. It was really good to see her again. With that glossy brown hair tumbling around her shoulders, her sparkling blue eyes and a soft, round figure that made him think things he really shouldn't associate with his oldest buddy.

Had she changed somehow since he'd seen her last? He didn't remember her being quite so...womanly. They'd been friends through elementary school and junior high. After he dropped out of high school, they'd reconnected when Grace was working at the cheap restaurant where he went for dinner after his ranch chores. They'd liked the same movies and she had a quick wit when it came to tearing apart the ones they didn't like. She'd also enjoyed horseback riding, and he used to take her out on the ranch where he worked on his days off. She was easy to talk to, and she'd had good advice when it came to his girlfriend problems.

After he and Tracy moved to Denver, he'd somehow lost touch with Grace. He'd tried calling a couple of times, but he'd gotten nothing back. And if he could read better, he would have tried to reach out online, but he struggled with reading, and he pretended he was just old-fashioned to hide that fact. It would have been nice to get some of her advice when things were falling apart with Tracy. Whatever—they'd drifted apart. But he'd missed Grace more than he should have, and more than Tracy liked.

"Daddy!" Poppy's tone got more reproachful. She was already used to making him jump.

Billy crossed the room to his daughter's side and looked down at the lines she was raking in the sand.

"Very pretty," he said.

"Read it!" she said excitedly.

His heart stuttered, and he forced another smile. Easy enough for Poppy to say, but he couldn't make out any letters in her raking, and even if he could… "Um…why don't you read it to me?"

"It says *Hi Dad*. See? And that there says *unicorn*. And that there says *pancake*."

"Yeah, yeah, there it is." He glanced over at Grace, and she was looking down into the sand, not at him, thankfully. Her eyebrows climbed, and her gaze flickered toward Billy.

"Very nice, Poppy," Grace said, but there was surprise in her voice. It looked like Poppy had done something right.

"I would have written a whole letter, but there's no space," Poppy said.

"Here." Grace grabbed a piece of paper and a pencil. "Do you want to try on this?"

"Okay…" Poppy settled down at a table. She'd written him a few stories over the last few days—but whether she could actually spell and all that, he had no idea. For as long as Billy could remember, whenever he looked at a page of writing, the letters just jumbled together without meaning. They got mixed up between the page and his head. There'd been a good reason he'd dropped out of school in the tenth grade—he couldn't fake it any longer.

"So, how much can she do, exactly?" Grace asked.

"I'm not sure," Billy said with a faint

shrug. "I don't even know where to start. I was hoping you'd have an idea."

"Does she just have an interest in certain words, and you've shown her how to spell them, or is this something more? Do you read to her?"

"No, I don't read to her a lot," he confessed. Not at all, more truthfully.

"Is she reading on her own?"

"She reads anything she can get her hands on, from the microwave instruction manual to the cereal boxes."

"Well, there are several tests I can give to find out her reading levels. What's she like with numbers and math?"

"She corrected the cashier at the grocery store the other day," he said.

"And she's four, you say?"

"Four," he confirmed.

"Wow." She shook her head. "That's something. You're going to have your hands full, Billy. The smarter they are, the more demanding they are. They don't know how to satisfy their own intellectual curiosity yet, and they wait for adults to provide it."

"Great." Billy scraped a hand through his hair. That was going to be a problem, because he wasn't going to be much use to the kid, unless he could show her how to fix an engine or ride a horse. He'd tried reading her a book the other day, just making up the story as he went along. He thought he was telling a pretty good one, but Poppy got furious with him for "messing up all the words." She wanted accuracy, and he couldn't give that.

"Daddy, how you spell *extra special beautiful*?" Poppy asked from her seat at the little table.

"Just do your best," Grace said. "Let's see if you can get close on your own, okay? I don't mind if you spell stuff wrong. It's the trying that counts."

That was a good answer—he'd have to remember that one. So far, Poppy didn't know how limited his own education had been, and he wanted to keep it that way. No man wanted to give up hero status in his own child's eyes.

"Sorry," Grace said with a bashful look. "I'm curious to see what she can do when you don't help her. I hope you don't mind."

"Not at all," he said. The truth was, he'd hidden his reading problem from Grace, too, and he wasn't in any rush to fess up.

"Does she get this from your side of the family?" Grace asked with an impish smile.

Billy barked out a laugh. "Now you're just being mean. And unless Carol-Ann was hiding some genius, I have no idea where that little brain cropped up."

"Her mom… Carol-Ann never mentioned it when she dropped her off?" Grace pressed.

"Nope. I have to say, I had more immediate questions than how well she read."

He could still remember that last goodbye between mother and daughter. Seeing the shock and heartbreak in his daughter's big blue eyes had shredded his heart, and he didn't even know Poppy yet. Carol-Ann had promised that she'd be back, but Billy had seen the lie in Carol-Ann's eyes. Was she telling the truth about Germany, or was she just walking away from her responsibilities?

Billy had been raised by an uninterested mother, so maybe he and Poppy had a few things in common. But he was determined he'd be the parent Poppy could count on for the rest of her life. No more betrayals. No more people she loved walking out on her. Billy was the end of the line here—and he'd be the superhero she needed to feel safe, whatever the cost.

"I'm done!" Poppy hopped up from her seat and brought the page over to Billy. He looked over it, pausing for the amount of time it seemed to take other people read a page of print, then passed it to Grace.

She took it from his hands, her soft fingers brushing his.

"This is very sweet," Grace said, then nudged Billy's arm. "Isn't it?"

"Yeah," he said with a curt nod. "Sure is."

He wished he could take it home and spend some time poring over it. Sometimes he could sort out the short words. Poppy had filled the page with her diagonally slanted lines of printing, and he wished he knew what she'd so lovingly put onto that page.

"Do you mind if I hold on to this?" Grace asked. "I'd like to show Mrs. Mackel."

"Yeah, sure," he said, pulling his eyes off the page, trying to push away that welling sense of disappointment. This was a good thing—Grace would show the principal, and the school would know just how smart his little girl was. Then *they* could give her that much-needed challenge that he didn't know how to provide.

"Thank you." Grace shook her head and

shot him a grin. "She sure loves you, doesn't she?"

What had Poppy written?

"I hope so," he said uncertainly.

"Well, I think we can see how much she does," Grace said, tapping the paper on her hand. "Poppy, this is really well done. I think you're going to have a lot of fun in our classroom. Are you looking forward to meeting the other kids?"

Poppy squirmed, glanced around the room and then cast Billy an anxious frown. "I want to stay with Daddy..."

Billy squatted down next to her and looked into those worried little eyes. She'd had her mom walk out on her recently. And then she'd watched a big fight between Billy and Tracy, and Tracy had packed her bags... It was no wonder she was anxious. Let alone the fact he was virtually a stranger.

"You're worried I'll leave and not come back," he said frankly.

Poppy froze, eyed him for a moment, then nodded slowly.

"Thing is, Poppy," he said quietly. "I'm your daddy. I didn't know about you before this, but now that I do, you don't have to worry about me taking off. I'm here to stay.

I'll always pick you up after school, and I'll make you your supper, and I'll tuck you into bed, and I'll probably always read the stories wrong, too. You can count on all of that."

"You mess up the words," Poppy whispered.

Billy chuckled and gathered her into his arms. She was as light and ferocious as a cat, and she inspired a protective surge inside him every time he looked at her. She was *his*.

"Do I?" he joked. "Well, I think my way is better."

"It's not," she said with a shake of her head.

"Still—I'm the one guy you can trust to never tell you a lie, okay? And I'll always pick you up after school. That's a promise."

Poppy was silent for a moment, and Billy stood up, lifting her with him. She was holding on to his shirt in one little fist. Neither of them wanted to let go of the other. He caught a mist of emotion in Grace's eyes as she watched them.

Grace…beautiful and smart, and always several levels above the likes of him. He'd known that from the start. Her dad was a doctor; her mom was an accountant. She'd been raised to expect the best out of life, and Billy had known from the start that he was a far cry from what Grace deserved. Hell, Poppy deserved more than he could offer, too, but that was life. Sometimes you got the short end of the stick. Right now, his deepest wish was to maintain whatever respect Grace still had for him, and hopefully both Grace and Poppy could stay in the dark about his limitations.

"We should probably head out," Billy said. "I think Poppy and I could use an ice cream."

Poppy's eyes lit up. This kid was easily bought, and that was a good thing. He needed every brownie point he could get.

"Thank you for coming by," Grace said, and her gaze caught his for a moment.

"Grace..." He paused in the doorway. "It's really good to see you again."

It was more than "good"; it was a strange relief, like coming home in a whole new way. He hadn't realized just how much he'd missed her over the last few years. She'd been an anchor in his life when he'd needed it most, and it looked like he was going to need her again. She cleared her throat and dropped her gaze, breaking the moment between them.

Maybe she hadn't missed him…

"We'll see you tomorrow, Poppy," Grace said.

Billy dropped his cowboy hat back on his head, and he headed out into those familiar old Eagle's Rest Elementary School hallways. Hopefully this school would do better by his daughter than it ever did by him.

CHAPTER TWO

GRACE PARKED HER car behind her mother's SUV and turned off the engine. Coming back to Eagle's Rest had been filled with reconnections, but meeting up with Billy was different. Billy was supposed to be safely out of the picture. She wanted to smooth layer after layer of life over the hole he'd left in her heart. He belonged to the past. Her mind was still spinning, and her emotions hadn't caught up.

"Just over two weeks left..." she murmured. And while before that had meant relief at getting back to her apartment in the city again—the quiet, her own routines—now it was taking on a whole new urgency. It had felt good to see Billy again—too good. And she'd come too far to let herself slip into that place where she didn't feel pretty enough or interesting enough to capture the heart of the one man she loved. Not again!

Grace got out of her car, slamming the

door behind her, and headed toward the side door. Someone had thrown down some salt, but the driveway and sidewalk were still slick. She could smell something cooking as she opened the door…but it wasn't the same, familiar smell of cooking from her childhood. This was different, and had been ever since her mother had retired.

"You're home," her mother said as Grace came inside and stepped out of her boots.

Connie Beverly was a short, round woman with eyes that crinkled up and sparkled when she smiled. She wore a loose sweater over a pair of leggings, an apron tied around her ample waist and a pair of slippers. She stood by the counter with a potato masher held aloft.

"Smell this," her mother demanded. "Seriously. Smell it."

"I *can* smell it," Grace chuckled, slipping off her coat. "That's not mashed potatoes."

"You're just being a cynic now!" Connie retorted, turning back to the bowl. "It's almost like mashed potatoes."

Grace winced. Her mother had been saying for years that she didn't lose weight because she worked full-time and she was too busy to bother. But this year, she'd retired and sworn that she would drop the extra weight.

Grace went over to the counter and looked down into the bowl.

"Mom, cauliflower isn't a carb," she said.

"That's the point. You smash the cauliflower up to look like mashed potatoes, and you don't miss the extra calories."

"It looks like sadness to me." And it smelled like boiled cauliflower.

"It looks like health and longevity." Connie smiled in satisfaction and turned back to her cautious mashing. "You should give this a try, Gracie. Our genes being what they are—"

"Mom, please…"

It was an old conversation. They came from a long line of "big-boned" women who never had any trouble finding husbands, and whose love language was cooking. Grace had never been thin, and neither had her mom. It was easy enough to love herself, but a little harder to compete with the likes of Tracy. There were times she wished she could be naturally slender.

"You're turning thirty next week," her mother reminded her.

"I know," Grace replied with a grin. "And

I'll turn thirty with real carbs, thank you very much."

"Well… I'll agree to that," her mother replied. "What's birthday cake if it isn't sinful, right? So, how was your day?"

"Good," Grace replied, and she flicked the switch on the electric kettle. "Actually, this afternoon, I saw Billy Austin."

"Billy Austin?" Carol turned from the sodden cauliflower and frowned. "He's back in town? Did you see Tracy?"

"Tracy wasn't with him. They broke up."

"Ah." Her mother's eyebrows climbed, and then she nodded. "What's he doing back in Eagle's Rest?"

"He found out he had a daughter, and the mother had some modeling plans in Germany, so she dumped the little girl on his doorstep. Tracy took a big step back, and he came home to raise his daughter."

"Billy's a dad!" Connie headed to the fridge and pulled open the door, staring into its depths. "How old is his daughter?"

"Four."

"Wait—the mother is a model? She's not from Eagle's Rest, then, is she?"

Grace had done the same math. "No, it

was that summer he spent working a ranch in the foothills. Remember that?"

"I remember the two of you missed each other more than you'd admit," her mother quipped.

"Apparently he wasn't quite so lonely," Grace replied with a wry smile, pushing back a sense of betrayal she had no right to. They'd been friends—nothing more. Her heart in knots hadn't been his fault.

"You were always too good for him," Connie said. "You know that. I told you so from the start."

Was she? Grace didn't believe it. Billy had been fun and sweet. He might not have finished high school, but he was a hard worker, and he'd worked his way up in the ranks of any ranch that employed him. Those strong hands and laughing eyes—they'd been enough for her.

"I remember Tracy told me that she was going to make a gentleman out of him—*My Fair Lady* style." Grace shook her head. "It doesn't surprise me that she left him at the first sign of a challenge."

"They deserved each other," Connie retorted.

"No, he didn't deserve that. If they could

have been happy, that would have been one thing, but as soon as Tracy found out about his daughter, she walked out on him."

"Maybe she'll come back."

"Maybe." But Grace's heart gave a squeeze at the thought. She wanted Billy to have a full and happy life, but somehow giving him up for Tracy was harder than it would have been to see him move on with some woman she'd never met. "Anyway, his little girl's name is Poppy, and she starts in my class tomorrow."

"Two weeks, sweetheart," her mother said. "You probably won't see him except for drop-off and pickup."

The kettle started to boil, and Grace pulled down two mugs. She could get through this, but it wouldn't be easy. The problem with Billy wasn't just her feelings for him. Grace had learned some valuable lessons through allowing herself to fall in love with a man who didn't reciprocate her feelings. No good could come from it! She'd spent too long hoping that he would suddenly see her in a different light and recognize that his best buddy was actually his perfect romantic match. Now she knew she'd never thought it all through.

What happened if he did see her differently? She'd still be the woman who hadn't been enough to draw his eye for literally years' worth of friendship. Yes, Grace was plump and round in an age of lithe models, but she didn't suffer from low self-esteem. Everyone had a type they were attracted to. She seemed to like lanky cowboys. And Billy liked the model type. He always had. There was nothing to apologize for here.

"How did you feel seeing him again?" her mother asked, passing Grace a tin of tea bags.

"I'm okay," Grace replied. "Billy was a good friend, and our lives have both moved on."

"Very mature of you," her mother said, shooting her a smile.

"Thank you. I thought so, too."

Connie chuckled. "What is his little girl like? Does she favor him?"

"You can see him in the shape of her face… His daughter is gifted, though."

"Are you serious?"

"It sure looks that way. She's four, and she sat down and wrote a letter to her father about how she liked his cowboy hat. She called it 'extra special beautiful.' She said how she'd never had a daddy before, but she said he could use his muscles to keep her safe, and she hoped he wouldn't go away like her mother had. She promised to be good so he wouldn't want to. It was heart-wrenching—and perfectly punctuated."

"At four," Connie breathed.

They exchanged a long look.

"He's overwhelmed," Grace admitted, and an image of Billy came to mind—those dark eyes, the large, calloused hands, and the tender way he'd held his petite daughter in his arms. Billy might never have loved Grace, but he certainly did love that little girl.

"Gracie, it's a good thing that you're going back to Denver," her mother replied. "He's a dad now, and he'll have to figure it out on his own. He's always been very comfortable leaning on you as his buddy, but you can't use up all your energy on Billy Austin again. You've got your own life to live."

"I'm not trying to rescue him," Grace replied. "I won't go back to that."

It wasn't possible to love a man into loving her, and she couldn't fill those gaps between them with her own hopes and dreams. She was going back to Denver to work her next job, and hopefully one of these days, she'd meet a guy who looked at her the same way Billy had looked at Tracy.

"Let's see if your father notices these aren't potatoes," Connie said, looking down into the bowl she'd been mashing.

"He'll notice," Grace said with a low laugh, and she looked down into the bowl. "I think they're getting soupy, Mom."

"Oh…" Connie sighed.

"You don't need to lose weight, you know," Grace said. "You and I are soft in all the right places."

"I'd like to have a waist, though," her mother retorted. "And I'm determined to get one."

Grace knew better than to argue with her mom when she was on a mission, but Grace's most treasured memories of her mother included her soft hugs, her delectable baking and the way her chunky jewelry used to clatter when Grace would fiddle with it as a little girl. And when Grace's father looked at her mother from across the room, Grace had always seen that look of devotion that she longed for from a man of her own.

It wasn't about weight, because her mother had always been a beautiful woman who could light up a room with her smile and her laughter. She'd had a soft figure, an ample bosom, and she'd always taken pride in her appearance. Her parents' marriage had been about two people who were so in love that they didn't need anyone else.

Grace went to a bottom cupboard and pulled out the bag of potatoes. "I'll just peel a few," she said with a grin. "You don't mind, do you?"

Connie looked down at the cauliflower mush in the bowl and smiled sheepishly. "I can have a cheat day, right?"

Grace would not eat cauliflower mashed into fake potatoes. Life was too short for that kind of sadness on a plate. Her life in Denver had been about more than moving on after Billy moved in with Tracy; it was about building the life she wanted—*asking* for what she wanted.

And tonight she wanted some comfort food and a cozy evening. It wasn't too much to ask.

"Is my ponytail straight?" Poppy asked as Billy pulled into a parking spot in front of the school the next morning. It had been a hurried morning. Poppy had refused to get out of bed, so getting her ready for school had been hectic. They hadn't had anything pressing to do since he'd gotten custody of her, and this morning—his first day back on the job at Ross Ranch—was a taste of real-life parenting.

Poppy didn't want to eat, didn't want her hair brushed, didn't want to wear matching clothes from the small suitcase her mom had dropped off with her. He'd given up on the last one, and this morning she wore blue tights, a pink summer dress and a second-hand Christmas sweater on top of it all. She said Mommy had bought her the sweater, and it seemed unnecessarily cruel to deny her some connection to her mom. It only occurred to him now that she'd probably be expected to play outside, and he didn't have snow pants for her.

Billy looked over at her for a moment, considering his morning's handiwork. He'd done his best.

"It's not perfectly straight," he admitted. "But it's not bad. You look good, kiddo."

With the rest of her ensemble, no one would be looking at her hair, anyway.

"I don't want to go to school," Poppy said, her eyes welling with tears.

"This is where you'll learn the fun stuff,"

he said. "A teacher can show you all sorts of things I can't. Besides, I have to go to work while you're at school. That's the deal I made with Mr. Ross."

Billy had worked at the Ross ranch before he left for Denver with Tracy, and now that he was back, Mr. Ross had been happy to offer him another job. Billy had built a reputation for himself based on his hard work. Mr. Ross understood the complication of having a little girl to take care of, so he agreed to flex-time employment—Billy would put in as many hours as he could while his daughter was at school, and he'd be paid by the hour. It was a generous offer, and one Billy didn't want to take advantage of.

Poppy was silent, but a tear escaped and trickled down her cheek.

"Did you know that I know Miss Beverly from a long time ago?" Billy asked. "She's my friend. So she knows how to find me if you get too lonely."

The poor kid had dealt with so many changes lately, and he didn't blame her for balking at this one.

"Let's go inside," Billy said. "I won't leave until you're ready, okay?"

"Okay," Poppy consented, then looked him over. "Your hat is dirty."

Billy pulled his hat off his head and saw a few pieces of hay stuck to some stitching. He plucked them off and dropped his hat back onto his head.

"We good?" he asked.

"You'll do," Poppy replied, and Billy chuckled.

"It'll be okay," he assured her. "You'll see."

The hallways were buzzing with students, and Billy walked Poppy through the school, toward Grace's classroom. Billy had gone to this school, and his memories were filled with frustration. Every year, the work got harder, and his reading remained a colossal struggle. Everyone else could read aloud and follow instructions, while he'd take half an hour to decipher two lines, and then forget what he'd managed to read. So he gave up and put his energy into coping—got other kids to help him do his work, groomed a cocky attitude, made nice with teaching assistants who helped him to keep up with the basics so that he could be pushed forward into the next grade.

The school repeatedly told his mom that he struggled with reading, but no one quite picked up on the fact that he *couldn't* read. He'd thought that was a victory. Now he wasn't so sure. If they'd figured it out when he was young enough, maybe someone could have helped him. But at the age of thirty, how was he supposed to admit to that?

Poppy's classroom was at the far end of the school, next to the double doors, and as Billy and Poppy approached, he saw Grace helping a student hang up a backpack almost as big as the kid was.

"Good morning," Billy said, and Grace looked up. Her soft chocolate waves were gathered back in a loose ponytail, and the first thing he noticed was the pink in her cheeks and the shine of her lip gloss. Grace had definitely changed over the last few years—she'd never been the type to wear makeup before. And there was something different about her clothes, too, although he couldn't quite put his finger on it. She wore a pair of fitted dress pants and a loose pink blouse, with a belt cinched at her waist. She didn't look like she was hiding in her clothes anymore. She stood out.

"Hi!" she said, rising to her feet. "Poppy, I have a hook all set up for you with your name. This is where you'll hang your backpack and your coat and your snow pants—"

"We, uh, don't have those yet," Billy said. "I'll pick some up tonight."

"I do have an extra pair she can borrow," Grace said. "She'll need them for recess. We have a special nature walk today, too, so..."

"Thanks." He nodded quickly. "And I'll make sure she has her own for tomorrow."

Billy already felt like he was falling behind as a dad. The other little girls were wearing matching outfits in pink and purple. He looked down at Poppy with her red-and-green sweater, the pink dress poking out the bottom, and he felt a wash of regret. He should have fought harder when she was getting dressed this morning. The kids were going to be cruel.

"You dressed yourself!" Grace said, looking down at Poppy with a big smile. "Didn't you?"

"Yep," Poppy said quietly.

"You look wonderful. I can always tell a kid who likes to choose her own clothes. That's great!"

Billy looked at Grace uncertainly. Was it great?

"I should have put up a bigger fight about that," he murmured, and Grace shook her head.

"They're four. The others won't notice. And when I see a kid who insists on choosing her own clothes, I know that she's got a strong spirit. That's a good thing, Billy."

"I hope so."

"Relax. It'll be fine." Grace put her hands on her hips and regarded him for a moment. "Are you going to stay for a few minutes, or leave now?"

Billy looked down at Poppy and saw she was glancing nervously at the other kids. "You ready for me to go to work, Poppy?" he asked quietly.

"Nope," she said with a shake of her head. "I don't know these people."

Grace smiled. "Your dad can stay for a little bit until you feel better, Poppy. Let's go inside and I'll introduce you to the other kids. Okay?"

Grace *was* different now, he realized. Maybe it was that she was the sun and the moon to a roomful of four-year-olds, but it leant her a certain air of confidence that she hadn't had in years past. He hadn't expected her to be any different from the pal he remembered when he heard that Grace Beverly was teaching this class, but his memories of her weren't like this. Grace had blossomed.

As she started the day with her students, Billy found one adult-size chair next to a window and took a seat. Grace walked Poppy around the room, introducing her to the students individually and keeping her hand in the little girl's the entire time. Poppy looked up at Grace with a flicker of a smile and big, adoring eyes. It looked to Billy like Grace was winning Poppy over.

"Good morning, friends," Grace said. "We have a new friend joining us today. Her name is Poppy, and I already like her! Don't you? Now, let's all come to the story carpet, and we'll get ready for the daily announcements and the pledge of allegiance."

The kids spun in their places, dug toes into the carpet and a couple sat down during the pledge of allegiance. Grace went around, gently tugging them back to their feet and putting small hands over their chests. As she helped the children into the proper, respectful position, she was saying the words aloud with the principal over the loudspeaker.

"…and to the republic for which it stands. One nation under God, indivisible…"

Along the wall under the window, where Billy sat, there were letters of the alphabet on separate laminated sheets. *Q. R. S. T.* Large letters, separated by inches of wall, made the letters distinct and different in his mind. They didn't jumble up like they did on a page, and Billy eyed them for a moment, mildly intrigued by his ability to differentiate them.

He understood the basic concept of letters, sounds and the combination turning into words. He looked around at the kids as Grace sat down in front of a large picture graph with different weather symbols on it.

"This morning is sunny," Grace was saying. "Who can find the picture that tells us that it's sunny?"

Most of these children wouldn't even know their alphabets yet, but they would be introduced to the basics this year. An idea was forming itself in his mind. He wasn't sure if he was crazy to even be considering this, but maybe he could start over.

Billy had given up on school and put his energy into avoiding the embarrassment. But maybe as his daughter learned, he could catch up on a few basics he'd missed, too. Maybe, just maybe, he could learn to read.

Billy pulled off his hat and looked down at it for a moment, trying to hide any expression that might be betraying his thoughts right now. He hadn't changed in his desire to hide his illiteracy, but if he could really buckle down and learn how to read at long last...

It could change everything! He could apply for higher positions at the ranch. He'd figured he'd never be anything more than regular labor, but if he could read, he might be able to work his way up to ranch manager eventually. A whole new world would open up to him, a world of instructions, information and upward mobility.

And at the end of a long day, he could sit down with Poppy and he could read her a book. Instead of pretending that he was teasing her, making up stories that only frustrated her because she wanted him to read the book properly, he could do just that— read his little girl a story.

Billy's heart hammered in his chest, and he realized that he'd zoned out there for a minute, because the kids were moving off to different corners of the room now, and Grace was coming toward him. Billy stood up, scanned the room and found Poppy at the puppet theater with another little girl, hand in hand.

"You could probably leave now," Grace said quietly. "Poppy has a friend. She'll be okay."

"Yeah, of course." He cleared his throat, feeling a little embarrassed not to have been the one to come to that conclusion first. "Sorry, I'll get out of your hair."

"Sometimes this is harder on the parents than the kids," Grace said, putting a hand on his arm. In that moment, she was the old Grace again—the confiding pal who always saw the best in him.

"I'll be back at three," he said with a small smile.

Poppy didn't even look up as Billy made his way out of the room, and he glanced back to see Grace turning toward her class, her figure outlined in the doorway. The same old Grace in so many ways, and yet she wasn't. Then the door shut with a decisive click, and he heard Grace's voice filtering out to him in the hallways.

"Michael P., let's keep our hands to ourselves, please!"

Maybe Billy was crazy to think he could learn how to read, because that classroom door had just closed on his opportunity. Who was he fooling? He wasn't a kid anymore, and he'd had his chance. Now it was Poppy's turn to learn "all the fun stuff," as he'd put it.

Still, he couldn't quite stamp out that little spark of hope. And he glanced over his shoulder as his cowboy boots echoed down the hallway.

Maybe.

CHAPTER THREE

As BILLY FINISHED up his work in the barn that afternoon, he glanced at his watch. It would be time to pick up Poppy from school pretty soon, and he'd been looking forward to it all day. He'd felt strange, disconcerted walking away from Poppy—like he was messing up in some fundamental way that he didn't even know about. But that seemed to be his general feeling these days. He'd never been "good enough"—not for school, not for Grace. And now, not even to be a dad to a kid like Poppy.

What did he know about raising a little girl, especially one this smart? What did he know about parenting, period? He'd been raised by a chronically overworked mother who was more interested in finding a new man than she was in raising her son, and he'd ended up raising himself. Not terribly well, either. Frankly he was as surprised as anyone else that he was a functional adult. If he'd ended up with a boy to raise, he might have had a better idea of how to do it based on his own pitfalls, but a little girl? That was a whole other world!

One of the other ranch hands had suggested that he ask his mom about raising a girl, and Billy had laughed out loud at that one. His mom had barely managed to raise him. She wasn't one to give advice about what kids needed. She'd been of the opinion that what didn't kill a kid could be considered a success. And maybe he had picked up a lot of life lessons along the way, but he'd missed out on some important fundamentals, too.

Billy hung his shovel on the wall just as his cell phone rang from inside his shirt pocket. He pulled it out and looked at the number before picking up the call. It was Mr. Ross.

"You've got a visitor," Mr. Ross said, then lowered his voice. "A woman from social services. She's here at the house, if you want to come on up."

He didn't have much choice, so Billy hopped into his truck and rumbled on up the gravel road. His stomach felt like it was in a vice as he drove along, wondering what to expect. He'd spent a good many years avoiding raising the suspicions of social services when he was a kid. His mom had warned him repeatedly that they'd take him away if he wasn't careful, so facing them now just felt ominous.

The main house was a two-story affair with a porch out front and a rustic fence running around the yard. Billy parked in the gravel patch just behind the house, trying to tamp down the uneasy feelings. Apparently social services had been involved with Carol-Ann in the past, so when she passed Poppy over to him, they were coming as part of the package. It only confirmed in his mind that Poppy was better off with him, as limited as his prospects were.

He turned off the engine and hopped out of the truck. Best to get this out of the way. His boots crunched over the snow as he headed to the back door.

"Here he is now," Mr. Ross said, pushing open the screen. "How ya doing, Billy?"

"Real good, sir."

He and his boss exchanged a look that didn't match their cheery banter, and as he passed into the house, Mr. Ross slapped him in the shoulder.

"One of the best workers I've got," the

older man said. It sounded slightly over-the-top, but Billy could appreciate the intent, at least.

The social worker was a middle-aged woman with a close-cropped hairstyle and a pair of prominent, artsy glasses. She smiled cordially and put out a hand.

"Mr. Austin, I presume?" she said.

"That's me," Billy said, pulling off his gloves and shaking her hand. "What can I do for you?"

"My name is Isabel Burns with Colorado Child Welfare, and we're just following up with you about Poppy," she said.

"Okay..." He eyed her for a moment, waiting for the blow to land.

"And I wanted to see if you need any support," she concluded.

"Like...what kind of support?" he asked. "I've got a job, and I can provide for my daughter, if that's the worry. I'm going to buy some snow pants for her this afternoon. I don't know what the school told you—"

"No, no, this has nothing to do with the school," she replied. "But I'm glad to hear she's enrolled. She's—" Isabel looked down at her computer tablet "—four years old. Am I right?"

"Yeah, four," he confirmed. "So, what do you need from me?"

"I'm here to see if *I* can be of any assistance to you," Isabel replied. "Do you have any other children?"

"No, Poppy is my only child," he replied. *His* child, and he didn't like people butting in, even when he felt ridiculously overwhelmed.

"So, she's in preschool, then?" Isabel asked.

"Yes, ma'am. Her first day is today."

"Wonderful. I have some information about community resources we have available for young families." She pulled a stack of brochures out of her bag. "Take a look through when you have some time. When was her last visit to the dentist?"

"I don't know," he confessed. "I've only had her for a couple of weeks. But I'll make a few appointments once things calm down a bit."

"That sounds good." She smiled again. "I'd also like to set up a visit when I could chat with Poppy, and with you. Just see how things are going for you both."

Billy repressed a grimace. "Sure. That would be fine."

"How about in…" She consulted her tablet again. "Two weeks? That would give you both some time to settle in, and you might have a better idea if you need any extra support."

"Sure. Two weeks."

Isabel pulled out a business card, scratched something on the back of it and handed it over. "Would the early evening, say around seven, be less intrusive to your schedule?"

"Probably," he agreed. "That would be fine. We'll be here."

"Wonderful." So much cheeriness, but he couldn't help narrowing his eyes.

"And if you have any questions, any problems, or think of anything that might help you out at all, don't hesitate to call, okay? This is my job—helping with these transitions. And my interest is in making sure that kids are getting everything that they need. I'm sure we both want the same thing there."

"Hey, I'm not the one who abandoned her," Billy said. "I want that on the record."

"Mr. Austin, I'm only here to help and provide support." Her tone grew firmer, and a little less cheery.

"Okay, then," he said.

"I look forward to seeing you both in two weeks."

Isabel moved toward the door and slipped back into her boots, and Billy stood there in silence.

"In that stack, there is a brochure about nutrition and sleep schedules for young children. I hope those will be helpful," she said.

"Yeah, thanks."

Whatever she was trying to do, it wasn't as reassuring as seemed to be her goal. With a wave, the social worker left the house and headed to a small sedan. Billy watched as the car pulled out of the drive and headed for the main road. He heard a shuffle behind him and turned toward his boss, mildly embarrassed.

"I'm sorry about that, Mr. Ross," he said.

"It's not a problem, Billy. You're going to make a fine father. I have no doubt about it. They'll see it and let you be."

Billy sincerely hoped that Mr. Ross was right. He actually did need help. He just didn't trust getting that help from child-welfare services. It might not be completely logical, but he was afraid that if he showed any weakness, it might give them confirmation that he wasn't a fit parent.

And it was more than the fact that whatever that link was between a father and his daughter, Billy felt it. She was his, and he could see evidence of that in all sorts of little mannerisms. But he'd also seen his daughter struggle with her mother's choice to leave her. There was no way he was going to let her feel that again. Poppy needed him, and he was going to be the best parent he could possibly be.

Billy looked at his watch.

"I've got to go pick up Poppy from school," he said.

"You bet," Mr. Ross replied. "Thanks for your work today."

So maybe Billy hadn't had much of an example of a good parent in his own life, but at the very least he could look at what his mother had done and take the opposite path. Poppy was going to come first —always. There'd be no competition between his daughter and his romantic life. He'd probably mess up a lot of things as he navigated the world of little girls, but he wouldn't mess up that one!

"NATHANIEL, YOUR MOM is over there," Grace said, pointing for the little boy's benefit. "Do you see her?"

"Mommy!" And Nathaniel was off, boots thunking against cement as he ran toward his waiting mother. Grace smiled and waved. Nathaniel was the last child to leave, except for Poppy, who stood next to Grace, her thin legs poking out of her winter boots, and her eyes wide with nervous tension. Grace reached out and smoothed a hand over Poppy's hair. She wished she could shoulder some of that anxiety for the girl—but that wasn't possible.

"There's your dad," Grace said as she spotted Billy coming across the snow, toward them, feeling a flood of relief at the sight of him. Poppy needed her dad, and Grace was a poor substitute right now.

"Oh, good..." Poppy breathed.

Grace could hear the solace in that little sigh, and her heart nearly broke. This child had been bravery itself today, making new friends while eyeing the door with a forlorn look on her face.

Grace waved Billy inside, a frigid wind whipping into the school and raising goose bumps on her arms under her blouse.

"There you are, kiddo," Billy said with a grin. "Sorry I'm a few minutes late. Somebody came by to talk to me, and *she just wouldn't leave.*"

A small smile turned up the corners of Poppy's lips. "Why not?"

"Some people, kiddo. Some people. Anyway, I'm here now." Billy looked over at Grace with a hesitant smile. "How'd it go?"

"Pretty well, I'd say," Grace replied, trying not to react to those warm brown eyes of his. "I got Poppy reading some picture books, but she worked through the pile pretty quickly. I had her read to me for a little while, and I can't find the top of her vocabulary yet. But at the same time, she's four, so while she needs a challenge, it has to be...age appropriate."

After watching that child stare at the door with a lonesome look in her eyes, Grace knew exactly what Poppy needed—and it wasn't anything a teacher could provide. Grace was on the outside of the circle.

"If she can handle bigger books..." Billy said with a shrug.

"She can handle the words and the paragraphs," Grace replied. "But the emotional intensity might be a bit much. Older kids need more of an emotionally intense plot. Little kids need more reassurance that their world is safe and secure."

"Ah." Billy picked up Poppy's backpack and put it over his own shoulder. He was silent for a moment, and Grace looked down at his daughter.

"You ready to go home, Poppy?" she asked.

"Yeah," Poppy said quietly, and she looked up at her father, looking deflated and tired.

"The…uh…the woman who came by the ranch was from child welfare," Billy said, and he met Grace's gaze, his expression hollow and tired, too. He wanted to talk, she could tell.

"Poppy, do you remember that book you liked about the bear family?" Grace said, turning to the little girl. "I wanted to show your dad. Could you run and find it? It's in the pile somewhere…"

"Okay…" Poppy looked up at her father.

"Yeah, I'd like to see it," he said with a nod. "Go ahead."

Poppy trundled back into the classroom, and Grace looked up at Billy. "Who called child welfare on you?"

"It's not that. Apparently they were involved a lot with Carol-Ann, so when she passed guardianship to me, they were already in the picture," he replied. "Anyway, the child welfare lady is coming back in two weeks, and I want to have something to show her—something to prove I'm the right one for my daughter, as stupid as it is that I even have to defend that...but Poppy needs to learn stuff that I can't teach her."

Billy was in over his head, and like he had done in the past, he was coming to her. There'd been a time when she would have done anything he asked...

"I'm not sure what you're worried about," Grace replied. "She's doing just fine. I mean, if anything, she's miles ahead."

"And she's bored," he said.

"You know what they say about reading to kids—" she began.

"No, she's really bored. She needs more than I can give her...intellectually. I don't know what to show her next, and she's constantly asking me to teach her something. Look, I can just feel it. She needs to learn stuff, and I'm at a loss here."

"I could recommend a tutor—" she started.

"Why not you?" he asked, and he met her gaze pleadingly.

"I'm not going to be here long-term," she countered. "I'm very, very temporary."

"For the next couple of weeks, then," he said. "I trust you, Gracie. If you could teach Poppy some extra stuff—satisfy that curiosity of hers—I think it would go a long way toward showing social services that they have nothing to worry about."

"You're going to be fine," she said, and she wished she sounded more certain. He would be...wouldn't he? This was his daughter—his family situation didn't include her. "I'll definitely give her some extra challenge in the classroom, and I can send some books home that you could read with her."

Billy swallowed. "So that's a no?"

No. That was the right answer here. She should turn him down and send him to a teaching assistant or some local tutor. But she'd always been his answer, his trusty friend, and while they'd been apart for a few years, falling back into their old patterns seemed as natural as breathing. That was the problem with Billy—he fit into her heart too perfectly, and she never could say no to him. Not that it made any difference in how he'd seen her. Billy admired her, trusted her... He even thought she was funny. He just didn't love her in return.

Just then Poppy came back with the book under one arm and a hopeful look on her face.

"I got it!" she said. "Daddy, you'll like this one. It's got a bear fixing a car, and you like fixing cars, right?"

"Yeah, I do," he said with a smile, then he looked over at Grace hopefully. She knew what he wanted, and if she hadn't spent the last three years trying to purge him out of her system, agreeing to teach that insatiable little sponge would have been a pleasure.

"You hungry, Grace?" Billy asked instead.

"Uh…" Grace shrugged. "I suppose."

"Why don't you come with us for an early dinner? My treat. Poppy and I like pizza, and I seem to remember you liked sausage pizza." He shot her a familiar smile. "Besides, maybe you'll give me some credibility with my daughter. I told her we were friends."

The sound of high heels echoing down the hallway made Grace look up, and she saw Mrs. Mackel coming toward them.

"Hello, Poppy," the principal said with a smile. "How was your first day?"

Poppy made a face. "I didn't like it."

"I'm sorry to hear that," the principal said.

"I have a feeling tomorrow will be better, though."

Poppy didn't answer, and Mrs. Mackel turned her attention to Grace.

"Do you have a moment, Miss Beverly?"

"Sure."

They stepped aside, and the principal handed her a slip of paper with a phone number written on it. "I just spoke with the principal at an elementary school in Denver. You applied for a job starting in September, I believe?"

"Yes—" Grace's breath caught in her throat.

"He was just checking on your references, and I gave him a glowing one. He asked that you give him a call. He sounded very interested in you."

A surge of delight throbbed through her heart, and she shot the principal a grin. "That is wonderful news!"

"I agree!" Mrs. Mackel said. "Whichever school gets you is incredibly lucky! I'm happy for you, Grace. I hope it isn't premature, but congratulations."

Grace would call the principal in question just as soon as she could, and she looked over to find Billy watching her quizzically. Mrs.

Mackel headed back down the hallway, toward the school office.

"You got offered a job?" Billy said.

So much for discretion. "I hope so... It looks that way."

"Where is the school?"

"Denver," she said. "But nothing is confirmed yet. I need to return a phone call."

"Yeah, you bet." He nodded quickly, but the glitter had gone out of his eyes. He pressed his lips together in a firm line. This was hers—she'd been looking for full-time work for a year now, and to finally have a request for her to call back after checking her references was a massive accomplishment. She'd never gotten this far in the process before. Not that he'd know that.

"Billy, I wasn't staying—" she began.

"Yeah, I know." He smiled, but it didn't reach his eyes. She didn't need him to understand this, did she? They couldn't be the pair of best friends they used to be...

"You did the same thing to me when you took off with Tracy," she reminded him with what she hoped was a teasing smile, but she wasn't sure she managed it.

"Hey, you've got to do what's good for you," he said, scooping up his daughter's hand in his broad palm. "I'm happy for you. I just wish I had you around Eagle's Rest for longer."

Why did she feel like she was abandoning him? It wasn't a fair emotional reaction to this. She didn't owe Billy Austin a blasted thing. She wasn't his fallback in time of need—she was a woman with a life of her own, and her life was moving forward at long last.

"So, what about that pizza?" he said.

Okay, it seemed they were over her news and back to dinner plans. She pushed down some irritation. She should say no, bow out… but she had a feeling that she'd have reason to celebrate, and there was no harm in some pizza, was there? She eyed Billy for a moment, then smiled. "Give me a minute to return this call, and you've got yourself a deal."

"Miss Beverly?" Poppy whispered, and Grace bent down to catch the girl's words. "Who's going to teach me calculus?" Poppy stared up with solemn sincerity.

Grace looked up at Billy and saw hope glimmering through his own solemn expression.

Maybe she could help him out for a couple of weeks. What could it hurt? If she refused, she'd only think about him constantly anyway. Besides, some time with him might help to break the spell. He was a man—nothing more or less—and a lot had changed since he had run off with Tracy. Maybe some time together could prove that to her, and she could shake her heart free of him for good.

"Well, tonight I can't show you calculus," Grace said, "but I can introduce you to fractions…"

"Fractions?" Poppy's eyes lit up. "What's that?"

"I'll show you with the pizza," Grace promised.

"So…" Billy caught her eye. "Are you saying you'll help me out?"

"Yes," she said with a small smile. "I suppose I am. For two weeks. But that's all we've got, okay? After that, you'll have to find someone else."

"Thank you. You're one in a million—you know that?" He shot her a grin, and she felt something inside of her melt.

"Yeah, I know," she replied with a shake of her head. She always had been, and Billy had never seen it. He might not deserve her help, but this wasn't only about Billy. Standing there, with a book about bears clutched in front of her and hope in her big blue eyes, was a little girl who wanted to learn.

How could Grace refuse?

CHAPTER FOUR

BILLY AND GRACE took separate vehicles to the restaurant. It felt so formal…but maybe he was reading more into this than was really there. Then, while he and Poppy drove to the pizza place, Poppy changed her mind.

"I don't want pizza," she said softly.

"Well, I do," he replied. "I'm hungry. Aren't you?"

"I want to go home…" she whispered.

"Kiddo, I invited Miss Beverly to come with us. If I tell her we changed our mind, it's going to really hurt her feelings."

Poppy was silent. She was tired—he understood that—but he couldn't cater to his daughter all of the time. Besides, he finally had a chance to sit down with Grace and talk, and he couldn't give that up. He needed to know what had happened, what had made her go silent for three years.

"It won't take too long," he said after a few

beats. "You'll feel better with food in you. You'll see."

When they arrived at the restaurant, Grace pulled into the parking spot next to theirs, and they went inside together. The hostess led them to a booth, and Billy let Grace and Poppy slide in first, and then he sat opposite Grace, glancing up at her uncertainly. She was standoffish, and he wasn't sure why. It wasn't like they'd ever had a fight. He and Grace had always been buddies, pals, confidants. If he could turn to anyone when he was in a bind, it was her. Or it had been her... Could a few years really change so much between two people who had once been close?

She'd agreed to give Poppy some extra tutoring, but it had taken a whole lot more convincing than he had expected or was completely comfortable with. Still, this wasn't only for Poppy—it was for him, too. He'd missed Grace more than seemed prudent to admit.

"Thanks for coming along," Billy said, shooting Grace a smile. "It's so good to see you again. You have no idea."

"Yeah. Like old times."

He hesitated. He wasn't sure what that look in her eye meant, but he glanced down at the menu the waitress had left them, pretending to peruse it. It would take too long to decipher to be any good to him, but that was why he chose this place. He knew what they served, and he always ordered the same thing, so he knew how much it would be.

"I don't have my glasses," Billy said. "Is this the same menu as before?"

Grace glanced down it. "Pretty much. Eagle's Rest doesn't change that quickly."

He was relieved. The restaurant was full that time of night, and a lot of the patrons were families with kids. They looked settled, confident. One dad was giving a boy a stern look and the kid was squirming. He hadn't gotten that far with Poppy yet. She hadn't relaxed enough yet to act up, and when she did, he had no idea how he was supposed to handle it.

"So, what kind of pizza do you want, Poppy?" Billy asked, turning to his daughter.

"Cheese," Poppy said, leaning forward on her elbows. She was so small that she sat up on her knees in the booth.

Billy shot Grace a smile. "I'll get her a personal-size cheese pizza, and you and I can order something else."

"That sounds good to me." Her smile

warmed, and they turned their attention to the menu.

"Do you still like sausage and tomato?" Billy asked.

"No, you like tomato," she retorted. "But add some mushrooms, and you have yourself a deal."

Billy met her gaze. "I missed this."

"Bickering over pizza toppings?" She smiled slightly.

"Yeah," he admitted. "We always did have fun, didn't we?"

"We always did," she said, and that reserved look in her eyes softened. "I missed you, too."

Did this count as making up for whatever he'd done to tick her off? He hoped so. The waitress came by with some crayons and activity sheets for Poppy.

"Those might be too old for her," the waitress said with an apologetic smile.

"She'll be fine," Billy replied, and slid the pages over to Poppy, who scooped them up enthusiastically. Then she opened her little box of crayons and set to work.

The waitress left with their order, and Billy leaned back in his seat.

"So, for that extra tutoring—when do you want to do it?" Billy asked.

"After school would be perfect," Grace replied. "But I think you should be there for the lessons. She's been having some real separation anxiety, and having you there would just let her relax a lot more. I mean…if that doesn't get in the way of your work schedule."

Actually, that was perfect for him. He'd have a chance to watch those lessons, maybe pick something up.

"That's fine for me," he said. "I mean, whatever's best for the kid, right?"

Grace smiled. "Right."

"So…starting tomorrow?" he asked hopefully.

"Sure. Just come by at three and we'll get started. I'll be able to show you a few things to give her some challenges at home, too."

"Okay." He felt a little rush of anticipation. "That would be great."

Grace looked over to where Poppy was working with her crayons, her gaze softening.

"So, fill me in…" Billy said. "What have you been up to?"

Grace's attention came back to him.

"Well, I finished my degree the same year you and Tracy left for Denver," Grace said. "And then I, uh—" She glanced down. "I went to Denver, too."

Billy frowned, her words sinking into his gut. "Wait, so you were in Denver the last three years?"

"Yes." She raised her eyes to meet his gaze again, and she looked almost defiant. "I've been substitute teaching, and Denver had more opportunities."

"Yeah..." Billy leaned forward, planting his elbows on the table. "So when I was trying to reach you, you were actually in the city."

"Yes." Pink tinged her cheeks.

"So how come we never saw you?" he demanded. "Why didn't we get together?"

"I was busy?" She shrugged weakly. "We all were busy, Billy. You and Tracy had your life together, and I was trying to do the same."

"Busy?" he shot back. "That's a cop-out, and you know it. I called you a few times. I even left voice mails, and you never called me back. I thought you were here in Eagle's Rest that whole time!"

"You could have tried to visit. You would

have found out otherwise," she replied with a small smile.

"Yeah, Tracy…" He stopped himself. How much to even say? Tracy had been jealous of his friendship with Grace. If he'd suggested going back to Eagle's Rest to see her, Tracy would have picked a fight. He'd learned pretty quickly that Grace was a sore spot for his girlfriend, so he tried not to rock the boat too much. Still, he'd called. He'd tried to reach out to his friend on his own.

"It's okay," Grace said. "Look—you and Tracy left for Denver for a reason. You needed a chance to just be the two of you."

"I never once said I wanted that!" he shot back.

"We don't always say what we want, do we?" she replied with a shrug. "I was giving you space."

Billy looked over at Poppy, who was busy working on a maze, her tongue sticking out the side of her mouth the way it did when she was concentrating.

So Grace had been ignoring him on purpose. And that stung, because when he'd dialed her number, it had been with a sincere desire to connect with her. She'd been his best friend for years, and he had needed more than just a girlfriend in Tracy—he'd needed his rock, his confidant. He'd needed Grace!

"Did Tracy say something to you?" he asked, still trying to sort this out in his head.

"She didn't have to." Grace licked her lips. "Billy, you were moving in with her. That's a huge step, and you had to expect there to be some changes that came along with it. What? Were we supposed to keep up like we used to?"

Yes. That's exactly what he'd hoped. They'd sorted out their friendship through his girlfriends in the past.

"Meaning what?" he asked.

"Movies together, cooking steaks at my place, calling each other day and night when we came across stuff we thought the other would like…?" She shook her head. "That would have been incredibly inappropriate. You needed to be doing that stuff with Tracy, not me."

"Fine. We could have adjusted out routines a bit," he conceded. "But you cut me off. Like completely. Are you saying that a civil cup of coffee was suddenly out of bounds?"

"I'm saying…" Grace sighed. "Billy, I couldn't be your third wheel."

"Third wheel," he scoffed. "You never

cared about that before. You were my best friend!"

"Tracy was different. I needed to take some space for myself, get my own life in order. I'm sorry. I know it was a little heavy-handed of me, but I didn't want to be your pal for the next decade while you moved your life forward with Tracy. You were right—it was time to grow up."

"So, you're saying you couldn't find a boy-friend with me around," he said with a small smile. "Am I that intimidating? Would he pale in comparison or something?"

Grace didn't look amused. "I'm saying that you had Tracy, and I needed to find my own significant other, too. So I did what I needed to. For me."

"Right." He nodded, sobering. A lot more had changed than he'd realized. Somehow, in the last three years of missing Grace, he'd never figured that she'd walked away be-cause it was best for *her*. "So, did you?"

"Did I what?"

"Find your guy." He eyed her, wondering why he felt a pang of jealousy, even as he asked it.

"A few." She laughed softly. "None that stuck."

"Okay." And he was glad to hear that, somehow. He knew it made him a Neanderthal to even feel this way, but Grace had always felt like "his."

"Look, I get it would be hard to watch me go start a life with another woman."

"Oh, really?" she said with a short laugh.

"It would be hard for me to see some guy take over…everything…when it came to you," he conceded.

"You'd have been fine," she said dryly.

"Oh, come on! We had all sorts of little traditions, didn't we? Like ice cream when one of us broke up with someone."

"When *you* broke up with someone," she countered.

"Fine, when I broke up with someone," he said. "And what about making steaks in the fry pan—that was ours."

"That was," she agreed. "Actually, that was mine. You couldn't fry a decent steak if your life depended on it."

He chuckled. "My point is, if I had to watch you move on… I might have felt a little territorial over your pepper-fried steak."

"My steak. Really." This time, there was a glint of humor in her eye.

"Hey, you make a fine steak, woman," he

said with mock solemnity. "And to have another man sampling that tender, perfectly fried goodness… I'm just saying, he might have felt it was weird if I demanded steak, too, whenever he got some."

Grace laughed and shook her head. It was a relief to see that tension break.

"I'm sorry," he added.

"For what?"

"For whatever I did or said that made you feel like you had to give me space."

Grace met his gaze, then shook her head. "Billy, it was just time. I needed a boyfriend, not a buddy. I needed a guy who wanted more than my steak."

Somehow she looked a lot less like a buddy now, though. Gone were the oversize T-shirts and the messy ponytails. She looked…feminine. Soft. These new clothes made a difference. He had to keep his eyes from moving down her figure. But that wasn't the right thing to be noticing right now, either, because he wasn't looking for romance, and even if he were, he wasn't about to mess with the best friendship he'd ever had.

The pizzas arrived, and Poppy looked moodily at the personal-size cheese pizza that Billy handed over to her. The medium pizza to be shared between him and Grace was put in the center.

"I don't want that," Poppy said, staring at the pizza in front of her.

"What?" Billy looked over at his daughter, and he could see her lip starting to quiver as she stared down at the steaming pizza. "You like cheese pizza."

"No! It's a little circle! I want a big pizza, in a triangle!" Poppy said.

"You can have some of ours," Billy said with a shrug.

"No!" Her voice was rising now, and spots of red appeared on her cheeks. Billy felt a wave of panic. What was happening here? "I don't want this!"

"Poppy," he said, lowering his voice. "Come on. It's pizza. Who cares what shape it's in, right?"

In response, Poppy started to cry—but not a quiet cry like he'd seen from her in the past; it was a loud, wailing cry that echoed through the restaurant.

"Poppy, seriously!" he snapped. "Stop that!"

That didn't seem to help, because Poppy threw herself back onto the bench and wailed all the louder.

"I don't want *that*!" she howled, and Billy

shot Grace a horrified look. Here it was—the misbehavior he didn't know how to handle.

"What do I do?" he demanded.

Grace shrugged. A lot of help she was right now! Billy could see the glares of other patrons boring into him, and he looked at the pizza, then at his daughter. Whipping out his wallet, he pulled out enough cash to cover the bill and then some, dropped it on the table, then reached over and scooped Poppy up the way he would a puppy. She flailed her arms and legs, connecting with the table and rattling the plates until he could stand up with her.

"Could we get this to go?" Grace asked, her voice rising above the din. The waitress removed the food from the table, and Billy could feel his anger simmering.

What on earth was this?

"Poppy!" he said firmly. "It's pizza, for crying out loud!"

Poppy was no longer willing to even use words, and she howled as Billy attempted to get her back into her jacket. It didn't work, and he ended up wrapping it around her burrito-style, and pinning her arms to her sides as she wailed into his ear.

The other diners glared in his direction, muttered, and one teenager seemed to be recording it on his cell phone. Great—now his parenting failure could be posted online somewhere. He stalked toward the door and marched outside, not even pausing to see what Grace decided to do. The cold air slapped them, and Poppy paused in her howling, took a few breaths and then started up again.

The door opened behind him, and Grace emerged with two pizza boxes. She shot him a serene smile.

"What *is* this?" he barked, struggling to keep a good hold on his daughter, lest he drop her in her wailing fit. Her face was blotchy and wet with tears, and she was surprisingly strong, arching her back against his grip as she drummed her winter boots against his thigh.

"That, Billy, is a tantrum," Grace said with a shrug. "Get used to those. They come with the territory."

He couldn't say that Poppy hadn't warned him before that she wasn't in the mood for this. But he'd wanted to see Grace, and even with this tantrum, it had been worth it.

GRACE WATCHED BILLY as he stood there with his daughter screaming in his arms. There wasn't much she could do—Billy was already doing it. She didn't envy him this part of the parenting job. But it looked like Poppy had just reached her limit of what she could take for one day, and Grace's heart went out to the poor kid. She wasn't very old, and her whole life had been turned upside down. This tantrum was due.

"She'll cry herself out," Grace said, raising her voice to be heard. "You're doing fine."

"I'm not doing anything!" he retorted, and Billy looked around, mildly panicked.

Grace just shrugged. It was hard to argue anything over that piercing wail, and Grace stood there with the pizzas balanced in front of her, the aroma of cheese, sausage and tomato sauce making her stomach rumble. Poppy might not have wanted that pizza, but Grace was starving.

After a couple of minutes, Poppy started to calm down, and then she subsided into some shuddering sighs and dropped her head against her father's shoulder.

"Are you cold, Poppy?" Grace asked quietly. She put the pizzas down on the hood of the truck and stepped closer to give Billy a hand.

"Let's get you into that jacket," she murmured, and Billy adjusted the girl in his arms so that Grace could maneuver Poppy into her coat and zip it up. Then Grace wiped the tears from Poppy's face and looked into those tired, sad little eyes.

"I don't want it…" Poppy whispered.

"I know, sweetie," Grace said softly. "I think you've had enough, huh?" Poppy didn't answer, and Grace looked up at Billy with a rueful smile. "I think our evening is over."

"Yeah… Sorry." Billy rubbed a hand over his eyes. "I didn't mean for all this to… I mean…"

"Billy, this happens," Grace said. "Welcome to parenting. I think you count as properly initiated now."

Billy laughed softly, and she felt a wave of relief. That's what she'd been aiming at—making him feel better. He met her gaze, and he shot her one of those boyish grins of his.

"Thanks, Gracie. You're the best."

Yeah. That's what he'd always said—and it had never meant what she wanted it to mean.

Grace tried not to think about Billy the next day, as she taught her roomful of rambunctious four-year-olds, but it didn't work. Dinner last night had been a little too much like old times, where they'd had so much fun together and even everyday occurrences had turned into something memorable.

Back then she would read too much into every little gesture and she'd jumped every time he called. She'd put her own plans aside if he wanted to get together, because she wanted to. He'd been her priority, even if she wasn't always his. His girlfriends had always come first—as was expected. They'd suggest some romantic date, and he'd cast Grace that boyish grin and say, "Rain check? You know I'm good for it." And she'd had to pretend she didn't mind. So when he did ask her to do something just the two of them, she made the time because she missed him.

Poppy's tantrum had broken off those old, familiar feelings—and Grace was grateful for that. She'd needed the reality check. This was *not* old times. Back then she could remember going home after hanging out with him, sifting through the details of her evening, wondering if he felt something more this time... When he gave her a hug goodbye, had he held her just a little bit longer? Or was that her imagination? Maybe he meant something more when he said, "You're the best, Gracie." Maybe he'd finally recognized that she was the one for him...

Dumb. That was what she'd been. She wasn't going to put herself through that kind of misery for any man ever again. She'd been stupid before—seeing romantic potential in a man who'd never seen it in her.

Because he hadn't needed years of friendship to see more in Tracy. Tracy had been new in town, and she and Grace had been chummy at their office job at city hall. They'd gotten along well, confided in each other over coffee after work. So Tracy knew that Grace was in love with her buddy, and that had hurt—Tracy's immediate and enthusiastic betrayal when it came to a chance with Billy. And it hadn't taken more than two or three times seeing Tracy for Billy to set his sights on the leggy blonde.

"What does she like? What would impress her?" Billy had asked. "Is she single?"

"Single? Yes...but, not really your type," Grace had hedged.

"Trust me, Gracie, she's my type," he'd said with a grin. "Come on. What's so wrong with her? Or is it me? Am I the wolf in this situation?"

By that time, Grace had seen some new

sides to Tracy's personality—including her ability to betray a friend.

"She's a bit selfish, honestly," she'd told him.

Tracy had been the kind of woman who snapped up what she wanted—friendships notwithstanding. She'd known what she could get, and she'd gone for it. Grace had been the idiot who just waited around.

"I like a woman who looks out for herself," Billy had quipped back. "So…are flowers too much?"

So Grace had done what any good friend would do, and she stood back and watched him fall in love with another woman. Not like she had much choice. Tracy was Grace's polar opposite. She was tall and thin to Grace's shorter stature and more generous proportions. She was fair and blonde to Grace's dark mane. Tracy knew how to flirt rather effectively, and Grace had never figured that out. Tracy was everything that Grace was not. Including thin.

That was when Grace realized what "falling in love" looked like with Billy. And all those nudges, laughs, shared jokes and late-night cell phone conversations between herself and Billy hadn't been love. Or even attraction on his part. It had been friendship. She'd been the fool who was waiting around for it to blossom into something more. He wasn't.

Their dynamic had to end. It was fine when she was young, single and didn't mind if she remained that way for a little while so long as she had Billy in her life. But she was old enough at that point to want a family of her own, and this close friendship with Billy hadn't been enough for her, either. She knew that using up her time with him would make her less available for the kind of relationship she did want. Besides, when she did find a good guy of her own, he wouldn't be okay with this cozy setup she and Billy enjoyed. How could he be? Tracy sure hadn't been. Their dynamic relied on Grace being in love with Billy!

So last night, after Grace went back to her parents' house and went upstairs to her old bedroom, she did the same thing that she'd done three years ago. She vowed to herself that this was it—no more pining for that man. Billy was a friend, and Grace wanted romance, marriage, a few kids of her own. And she wasn't going to get her wishes fulfilled with Billy Austin.

The school day drew to a close, and Grace saw her students off. She stopped to talk to the mother of one little boy who had wet his pants, and the mother of a little girl who was very upset because "Daddy smokes cigarettes and he's going to die!" She must have overheard something at home, because that wasn't a topic they covered this early in school. When the last of the children were gone, Grace went over to sit down next to Poppy at the sand table.

Poppy looked down at the lines she'd drawn in the sand—childish block letters that started out large and squashed down to small and skinny the closer she got to the other side. *Extra special beau*— That was all that fit.

"How was your day, Poppy?" Grace asked.

"Not good." Poppy looked up at Grace somberly.

"No?" Grace said. "I'm sorry."

"I miss my daddy," Poppy sighed, and looked forlornly toward the door. Grace followed her gaze.

The door swung open and Billy appeared, his cowboy hat tucked under one arm. He peered inside with a cautious expression, and Grace felt a wave of relief of her own. He was back…and she was happy for Poppy, not for herself. At least that was what she told herself.

A smile erupted over Poppy's face and she bounced to her feet. "There's Daddy!"

"Hey there, kiddo." Billy came into the room, and he looked relieved to see his daughter, too. He bent down and gathered her up into a hug. "So, how was your day?"

"Terrible," Poppy said, her voice wavering. "Just terrible."

"What happened?" Billy looked a little panicky, and Grace couldn't help but smile at that. He'd been taken off guard by that tantrum last night and seemed to be mildly traumatized still.

"I missed you!" Poppy declared. "That's what happened!"

Billy's shoulders lowered and he nodded a couple of times. "Well, I'm here now."

He put Poppy down and let himself be tugged into the room, and he shot Grace a relieved smile as Poppy pushed him toward a tiny, child-size chair.

"So, how was *your* day?" he asked Grace.

"I signed the papers to accept that teaching position in Denver starting in September," she replied. "I'll be teaching first grade."

"Yeah?" Billy paused, then nodded. "That's great. Really great."

She wished it felt better. "A full-time teaching position is hard to come by these days, so it's a big relief."

"Yeah, I'll bet." Billy met her gaze. "I'm proud of you." His lips quirked up into that heart-stopping grin of his. "Miss Beverly."

His use of her name sounded almost flirtatious, and she met his eye for a moment. She wasn't interested in playing this game. Flirting might pass the time for him, but it only made things harder for her.

"Thanks," she said.

"Seriously," he added.

She smiled faintly. "Yeah, I'm happy with it, too." She looked toward Poppy, who was watching them quizzically, and forced a cheerful smile to her face. "So, are you ready to learn some fun stuff, Poppy?"

"Yep," Poppy agreed.

"Why don't we start with some reading?" Grace suggested. "I've got some fun new words you might like."

She glanced back at Billy and found his eyes locked on her. Heat came to her cheeks, and she turned back to her student. Grace had put together a spelling list for Poppy.

She'd been so keen to know how to spell *extra special beautiful* that Grace had to wonder if she'd enjoy *caterpillar* and *unicorn* just as much.

"Let's go to the whiteboard," Grace said. "I have some magnetic letters that spell a word. It's a fun word! I think you'll like it."

Grace held up a paper bag temptingly, and Poppy's eyes widened.

"Okay!" Poppy skipped up to the board, and then Grace opened the bag and handed her the letters. "Now, I want you to find a letter *C*, and stick it to the board."

Poppy took her time sorting through the letters. She pulled them out, sticking them to one side of the board, frowning at each one. But when Grace glanced over at Billy, she noticed that he was staring at the letters with the same level of intense scrutiny.

"First a *C*…" Grace prompted, and Poppy pulled out a *C* and put it in the center of the board. "Now an *A*…"

Grace walked her through it, and the girl's eyes lit up. "That's how you spell *caterpillar*?"

"Every time," Grace said with a laugh. "I thought you might like that one. Now put those letters back in the bag, give it a good shake and let's see if you can spell it again on your own."

Poppy seemed to like this game, and Grace looked over at Billy again with a grin.

"You tired or something?" she asked.

"Why?" He pulled his attention from the board.

"You're focusing on the board like it's a black hole," she said. "Long day?"

"Uh…" He smiled sheepishly. "Yeah. I guess I'm tired."

"You looked spooked last night," Grace said.

"That was the first tantrum," he said with a small smile. "Took me off guard."

Grace shot him a grin. "You survived."

"I shouldn't have pushed dinner," he said. "I knew Poppy was tired. I did exactly what my mom always did—put my own social life ahead of my kid."

"You're being a little hard on yourself," Grace said. "You took your daughter out for pizza. I mean, not exactly torture."

He shrugged, and then fixed his attention back on the whiteboard once more.

"Cat-er-pill-ar," Grace intoned slowly for Poppy's benefit, then turned back to Billy. "Anyway, about teaching children this young. It can be easier for little kids to deal with letters in a tactile way. It's hard to focus on just a squiggle on the page. I know that Poppy is already really advanced, but holding letters, arranging them…that can be a nice way for a child her age to learn."

"Yeah…" Billy nodded a couple of times. "That…um…makes sense. I might try that with her at home. Where do you get those letters?"

"I have an extra set here if you want to borrow them," Grace said. "They're really useful."

What was with him? Billy had closed off and looked almost uncomfortable, and his gaze was fixed on that board with the letters that his daughter was lining up to spell the word *caterpillar* for the fourth time.

"Can you rearrange those letters to spell other words?" Grace asked. "I bet you could!"

Billy pulled his attention from the board as Grace handed him a plastic box of magnetic letters. He looked down at it for a moment, then nodded quickly.

"Thanks."

"Billy, what's going on?" she asked.

"I'm going to do better than my mom did with me," he said seriously.

"You already are," she said. "Look, I know that teaching a little girl can be a bit daunting, but this makes it easy." She tapped the box in his hands. "Just stick them on the fridge."

"Yeah, yeah, of course." He opened the box and picked up a letter, scrutinizing it for a moment before putting it back. "This just might work…"

It was sweet, really. He was taking this so seriously. He was a first-time parent, tossed into the deep end with a four-year-old girl. So she could appreciate how intimidating that would be. She was used to kids from her job, but Billy wouldn't be. He was used to horses and cattle—a whole different ballgame.

"Don't you remember being a little kid with magnetic letters?" she asked.

"No, I remember being a little kid, watching TV until my mom got home, and being afraid if anyone came to the door because it might be child welfare. That's the kind of thing I remember."

"At four?" She eyed him for a moment.

"Older probably, but still."

Grace heaved a sigh. "Your mom had to work—"

"No, she was dating some loser or another," he replied with a bitter smile. "Every romantic prospect came before I did. And I had to call them all Uncle."

So pizza with her and his daughter brought back those memories? That thought was a heavy one, and Grace looked back toward the whiteboard, where Poppy was sorting through the letters.

"How's your mom doing?" Grace asked quietly, turning back to Billy.

"Fine." His answer was clipped and tight. He didn't want to talk about this. Grace remembered that he and his mom had always had a tense relationship.

"Have you seen her yet?" she pressed.

"Yeah, of course," he said. "I stopped by the bar and she came out to the parking lot to see Poppy. But…no, I haven't visited her properly yet."

"Isn't she why you came back?" she asked, keeping her voice low. "You came for family, right? Who else have you got?"

"I used to have you," he said.

"I'm not family," she said, slightly irritated. He wanted more from her than was fair to ask.

"I know. Sorry, I just…" He dropped his gaze to the box of letters in his hand. "But you're right—I need to reconnect with my mom. Who knows? It might even be good for me."

"Look, Miss Beverly!" Poppy said. "I've got some little words. But I don't want this one anymore. I want a new word!"

She glanced toward Billy, and he shrugged. "Teach the kid a word, Miss Beverly."

She forced a smile. That was why they were here—this was about Poppy.

"Then you need to pull out the letter *U*," Grace said, walking closer to her student. "This is a great word. You're going to love it."

And Billy's attention went back to the board with that laser focus of his. He was going to have to learn to relax—there was no way around it. But what did she know about adjusting to surprise parenthood? She didn't have kids of her own. This was Billy's challenge.

Even with everything that Billy was going through right now, it wasn't all about him. Grace wasn't willing to be the emotional support he needed. She'd been the one he could count on for too many years, and it hadn't gotten her what she'd longed for. He'd just have to stand on his own two feet, like she'd been doing all along.

CHAPTER FIVE

BILLY TOOK THE box of magnetic letters home that night, and he put them on the counter next to the fridge. He sorted through them, holding one letter at a time, enjoying the fact that, individually, the letters made sense. If he put some together, with some space between, he could make out some short words, too. He'd noticed that in the classroom—that those silly magnetic letters seemed to help, somehow.

And he felt foolish, because they were a children's tool. Still, he'd wanted to pick up something while his daughter learned, and it seemed that he had.

Grace had mentioned his mother this afternoon, too, and that had gotten him to thinking. He'd seen her since he'd come back to town only the once, when he'd stopped by to say hi at the bar where his mom worked these days, but he hadn't invited her over. He felt a twinge of guilt. She was his mother, after all. He didn't hate her; he just wanted to parent better than she had. Plus, she still seemed pretty busy with her own life. She'd called him once after he'd returned and they'd had a short conversation where he promised to come see her soon, so maybe it was time he made good on that.

Finally Billy picked up the phone, called her and invited himself and Poppy over for the next evening.

Heather Austin lived in a little rental house in an older part of town. It was a bungalow with brown siding and a carport that was filled on one side with chopped wood. The other side had an assortment of boxes, and Heather's little blue sedan sat out on the drive. Billy parked behind it.

"Here we are," Billy said. "You remember meeting Grandma, right?"

Poppy was silent, and Billy heaved a sigh. His tense relationship with his mom had gotten worse after he'd left town with Tracy. Mom hadn't liked Tracy much, and that had ticked off Billy something fierce. Looking back on it, maybe she'd had a point, but his relationship with his mom hadn't been strong enough for him to hear it. Now he was back, without Tracy, and he wasn't sure how he felt about all this. It would have been easier on his ego if things with Tracy had worked out. At least he wouldn't have had to tell his mom she'd been right.

Billy got out of the truck and opened up the back door to help Poppy down. She was wearing snow pants now and a matching winter coat—all in pink. She'd chosen them herself, along with a toothbrush, and Billy finally felt like he was getting things together. He took her mittened hand and they tramped through the heavy snow together, toward the front door. But before they got to it, it swung open and his mom beamed at them in welcome.

Heather was a petite woman. She wore a low-cut pink sweater that revealed some cleavage and part of a tattoo across the top of her chest. She wore jeans about one size too small. Her hair was cropped short in a spiky modern do, and her makeup was subdued.

"You're finally here!" Heather said. "Well, get on in here, you two."

"Hey, Mom," Billy said, bending down to kiss her cheek as he walked inside. The house was warm and smelled of roasting chicken. As Billy peeled off his winter coat, his mom helped Poppy to get out of hers.

"Do you know who I am?" Heather asked softly.

"You're my grandma," Poppy said solemnly. "I've never had one of them before."

"You're my first grandchild, too," Heather said, then glanced up Billy. "She looks like you, Billy."

Billy looked down at the little face with the big blue eyes. People seemed to say that without much thought. He'd never been blonde in his life, and his eyes were dark.

"Well, let's get you inside, little miss," Heather said. "We have lots of getting to know each other, don't we?"

Poppy reached up to touch the tattoo near Heather's collarbone, and Heather chuckled, bending down to give Poppy a better look.

"That was my birthday present to myself when I turned thirty-five," she said. "It's a long story, and it includes some bad choices, so I won't tell you until you're older."

"Mom…" Billy said warningly.

"I said I wouldn't tell her!" Heather protested, then winked at Poppy.

His mother seemed softer now. Maybe she was more suited to grandmothering than she was to being an actual mom.

"So…how are you, Mom?" Billy asked.

"I'm doing great," she said. "Tips are fantastic these days. I don't know what it is—maybe it's the bulb that burned out by the bathrooms."

"Mom, little ears," he said irritably.

"Grandma looks younger than she really is in dim light, sweetheart," Heather said, bending down to Poppy's level. "And when Grandma looks younger, men tip better."

She tapped Poppy's nose with one finger and gave Poppy a wise look. Poppy stared up at Heather in silence for a beat, then looked over at Billy questioningly.

"How about we not talk about the bar in front of Poppy," Billy said, and Heather shrugged her assent.

"It never hurt you to know how the world worked," she said.

Hadn't it? He'd known far more than he should have. His mother's parenting approach had been one of complete honesty, whether it was age appropriate or not.

"Poppy has just started preschool," Billy volunteered. "And she's got Miss Beverly for a teacher."

"Beverly…as in Gracie Beverly?" Heather's eyebrows shot up. She headed over to peek inside the oven, then turned down the heat on a bubbling pot on the stove.

"Yeah, she's back in town for a few weeks, covering a maternity leave," Billy said.

"If they don't come to the bar, or I don't run into them at the grocery store, I have no idea," Heather said. "Oh, sorry." She pinched her lips shut for emphasis. "No talk of the bar."

"I know about bars…" Poppy said softly.

"What's that?" Billy looked down at Poppy.

"I know about bars," Poppy repeated quietly. "My mommy used to take me to the bar and I waited in the car with my teddy bear."

Billy's heart clenched, and he darted a look at his mother. She stood looking down at Poppy with a grim expression on her face.

"Your mother would leave you in the car when she went into the bar?" Heather asked.

"Uh-huh. I was a good girl. I stayed under the blanket. Except for once, and the police lady found me and Mommy got into trouble." Poppy's eyes filled with tears. "And that's why she went away…"

"No, no!" Billy bent down, but he had no words to comfort his daughter. He didn't understand why Carol-Ann had chosen some modeling gig over her little girl to begin with, and he didn't know how to fix any of this. She'd been leaving Poppy alone in the car while she drank at a bar? The realization was startling. Who did that?

"Let me tell you something, little one," Heather said. "Some people are just messed up. And it sounds like your mother was one of them."

"That's what you've got?" Billy demanded, shooting his mother an exasperated look. Insulting her mom didn't seem like it was helpful right now.

"It's the truth!" Heather retorted. "What else are you going to say? Oh, I know..." Heather looked down at Poppy with a smile. "That'll never happen to you here. Your dad doesn't even drink."

Poppy was silent, her blue gaze moving between Heather and Billy, and Billy heaved a sigh. His daughter had been through more in her few years than he had realized. For all of his resentments when it came to his own mother, Poppy had had it worse.

"Now, I'm making chicken dinner, Poppy. Do you like chicken dinner?" Heather went on.

"Yeah!" Poppy said, some of the life coming back into her.

"Are you a good potato masher?" Heather asked. "Because I need a very good potato masher to help me."

Billy grabbed some plates from the cupboard to set the table while his mom drained the potatoes, tied a too-big apron around Poppy's waist and armed her with a metal masher. This house was a new place—she'd lived in an apartment when he left for Denver. He glanced around the little house, taking in the familiar details, like the old tin tea canister on the counter, the same old CorningWare dishes they'd always had and the same brown recliner Billy used to sit in and watch TV while his mom was working a late shift.

It had been a lonely childhood. He'd raised himself more than anything, and his mother had done her best, but... Billy sighed.

"So, how is Grace?" Heather asked once she got Poppy started with the mashing. She turned toward Billy with a small smile.

"Fine." Billy shrugged. "Great, actually. She's got a new job lined up in Denver, and... yeah, she's great."

He didn't want to say how good it was to see Grace again, or how relieved he was to just sit with her in the pizza place and talk again. She was a relief to be around—no posturing or flirting. Grace was comfortable, a big part of "home." But he'd already started messing things up as a dad because he wanted to be around her so badly, so she wasn't his favorite topic. If he was going to do better than his mom had, then he'd better stop chasing down his own comfort.

"You mentioned that Tracy is out of the picture now," Heather said.

"Yep." He gave a curt nod.

"I always said you should have been with Gracie," Heather said.

"What?" Billy retorted. "No, you didn't. You just said that Tracy was awful."

"I did too tell you that you should have been with Grace. I told you that she was the one girl who treated you nicely and didn't want to use you for something."

"You thought every woman was beneath me, Mom," he said with a short laugh.

"Was I wrong about Tracy?" Heather retorted, her eyebrows raised.

Billy sighed and turned his attention to the contents of the house. There was a new couch—completely mismatched from the recliner—and what looked like a fancy surround sound system.

"You've got some new stuff," Billy commented.

"Well, Gerald takes good care of me," Heather replied.

"Gerald?" Billy frowned. "Who's he?"

"My boyfriend," she said. "He wanted to be here tonight to see you two, but I said it was probably better if I did this alone."

"Good call," he muttered. This was a time for family, not whatever interloper his mother happened to be dating.

"Gerald is a nice guy, Billy. He got me that speaker system for when we watch movies here at home, and he even got the brakes fixed on my car. He's generous."

"Does he live here?" Billy asked, glancing around the house. There was a lot he didn't know about his mom's life now.

"No," Heather replied. "He doesn't. But he's nice. I think you'd like him."

"Hmm."

He'd heard all this a hundred times before. She kept meeting them, and they kept breaking her heart. It shouldn't be a twelve-year-old boy's job to comfort his mom and tell her that she'd meet a better boyfriend than the last one who didn't work out. A sixteen-year-old shouldn't be kicking some drunk jerk out the apartment. A nine-year-old shouldn't be waiting up for his mom to get back from a date after midnight. And then when she did get back, he'd pretend he was asleep on the couch, and she'd kiss his cheek and tiptoe past him to her bedroom. Then Billy would be stuck with his lie, and he'd have to stay there in the dark living room, staring at the curtains and wondering when he could creep back to his own room and the comfort of his bed...

"We've been dating now for almost a year," his mother said, pinning a hopeful look on him. "He's nice."

"You said that already," he replied.

"I was hoping you might want to meet him." She smiled hesitantly. "He's a good one, Billy. Finally."

"Nah," he said with a shake of his head. "I'm busy, Mom. I'm raising a daughter of my own now, and I'm not interested in whatever guy you're dating. Sorry."

He could see the pain in her eyes as he said the words, and he felt like a jerk. But it was true—he'd been through countless boyfriends with her, and it had always been the same. Besides, this was about family—a new granddaughter—not about some outsider who'd smile too big and make uncomfortable jokes that his mother would laugh too hard at.

"Why not?" Heather pressed. "I've met his kids. They're nice. He even has grandkids, and I've met a couple of them, too. It would be appropriate if he could see my son I've been talking about all this time. And Poppy, too…"

"I'm not confusing Poppy any more than she already is," Billy said, keeping his voice low. "Forget it, Mom. I'm glad you like this guy. I hope he works out. But I'm not raising Poppy like you raised me."

"Like I raised you…" she said, breathily, and then she ground her teeth together.

"She's not meeting your boyfriends. I'm glad you've got someone, but Poppy is going to have a little more stability."

"Oh…" Tears misted Heather's eyes. "Okay then. Gotcha."

His mother turned away from him and took the masher from Poppy's hand to finish the job herself. A wave of regret crashed over him, and he heaved a sigh. His anger was rooted in that impotent protectiveness he felt for his mother. It hadn't mattered how much he wanted to save her from heartbreak, she'd waltzed right back into it. And it had never mattered if Billy wanted to shelter her from more disappointment, because he couldn't stop her, or the idiots she dated, from starting up all over again. He'd loved his mother so deeply and wanted to shield her from every hurt, but he'd been a kid and had no power to protect her. Now that he was an adult and might actually be able to do something, he realized he had no right to interfere.

But Poppy—she'd be the one who'd be caught in the middle and have her little heart torn out every time Grandma cried over some lost boyfriend. And Billy *could* protect his daughter. That was where he had both the capability to shelter her and the right to stand between her and the confusing adult world.

"Chicken dinner!" Poppy sang out as she hopped down from the kitchen chair she'd been standing on to reach the counter, and Heather gave the bowl another going over with the masher before she carried the potatoes to the table.

Billy felt bad. He hadn't meant to insult his mother, but there was so much they'd never needed to talk about that was bubbling up now that Poppy was in the picture.

"Mom—" Billy started.

"Son, would you please get the chicken out of the oven?" Heather said briskly.

"Yeah, sure." He grabbed a pair of oven mitts from the counter and pulled out a perfectly roasted chicken. He carried it to the table, where a cork pad waited.

"We're going to say grace before we eat," Heather said.

"Since when?" Billy asked with a short laugh. Was this from her boyfriend?

"Since this is my home and I'm still your mother!" Heather retorted. "Now sit down."

Billy did as he was asked, and he looked across the table at Poppy, who watched him with wide eyes. This was a whole new dynamic for her to witness. Whatever—he couldn't change people. He met Poppy's serious gaze and winked at her. A smile crept over her face. Heather might be his mom, but Billy was now a dad. He couldn't protect Poppy from everything, but that didn't mean he wouldn't try.

By MIDMORNING, GRACE knew she needed to meet with the mothers of two of her students who needed some extra help. One wasn't potty trained yet, and preschool wasn't the place for potty training. The other was a biter. Her job was to help the kids conquer their challenges, but some challenges required a little more parental participation than others.

Still, if she was meeting with parents for more than a quick chat, she wouldn't be able to give Poppy her lesson right after school, so she called Billy at morning recess. She'd normally just text someone, but Billy was quirky that way—he never answered texts or even bothered to check them. He'd always figured if something was important enough, the person would call. She'd always teased him that he was an old guy in a young body.

She dialed his number.

"Yeah," he said—Billy's way of picking up.

"Hi," she said. "How's it going over there?"

"Hey, Gracie." His voice softened, and she shut her eyes, trying to steel herself against that flood of emotion she no longer wanted to feel.

"I have some meetings this afternoon," Grace said. "So I need to cancel our tutoring session."

"No problem," he said. "Why don't you come over here when you're done? Come for supper. I'll surprise you with something good."

She was curious to see where he was staying—if she were being brutally honest. A man's home was personal. It said a lot about him, and in some ways, this felt like old times—when she was welcomed into his personal space, and she'd feel closer to him than ever before...

But not this time around. Billy would offer dinner. He'd cook up something delicious and insist she try it. He'd pick up some ice cream she wouldn't be able to refuse, and they'd sit with the tub between them and two spoons... She could already see where this would go.

"No," she said, more curtly than she'd intended, and then she cleared his throat. "Not for supper."

"No?" He didn't sound daunted. "After supper, then?"

"I could do that," she agreed. Why was she agreeing? But saying no—it was hard with Billy. "How about seven?"

"Seven works." His voice was so deep and warm, and she hated that. She couldn't be the only woman who melted for it, and reminding herself of that seemed to help.

"What's the address?" she asked, and as he recited it for her, she jotted it down. Poppy still needed her lessons, and even if she was looking forward to seeing Billy this evening, she'd steel herself against his charms. Their relationship didn't mean the same thing to him as it did to her.

So after her meetings and a quick supper at home with her parents, Grace headed back out into the cold winter evening. She put the address into her GPS and followed the mechanical voice out of town and toward the foothills.

As she pulled into the long drive that led up to the Ross Ranch, she glanced down at the directions around the property. He was staying in a cabin just behind the canteen, rather than in the main house. She stopped twice to get directions from various workers, and when she finally pulled up to the cabin, she heaved a sigh.

The curtain in the window flicked and Poppy looked out. She waved happily. Then Billy's face appeared far above hers and he shot Grace a grin as she got out of her car. The front door opened as she came up to the step, and Poppy hopped joyfully from foot to foot in the warm glow of the doorway.

"Hi, Poppy," Grace said. "Are you ready to learn?"

"Yep!" Poppy said. "I'm ready! I had my supper, and I brushed my teeth, and I took my bath, and now Daddy says I can learn stuff."

Billy tugged Poppy back out of the doorway to let Grace inside, and as Grace took off her boots and coat, Poppy danced around in excitement. Grace looked around the cabin—it wasn't very big. The main room included a sitting area and the kitchen, and there were two closed doors that she imagined led to bedrooms. It was cozy, and she could still smell the aroma of supper in the air—mac and cheese, if she wasn't mistaken.

"Did you find it okay?" Billy asked, holding up his cell phone. "I was prepared to come out looking for you, if I had to."

"I asked a couple of different cowboys for directions," she said with a shrug.

"Long day?" Billy took her coat and hung it up for her. He then headed for the kitchen side of the room. He had a simmering pot on the stove, and he poured the steaming water into a teapot.

"Yeah. I had a meeting with some parents. That's never easy."

"No?" He shot her a rueful smile.

"Not you, of course," she added cheekily. "You're the exception."

"Aren't I always." He chuckled. "Sorry, I don't have a kettle. One more thing on my list of stuff to pick up the next time I'm in Walmart."

"No worries," she said. But from the look of it, Billy had been picking up stuff for his daughter—the new snowsuit, a pair of fluffy slippers, what looked like a new stuffed dog on the couch. He'd just had to prioritize, and she could understand that. He was a dad... It was both strange to see Billy in this role, but also right. He'd always had a soft heart.

That old pang of familiar longing rose up, and she did her best to push it back down. She wasn't here to joke and cozy up with Billy like old times. She was here for her pupil, and she wouldn't get distracted.

"I've got some books we can read together today," Grace said, picking up her bag and opening it. "I think you'll like these ones, and I thought you could read them to your daddy—to give you both some practice at that."

Billy eyed her for a moment, then tossed a tea bag into the teapot.

"Don't worry about me," he said. "You two can get started."

"Daddy reads them wrong," Poppy said. "Every time."

"Does he tease you?" Grace asked with a laugh. She'd never seen Billy read a book in her life, but she was pretty sure he could make an exception for his little girl. Besides, reading together would help the two of them bond.

"Yeah, he teases," Poppy said with a sigh. "He should read them right, shouldn't he, Miss Beverly?"

"I'm going to have to insist, Billy," she said with a grin of her own. "Come on. When Mrs. Powell comes back from maternity leave, she's not going to have as much free time as I seem to have. She'll have a new baby waiting for her at a day care, remember? So I'm going to have to show you how to give Poppy a bit of a challenge."

"Uh, yeah…" Billy nodded, grabbed a couple of mugs and filled them with tea. "You want sugar?"

The mugs steamed temptingly.

"Sure," she said.

Billy scooped a couple of teaspoons of sugar into each mug, gave them a stir and then brought one over to her. He sank into the couch, next to Grace, and she took a sip, glancing over at him.

"And your dad won't tease you this time," Grace said with some mock firmness. "Right, Billy?"

Billy smiled ruefully, but didn't answer.

"So, this first book is about a princess," Grace went on, putting her mug down on a side table. Billy was so close, his muscular arm just inches from hers. He smelled musky and warm, and she felt that old temptation to just lean up against his rock-hard shoulder...

Instead Grace patted the space on the couch between her and Billy. "Do you want to come sit here, Poppy?"

Poppy squeezed in and picked up the book. A small child was about as good of a buffer zone as a woman could ask for, and Grace looked over Poppy's head at Billy, who was staring down at the book, his expression granite. Poppy scanned the first page, flipped it, scanned the next...flipped again.

"Poppy, we're going to read out loud," Grace said.

"I just wanted to see how it ends," Poppy said, and Grace shook her head and laughed. This little girl was so bright, and she wanted to keep rushing on ahead. Teaching a gifted child to slow down and go deeper—that was the real challenge.

Billy leaned forward, resting his elbows on his knees, and he pressed his lips together. His gaze flickered from the page to his daughter, then back to the page again. He looked...daunted. For once Billy Austin had met his match...in a four-year-old.

"I might not be good at this," Billy said quietly, and he shot Grace a pleading look over Poppy's head.

"Oh, this is the easy stuff, Billy," she said. "You aren't dealing with boyfriends and body-image issues. This is story time. It's fun."

"Yeah, right." He didn't look convinced, so Grace plunged on.

"You'll want to have her practice reading by pointing to each word. I've noticed that she'll speed ahead to figure out what happens, but she'll miss out on details. It's a common thing for exceptional readers—sometimes they need help slowing down, ironically enough."

"Uh. Yeah. Okay." Billy cleared his throat.

Was it her? Was he less comfortable around Grace than he'd been before? Maybe she was expecting too much. She'd been blaming him for acting like nothing had changed, but maybe Grace was the one with the problem there.

"Billy..." Grace eyed him curiously. "Is it weird because I'm here? I mean, I could just leave the books, and you and Poppy could—"

"No," he interrupted. "Let's start."

The little girl wriggled around a little bit and flipped open the cover. It was a picture book—not a very high reading level, but the story had some depth to it, and Grace was hoping to introduce Poppy to the idea of deeper reading.

"So, Poppy, let's start on the first page, and your dad is going to put his finger under each word as you read it. That means you have to read as slowly as he moves. Okay? That's going to be hard for you, I think."

"I have to go slow?" Poppy grimaced.

"Just for a page or two," Grace said. "Then you can read as fast as you want."

"The Princess Who Hated Pickles," Poppy read as Billy moved his finger under the title. "By Francine Wells. Illustrated by..."

"We could probably just move to the first page," Grace said with a chuckle.

Billy's face colored and he flipped the

page. His finger moved under the words, but he didn't slow or pause in the intuitive places, so Poppy read on as he moved his finger beneath the lines. He seemed to be pointing to the words almost blindly. What was happening here? Was he that uncomfortable? Or was there a bigger problem?

After a couple of pages of the same behavior, Grace put her hand on top of Billy's. He froze.

"Okay, Poppy," Grace said. "Now I want you to move your finger under the words for your dad to read, okay? But you need to move along slowly enough so that when he reads, it sounds normal, okay? Can you do that?"

Billy pulled his hand back from under her touch.

"Maybe you guys can carry on here—" he started.

"Daddy!" Poppy pleaded. "Come on. You have to do it, too!"

Poppy put her finger under the first word on the page. Billy looked stricken—horrified, almost—as her finger moved along the sentence.

"Daddy, come on!" Poppy pleaded.

"The…um…princess decided she didn't

want to marry a prince after all. She liked mechanics better," he said.

"Daddy, that isn't right at all," Poppy declared. "You've got to do it right. Tell him, Miss Beverly! Tell him he has to do it right!"

Billy's gaze flickered up toward Grace hesitantly. He hadn't been teasing. She could tell. He looked nervous, uncertain, even.

"Hey, I think a princess and a mechanic make a pretty good match," Billy said with an exaggerated smile and shrug. But the joke came a few beats too late.

"Miss Beverly!" Poppy said, tears coming to her eyes. "He's teasing again…"

But Grace had recognized something she'd never noticed before in all their years of friendship.

"Billy, what do you see when you look at that page?" Grace asked softly.

"It's just a silly little story. I make it more fun," Billy said, but his smile faltered. "I'm just playing around. Sorry, Poppy. You guys go on. I'm not much into princesses, I guess."

Poppy stared at her father with big, tear-filled eyes, and Grace saw Billy wince as he looked at his daughter's disappointed little face. He didn't mean to pester her and tease. He didn't *want* to. And she suddenly knew why.

"Poppy, why don't you read ahead and see how it ends," Grace said. "Maybe your dad could show me where the milk is in the fridge."

Grace stood up, grabbed her mug of tea and headed toward the tiny kitchen. When she got to the fridge, Billy came up behind her. He stood close enough that she could feel his presence, and when she turned, she had to tip her chin up to look him in the face. He shot her a guilty look.

"Billy, what do you see on that page?" she asked quietly.

"I…um…" Billy swallowed, and he met her gaze for a moment.

"Just tell me," she whispered.

"It kind of swims around. Maybe I need glasses."

"No, glasses would be if the words were blurry," she countered. "But you say the words swim. Do the letters seem to get jumbled up on the page?"

He was silent.

"You understand the basics of reading, right? But something happens to the letters on the page—" She was reaching here, and she knew it. But she'd studied this—and dyslexia was incredibly common.

Billy shot her a tortured look that clamped around her heart. He shrugged. "Yeah, it kind of gets all mixed up there, and it takes too long to make sense of it, and…"

His voice trailed off, and crimson colored his cheeks. He dropped his gaze and rubbed a hand over the rough stubble on his chin.

"You have trouble reading," she concluded quietly. "I never realized… I feel like I should have…"

And suddenly all sorts of details came flooding back to her—details that now made perfect sense, like how he never looked at a menu or tried a new restaurant. He never texted. He claimed to need glasses, but never got them. He preferred movies, and whenever he needed to look something up online, he'd pass Grace his phone and ask her to do it for him. There was always a reason—he was driving, he couldn't see the small lettering… He'd gotten adept at avoiding reading, and somehow Grace had missed it. She had been his best friend and had been taking college courses online to become a teacher, and she'd never noticed!

"Dads are supposed to read stories," he said, his voice low. "It's what they do."

"One of many things that dads do," Grace countered.

"Yeah, that, and make the money to give their children a good life..." His voice tightened, and he swallowed hard. "But the main one—bedtime stories—I'm no good at it. And my own kid thinks I'm an idiot."

CHAPTER SIX

GRACE LOOKED OVER to where Poppy sat on the couch, the book open on her lap. She could see Billy in that little girl's form. She had the same pensive look that Billy got when he was frustrated—the drilling gaze, that way of chewing the inside of her cheek.

Poppy slapped the picture book shut and heaved a loud sigh. She looked over at the bag of books on the floor, where Grace had been sitting. Grace could feel the girl's curiosity emanating from across the room, but Poppy didn't move toward the bag. She sat motionless, staring at the bag, chewing the side of her cheek.

"You can see what other books I brought," Grace said, raising her voice so Poppy could hear her. "Go ahead!"

Poppy looked back at Grace solemnly. "But maybe I should save them, so I don't run out."

"Sweetie, there's a whole library filled

with books. You don't need to worry about that."

"Yeah?" Poppy brightened. "Okay!"

Poppy squirmed off the couch and landed on the ground, next to the book bag. Along with the picture books, Grace had brought a children's classic, *The Secret Garden*. She wasn't sure if Poppy would have the attention span for such a long book, but she'd figured Billy could read it to her... Billy pulled a hand through his tousled hair. "Let's not talk about this. I never meant for you to know. I'll figure something out."

He was pulling away from her.

"She doesn't think you're an idiot," Grace interrupted.

"No, she thinks I'm a jerk who keeps teasing her," he retorted. "And I hate that, too. Because teasing her is the only way I can distract her from the fact that her dad can't even read those little picture books she whips through in a minute flat."

"Dyslexia isn't about intelligence," she countered.

"Tell that to a four-year-old," he muttered.

"I think you should!" she said. How long did he think he could hide this from a curious little girl? Kids picked up on way more than adults ever realized.

"Gracie, you always mean well," Billy said, those dark eyes fixing on her. "But no."

"Would you rather drive her crazy with teasing?"

"I don't know!" he snapped. "But I know for sure, I don't want to tell *my kid* that I can't read!"

Grace blinked, then pressed her lips together. His kid. Yes, that was what this came down to. Grace didn't have any say in this. She'd never been a part of the romantic side of his life, and when a child emerged, she wasn't a part of making these decisions, either.

"Fine—the parenting is your call," she said after a beat of silence. "But how did I not know this?"

"I didn't want you to." His voice was low and gruff.

"You couldn't trust me?" she asked quietly. "I was… You and I…" How to even encapsulate their relationship in a few words? They'd been everything to each other—at least he'd been to her. She'd have helped him.

"Look, a guy doesn't tend to advertise something like that," he said with a shake of his head. "I'm not a moron. I work with my hands. I don't need books out there, in the saddle. I use my instincts! I'm a good cowboy."

"I know." Grace eyed him uncertainly.

"For the record."

"I'm not sure I want to know this, but—" she swallowed "—did Tracy know?"

"Yeah."

Grace tried to hide the sting of his answer, and she dropped her gaze, trying to tamp down the hurt so he wouldn't see it. He'd told Tracy...not her. Tracy was the one who was selfish and coy, who hadn't been willing to stand by him if it meant being a stepmom, and he had opened up to *her*?

"And you wouldn't tell *me*?" Grace couldn't help the bitterness that oozed out of her tone.

"She only found out once we were in Denver," he replied. "She kept pestering me about why I did things the way I did, and I couldn't take it anymore. I mean, I was supposed to tell her anyway, wasn't I? We were living together! That's what couples do— they share their stuff."

"I guess it isn't my business..."

Tracy had a part of Billy that Grace had

never had access to—his romantic side. She got to share a life with him, a home, a bathroom, even! What Grace wouldn't have given for a chance at sharing some simple couple routines with him—a favorite cereal, or doing the dishes together. But he'd looked right past her and he'd given those things to Tracy, so why not his deepest secrets, too?

"When I told her, she was mad because I couldn't go for the better-paying jobs, and rent was expensive, and she was stressed out—"

"It isn't your fault, though," Grace interrupted.

Billy bit the side of his cheek, his gaze turning inward for a beat or two. Grace watched him, wondering why he'd been so blind to Tracy's true character. Were long, slim legs and that tiny waist of hers really worth it?

"I should have told her sooner, she said." Billy shrugged. "I guess, if she'd had all the information, maybe she could have thought better of moving in with me."

"That's what she said?" Grace asked.

"Of course not..." He sighed. "Look, I tried calling you then, because I wanted..." He stopped, licked his lips.

"Wanted what?" she breathed.

He didn't answer right away, but he smiled weakly. "Moral support, I guess. You didn't pick up. Or call me back."

"I know…" Still, he'd told Tracy first. "She didn't deserve your secrets, you know. You could have told me, Billy…"

"Why?" he said with a shake of his head.

"I could have helped!" she shot back. "I'm a teacher, for crying out loud!"

"Teachers tried," he replied.

"You could have told me so that I'd have at least understood," she pressed. "Of all people, I really cared!"

"Maybe I didn't want to be one of your students," he shot back.

Grace stared at him, then shook her head. "What misery that would have been," she said, irony dripping from her tone. "I'm a good teacher, you know."

"I'm not a kid, Gracie." And he looked at her with agony shining in his eyes. "I liked things the way they were between us— friends, equals. We were special, you and me. I didn't want to become the project you were trying to fix."

"Students aren't projects," she argued. "You never would have been that to *me*."

"Yeah? Well, they aren't buddies, either. There's this...distance...between a teacher and a student. It's all professional—big smiles, hearty encouragement. I wasn't going there with you."

She saw hot defiance in his dark eyes. He hadn't wanted that distance between them... but he also hadn't wanted to close that gap, either. He saved that for other women.

"At least I cared!" she whispered hoarsely.

Billy's gaze softened, and he reached out and moved a tendril of hair away from her face so tenderly that her heart skipped a beat. His rough fingers brushed against her temple.

"I should have told you," he murmured. "Thing is, I might not be educated, or smart, but I'm definitely a man. I just wanted to keep feeling like one." His voice was so low and deep, she almost didn't hear it. His fingers still brushed against her cheek...

Three years ago, she would have moved right into the moment and seen if that tenderness might turn into a kiss, but not anymore. Grace dropped her gaze and stepped back, her face cold where his hand had been.

He dropped his hand to his side and heaved a sigh.

"Sorry," he murmured.

"For what?" she asked, forcing lightness to her tone.

Across the room, Poppy had found the copy of *The Secret Garden* and was hunched over it.

If Grace had been the one who cared about him all along, then why hadn't he ever looked deeper? That was the problem—it always had been. He wanted her support, her friendship, to be her priority... He just didn't want to tell her too much.

Was that what friendship was to him? Because in her heart, she'd sailed right past friendship. What she'd offered him—that hadn't been simply being his buddy, and she had no one to blame for that but herself.

Now he needed her. Now he had no one else to distract him. But give him another leggy blonde, and he'd be gone again. She wasn't stupid, and she wasn't about to let him feel all male and testosterone-driven with her.

"Gracie..."

She looked back over at Billy to find him watching her with a tentative look on his face.

"I can teach you to read," she said quietly. That was something she could offer for the sake of their friendship. "I could do it at the same time I'm teaching Poppy. I can get you started at least."

"I don't want to be your student," he countered.

"It isn't the same," she said. "This would be…a friend lending a hand. Nothing more. I'm not going to be here more than two weeks. It's like you teaching me to ride a horse."

"Excepting reading isn't a hobby," he said.

"To a lot of people it is. I can teach you. If you want."

"Yeah?" He frowned slightly, looking toward his daughter once more. "You think I could learn?"

"I'm positive."

Billy's eyes were trained on his daughter as a myriad of emotions battled across his face. He didn't feel for her the way he'd felt for Tracy, or even Carol-Ann. But he needed her right now, and she didn't require payment in the form of some temporary romance. It wasn't her job to make him feel like a man, but she could teach him how to read.

"Okay," he said at last. "I'll do it for Poppy. I'll give it a try."

For Poppy. It was a good reason. He'd kept his secrets all those years, and in fairness, she'd kept hers. She'd been in love with her best friend, and since when was that ever a good idea?

THAT EVENING AFTER Grace left, Billy sat on the couch, waiting while his daughter changed into her pajamas. He leaned forward, resting his elbows on his knees. What had he done tonight? Images of Grace were still seared into his mind, but this wasn't the Grace from years of friendship.

Not that it should even matter right now. What did he have to offer a woman like Grace? He'd outed his illiteracy. That was the first dumb thing he'd managed. And secondly he'd looked down into Grace's eyes, and he'd seen something he hadn't seen before—

"Don't be an idiot," he muttered to himself.

Grace had never been the girlfriend type. She'd been his buddy, but she was dressing differently now, and there was a different air of competence about her that he couldn't ignore. She wasn't the same old Gracie. She'd always been soft, and suddenly those soft

curves were drawing his eye in a way that
had never been part of their friendship in the
past. He'd always thought she was pretty and
figured the guy she landed would be a lucky
devil, but he'd never considered her for himself. But when he looked down at her there
in the kitchen, he'd been imagining kissing
her—stupid as that might have been. He was
a brand-new dad, and already messing things
up with his daughter because he wanted to
spend time with Gracie—this was not when
he should be messing around with romance.
His mother had proven just how disastrous
that could be for a kid. It sounded like Carol-
Ann hadn't been much better.

But three years had changed Grace from
a buddy into a woman. How had that happened?

Grace had left a few minutes ago, after
reading a chapter of *The Secret Garden* aloud
to Poppy. His little girl had settled right down
and leaned against Grace's shoulder in such
quiet happiness. This kid loved being read to.

And now Billy was left with the memory
of Grace rattling around in his head. And
not just the comfort of her friendship. Tracy
had always been jealous of Grace, and he'd

never really understood why... But now he thought he could see it.

Poppy came out of her bedroom clad in her new unicorn pajamas. She had a book under one arm and the blanket from her bed clutched in the other hand.

"I want to read this one," Poppy said, holding up the book. She passed it over to him and squirmed up onto the couch, next to him.

"Okay. But you never like how I read," he said, grabbing the blanket and draping it around his daughter.

"You need the blanket, too," Poppy said, nudging a corner onto his knee. "Then we'll both be cozy."

"Okay, we'll both be cozy." Billy looked tenderly down at his little girl. She wouldn't stay this small—that's what everyone kept telling him. In the short time she'd been with him, he'd already noticed signs of her getting older, slightly more mature in her views of things. Her vocabulary sure was growing!

"Now, you read the story, Daddy," Poppy said. "But no silly business. You have to read it right, or I'll tell Miss Beverly."

"You'll tell on me?" he chuckled.

Suddenly her lip quivered and she shook her head. "No, I won't tell on you..."

Her eyes were wide and her cheeks paled. How many times had her mother asked her to keep secrets? He had no idea, but if she'd been left inside a parked vehicle while her mother went into the bar, then he had a feeling there were more secrets this girl had been keeping. He'd gotten some lectures of his own as a kid. *Don't tell anyone you're home alone in the evenings, son, or they'll take you away from me!* And he'd been scared to death of someone finding out how much his mom left him on his own. Moms didn't have to be perfect, or even functional, for their kids to love them with their whole hearts.

"Poppy, you don't have to worry," Billy said. "You're with me now, and no one is going to take you away. Is that what you're afraid of?"

Poppy was silent. She dropped her gaze to the book and started to pick at the corner with her small, pale fingers.

"I'm not ever going to ask you to keep secrets," Billy said. "Not a single one. Okay? Because I'm not going to do anything that would get me into trouble. So you can tell Miss Beverly anything you want. I'm a good dad, and I'm going to stay that way."

Poppy eyed him for a moment. "Mommy went away, though."

"Yeah," he said softly. "But we're going to call her tonight and see if she can talk a little bit, okay?"

"We'll call Mommy?" Poppy asked, brightening.

He'd tried calling Carol-Ann a few times on the cell number she'd given. They'd talked once when Poppy was asleep already. It had been one of those one-sided conversations in which Carol-Ann shouted into her phone, the sound of a party blaring behind her.

"But story time first," Billy said. "You've got to read to me."

"No, Daddy, it's the other way around," Poppy said solemnly. "You read to me. That's how it works. I know that because, in stories, the daddies always read to the children. That's the way it works."

He looked down at her for a moment, uncertain of what he'd even do. But then, before he could think better of it, he said, "I don't know how, Poppy."

"Yes, you do!" she said with a shake of her head. "You just read it right, and stop being silly!"

If only it were that easy. He wasn't the

kind of guy who pestered a little girl for entertainment. He loved this kid, and he wanted to do just as she asked.

"When I was small like you, I didn't learn to read," he said slowly. "And when I went to school, it didn't… It was hard."

Poppy frowned, looking up at him.

"See, Poppy, when I look at the words, they get all jumbled up for me, and I've been making the story up instead of reading it because—" a lump closed his throat "—because I can't."

"Daddy, you don't know how to read?" Poppy whispered.

Billy's heart ached, and he looked away from her. "Nope."

"I can show you how," Poppy said hopefully. "It's easy!"

"Well…" Billy rubbed a hand over his chin. "Miss Beverly says she can show me some tricks that might help while she's teaching you. Would you mind sharing Miss Beverly with me?"

"Okay." Poppy slid closer to Billy again and leaned her cheek against his arm. "We still need a bedtime story, though, Daddy."

"How about I tell you one?" Billy said

hopefully. "Then you can read your book in bed."

Poppy nodded, and Billy slid his arm around her, racking his brain for a story.

"Once upon a time, when I was a little boy," Billy began, "there was a boy in my class who used to pick his nose."

"You aren't supposed to," Poppy said.

"Well, I know that, and you know that, but this kid didn't," Billy said with a low laugh. "And one day, he was caught picking his nose by a big bully."

"Was it you who picked your nose, Daddy?" Poppy asked solemnly.

Billy eyed her for a moment, then sighed. "Yes."

"Okay, go on. What happened?"

Billy chuckled. He might not have stories from books in his head, but he had a whole lot of life experience. He still had wisdom to pass along to his daughter, and some of it was pretty simple, like don't pick your nose in first grade.

After he told his story, he grabbed his cell phone and dialed Carol-Ann's number. It rang five times, and then she answered, sounding groggy.

"Do you know what time it is?" she growled into the phone.

"Carol-Ann, it's Billy," he said.

"Oh." Her tone softened somewhat. "It's like…three in the morning here, and I am seriously hungover…"

"Sorry." He winced. "Poppy wanted to say hi."

"Yeah?" Carol-Ann sighed. "Okay. Put her on. But tell her to talk softly. My head is going to explode."

Billy passed the phone over to his daughter, and Poppy put it against her ear, tears welling in her eyes. "Mommy? It's me. I miss you. When are you coming back?"

There was a pause while Poppy listened, holding her breath.

"But I miss you," Poppy whispered. "I don't want to see you on TV. I want to see you here!" Silence again as Poppy listened. "But I miss you…"

Poppy's tears fell and she threw the phone back at Billy, then ran to her bedroom, her quilt dragging after her. Billy watched his daughter go, then picked up the phone.

"Carol-Ann?" he said. "What did you say to her?"

"I said I have a chance to be something,"

Carol-Ann said. "Billy, I wasn't much of a mom back in the States, anyway. You might as well know it. But explain it to her. It's better this way—I'll have a real chance at a career in modeling. That doesn't come easy. Maybe you can send her out on a plane in a few months to visit me."

Sending his four-year-old on a plane to Germany. Yeah. Not likely.

"She needs to see you," he said. "Pictures even. Maybe you could text me some selfies or something, and I can at least show her pictures of her mom."

"Yeah, I'll do that," Carol-Ann said. "And send me some pictures of her, too! I know this is going to be a hard wait, but it's worth it…"

"I don't think it is," he said quietly.

Carol-Ann was silent. "Fine. Whatever. I'm going back to sleep. Tell Poppy I love her."

Love—it was more than a word; it was an action. And Carol-Ann had no idea what love was if she could walk away from her four-year-old for a modeling gig. His daughter was going to carry the scars from this for the rest of her life.

"I'm going to fight you for custody when

you come back," he added quietly. He hadn't planned on threatening her with this, but he realized in the moment that it was true. When Carol-Ann came back to the States, there would be no picking up where she had left off. Poppy needed a safe home, with a parent who would put her first. And now that he knew about his little girl, he wasn't going away again.

"Stop being dramatic," Carol-Ann sighed. "I'll send pictures, all right? When I get up. In the morning. Thanks for everything, Billy. I appreciate it."

Billy hung up the phone without another word. Then he pushed himself to his feet and headed for Poppy's bedroom. He paused at her door and knocked on the frame softly.

"Hey, kiddo," he said. "Can I come in?"

Being a dad was going to be more than buying snow pants and figuring out how to do her hair. It was going to mean manning up in every way possible for her. He'd be the father she needed. He'd make up for Carol-Ann's insufficiencies and he'd give Poppy all the security and love that made for a good childhood.

This wasn't about child welfare services anymore, if it ever was. This was about his daughter. And one of these days, he was going to read his daughter a bedtime story. Poppy deserved the whole package.

Maybe Grace was right—he should have opened up to her sooner. Maybe she could help him to be the father he longed to be, if he could just keep things balanced properly. He needed his friend.

CHAPTER SEVEN

GRACE STOOD IN the lineup at Dark Roast, Eagle's Rest's best coffee shop. The hiss of a milk steamer floated across the shop, and the comforting aroma of coffee wrapped itself around her. It was Saturday morning, and she hadn't slept well the night before, her mind spinning over yesterday's revelation. Billy couldn't read…and she felt somewhat responsible for not having noticed. She'd always thought of herself as a natural teacher, but to have missed something so glaring in her best friend? It was humbling, both in her teaching instincts and in what she thought about their friendship. She wouldn't have been able to keep that kind of secret from him, though she'd hidden her unrequited love. That was another kind of secret altogether.

And then there was that moment by the fridge when he'd admitted he should have told her… Had there been something more to that? She'd seen the warmth in his eyes, and then there was the way he'd touched her face…

Why was she letting herself do this again? There had been other times when they'd had a connection like that, and it had never blossomed into anything. She was irritated with herself for even allowing herself to overanalyze the situation. Not again. She was supposed to be past that.

The line moved forward, and Grace scanned the menu board. She always ordered the same thing—chai tea with cream and sugar, and a bagel. It was comfort food, and this morning she needed it more than ever.

She pulled a hand through her hair and loosened her scarf. She wore a pair of leggings this morning, embroidered up the calf with twining crimson roses. She'd paired them with an oversize charcoal-gray sweater and a crimson scarf at her neck. She used to wear a lot of black—but not like this. Before it was jeans, and T-shirts and hoodies in muted colors that wouldn't draw attention. Now if she wore black, it was to offset a favorite scarf or to make a jeweled belt sparkle. Her time in Denver had opened her eyes to a lot of things—namely, that her size wasn't a liability. She could dress well, look fantastic and draw the male eye just as well as thin women could. It was all about confidence…and shopping in the right stores that she hadn't had access to here in Eagle's Rest.

Was that the difference in her that Billy had noticed—something as shallow as fashion?

"Gracie?"

Grace looked up to see an older woman just leaving the front of the line with a to-go cup of coffee in her hands. Grace knew her immediately—it was Heather, Billy's mom. She didn't have any makeup on other than mascara, and she looked tired. Her hair was styled into her regular spiky do, and she wore a pair of jeans and a bulky coat.

"Hi, Miss Austin," Grace said with a smile.

"Oh, come on, we're adults now. When are you going to call me Heather?" Heather stopped where Grace stood. "I heard you're teaching my granddaughter."

"I am." Grace smiled. "She's a real cutie. Congrats on the surprise grandchild, by the way."

Heather rolled her eyes. "That was a

bombshell. But she's a cutie, all right. You want to stay and chat a bit?"

"Sure," Grace said. "Let me just order, and I'll come over."

Heather headed for a table, hanging her purse over the back of a chair, then peeling off her jacket. Grace didn't have much else to do today, and while chatting with Billy's mom didn't exactly equal avoiding her feelings for the man, it was better than sticking inside her own head.

Once she had her order, she headed back to the table where Heather was waiting.

Heather hadn't changed a bit in the last three years, which was comforting in its own way.

"So, tell me everything," Heather said as Grace sank into the chair opposite her. "How have you been? Broken any hearts lately?"

Grace chuckled. "Not really. But I've been good. I'm a teacher now, as you know."

"And how is…my granddaughter?" Heather asked, her smile slipping.

"Uh—haven't you seen Poppy?" Grace asked.

"A couple of nights ago, I got my first proper visit with the kiddo," Heather said.

"She's adorable—looks so much like Billy at that age, except blonde, of course."

"What's going on between you and Billy?" Grace asked. "If I can even ask that…"

"Nothing! Everything's…" Heather stopped, a blush creeping onto her face. "Okay, I know, I know. Billy's being distant, and it hurts. He's decided that I shouldn't mention my work in front of the kid. It's dumb, but I'm trying to cooperate. Heaven forbid she know that adults consume alcohol. Poppy has a grandmother with a job. You'd think that would be something to be proud of."

"He might have a point, though," Grace said. "It might not be age appropriate to talk about the bar."

"I raised him, and he turned out great," she retorted. "I didn't hide things from him. He needed to know how the world worked, and he also needed to trust me to give him accurate information. I never lied to him. Not once. But now he's all determined to raise his daughter better than I managed with him."

"He said that?"

"Between the lines." Heather sighed, and then she took a sip of her coffee. "I did my best with him, you know."

"I know," Grace said. "And Billy adores you. You know that."

"Billy's deeply angry," Heather replied. "He's got some big surprises coming his way if he thinks raising a child on his own is easy. I didn't have family around. I had to work, support the two of us and try to put my own life together while I took care of him—"

"Heather, he loves you!" Grace insisted. "And you're right—he's brand-new to being a dad. Maybe it's like how everyone is an expert parent before they have kids."

Heather shrugged. "I can only hope. He never came back to visit me once. All that time in Denver, and Tracy was all he needed. Do you know what it's like to have your son at the center of your world, and then have him just walk off like that?"

Grace dropped her gaze. She'd felt the sting of his romance with Tracy, too, but for different reasons.

"Sorry to complain," Heather said with a sigh. "Mostly I was hoping you could tell me about Poppy. How she's doing… How she's adjusting. All I know is that she's ridiculously smart."

"She is," Grace confirmed. "She loves books and stories. And numbers… She loves carpet time in the classroom. That's where I read them stories. I hold up the book so that the kids can see the pictures, and she always leans forward so she can read ahead." Grace chuckled. "I don't think I've found anything she doesn't like yet."

Heather smiled uncertainly. "So…what do you buy a kid like that? For a present, I mean. I want to buy her affection."

Grace smiled at the dry joke. "She loves books. I've been bringing books from the school, but obviously she can't keep those."

"Books." Heather nodded a couple of times, and Grace could tell that wasn't the answer that she'd been hoping for. "I've never been much of a reader. I wouldn't even know where to start. She's going to find out I'm not like her, and combine that with whatever her dad is telling her about me—"

"Billy isn't trashing you," Grace interrupted. "I'm pretty sure he isn't, at least. He's really overwhelmed. Poppy is gifted, and he's been trying to find out what she needs."

"What *does* she need?" Heather asked, and she fixed her eyes on Grace's face imploringly. "Because I'll buy it for her. Anything."

Grace regarded the older woman for a moment, then shrugged. "You want my opinion?"

"Yes!"

"She needs a grandma."

Tears misted Heather's eyes. "I'm not sure I'm much good at that. I've never been the knitting and baking type."

"She needs to belong," Grace said. "She needs to be loved. She needs to feel like she's part of a family—because from what I can tell, she was neglected a lot by her mom."

"We got that impression," Heather said breathily.

"I'm going to go out on a limb here and say that Billy needs you, too," Grace said. "Maybe he's upset about some stuff right now, but that doesn't change that you're his mom, and he needs someone to tell him he's doing a good job."

"If he'd even let me…" Heather sighed. "It's okay. This isn't your problem, Grace. Sorry to unload on you."

Grace shrugged. "He dumped me for Tracy, too. I mean, not romantically, obviously, but he slid off with Tracy, and he didn't seem to even see the rest of us anymore."

"What?" Heather frowned. "I always figured your friendship would outlast whatever woman he was dating."

"In all honesty, I kind of backed off once he got really serious with Tracy. But it changed things. He opened up to her in ways he wouldn't with me—and maybe that was just natural."

"Tracy was different, wasn't she?" Heather said thoughtfully. "You know why?"

Grace shook her head.

"Tracy wasn't afraid to chase him down. I mean, bad for him or not, she was pretty up-front about what she wanted. The others waited for him to pursue." Heather sighed. "I wish he would have listened to me. I could have saved him from a whole lot of heart-break."

That was true—Tracy had definitely made her feelings clear.

"Well...you learn more from life experi-ence than your mom's advice, right?" Grace said ruefully. "But it made me realize that I'd better get my own life together. Billy is too easy to..." She stopped. She was saying too much.

"Oh, he wraps us all around his little fin-ger," Heather said with a small smile. "He's always been adorable that way."

Grace met Heather's gaze and shrugged. "All I'm saying is, he comes back around. It's his way."

"But will you stick around long enough for him to get back your old friendship?" Heather asked, and Grace felt her cheeks heat. "So, you won't."

"No." Grace dropped her gaze. "I need a husband and family of my own."

"Understood," Heather replied, taking another sip of her coffee. "I'm the one person who can really understand that. Finding a good guy can be hard work, and frankly Billy always stood in the way of that for you. Not that he'd actually say anything to other guys, but he made his presence in your life pretty palpable."

"Yeah…" He'd been territorial, and she'd never minded because she'd known that under that protective stance was a deeper emotional connection.

"You'll land a great guy," Heather said with a grin. "I did—at long last! You're beautiful—always were. But now you're positively glowing, Gracie, so keep doing whatever it is you're doing. It's working for you."

"Thanks," Grace said.

Heather glanced down at her watch. "I've

got to get going. I have some errands to run before my shift this afternoon, and I'm cutting it close."

"Thanks for the chat," Grace said.

Heather gathered her things and put on her coat. "If you think of anything else my granddaughter needs, let me know, okay?"

"Will do." Grace lifted her cup in a farewell as Heather headed toward the door.

That hadn't been the first time she was told that she was glowing in the last few days, and she was mildly afraid that the "glow" came from her own delusion with Billy all over again. He made her feel safe and secure, valued and fun. He woke her up in ways that no one else—friend or lover—ever could.

If she'd started to glow because she'd been hanging out with Billy on a daily basis, then it was a sure sign she needed to get her emotions under control. His mother was right—Billy could wind any woman around his finger. Grace couldn't do this again. She'd been right three years ago to distance herself from Billy, and Tracy's dumping him didn't change a thing. Grace still needed to build her own life and find her own happiness.

Her crush on Billy had gone on long enough.

BILLY PUSHED THE cart through the Walmart, with Poppy in the main section of the cart, being too big to fit into the toddler seat. But she'd wanted to ride all the same. Her boots dripped melted snow down through the slats, and Billy felt his anxiety rise as he headed through the menswear department, past the women's and toward the kids' section. Other dads would know what they were doing—or at the very least would have the instructions given by the moms. But Billy was on his own here. Poppy had worn holes in the knees of her favorite tights, and she wanted another pair. She also needed socks, some long johns to keep her warm in a Colorado winter and another couple of long-sleeved shirts.

"What size are you, Poppy?" Billy asked.

Poppy shrugged. "I don't know. I'm big enough."

"Huh." He eyed her speculatively. "Come here. I'm going to check the tag on your shirt."

He stopped the cart and checked the tag. If there was a simple *S*, *M* or *L*, he'd be fine. How did kids' sizes work? But whatever had been written on it had been washed off in the laundry long ago. He sighed.

"How much do you grow?" he asked, shooting her a teasing grin.

"Daddy, I don't know these things," Poppy said seriously. "But I need tights!"

"Yeah, tights. I know."

He glanced around the store. There were a couple of workers—both dashing in opposite directions. He stopped at a wall covered in packages of girls' socks and underwear. An older woman was watching him with pursed lips, and he wheeled the cart determinedly past the underwear. Yeah, his kid would need this stuff, but he wasn't exactly comfortable shopping for it on his own yet.

In the past, he'd called Grace when he felt out of his depth, but was that an option anymore?

"Hold on," he said. "I'm going to try something."

Billy pulled out his phone and dialed Grace's number. Maybe she could help him make sense of this. Once he knew what he was looking for, maybe he could get Poppy to read labels and look for the right sizes herself. Some independence was good for kids, right?

The phone rang twice, and then Grace picked up.

"Billy?"

"Yeah, it's me," he said. "How busy are you?"

"Um." There was silence for a moment. "I'm not doing much. Why?"

"Thing is, I'm at Walmart, and I have to pick up some stuff for Poppy, and I don't know how to shop for things like tights. I was wondering if you might want to give me a hand?"

He winced, waiting. In years past, she would have been here in a heartbeat—he'd always been able to count on her for pretty much anything. But now things were different, and he knew he didn't have the right to favors anymore.

"Why don't you call your mom?" she asked. "I have a feeling she'd like to be needed."

"She's working this afternoon," he said. "So I called you."

Not his entire reason, but it would have to do.

"I'll come, but only if you make me a deal," she said.

"Okay?"

"I want you to call your mother up and ask her for help with something," Grace said.

"With what?" he asked with a frown.

"Anything. She needs you to need her, too, Billy, and I'm not going to be around for long, so you'd better get your support network up and running."

He sighed, and shut his eyes for a beat. His relationship with his mother was complicated, and no one seemed to understand that.

"Fine," he agreed.

"A grandmother can be incredibly useful, you know," she added.

Yeah, he was clear on that. But his relationship with his mom was strained for some good reasons, and he'd called Grace because she was he first one to pop into his head—the one he wanted to see, if he had to be honest. The one he'd been missing for the last three years.

"Are you coming or not?" he asked irritably.

"I'm just coming out of the hardware store," she admitted, and he could hear the rueful smile in her voice. The hardware store was right next to Walmart. "Dad needed more duct tape, and I needed to get out."

"Good. So I'm not actually bugging you. Come to the kids' department. I'm the one standing around, looking confused."

"I'll be there in five minutes."

Billy hung up and looked down at Poppy, who was gazing at him curiously. The older woman had circled around, but she still seemed to be watching him. He met her gaze, and the woman quickly looked away.

"Miss Beverly is going to give us a hand," Billy said.

Poppy nodded sagely. "That's probably a good idea."

Billy wandered up and down a few aisles—most of which seemed to have baby stuff—until he spotted Grace. She was dressed in a pair of close-fitting gray pants, knee-high black leather boots and a red woolen winter coat that reached just past her hips. She looked...intimidatingly good.

She looked like a woman who had her life together, who dressed to impress. He'd never associated that with Grace before, and he felt the disparity between them right now. But when she shot him a grin, it was the same old Grace, and he felt the smile forming on his lips in return.

"So, you're lost in the kids' section, are you?" Grace said as she walked up. She hitched her purse a little higher on her shoulder and gave Poppy a smile. "Hi, Poppy."

"Hi, Miss Beverly," Poppy said with a shy smile.

"Yes, I'm lost," Billy admitted. "Thanks for coming."

"So, what are you looking for?" she asked.

"Tights. I need new ones," Poppy said from her spot in the cart. "And I need long johns, Daddy says, so I can be warmer. And I want a hair band."

"A hair band?" Billy said, looking down at his daughter. "Since when?"

Poppy's list just seemed to get longer, and his anxiety rose another notch. Not only did he have no idea about girl things, he didn't have a lot of extra money, either. Ranch hands weren't paid a whole lot.

"Since now," Poppy replied. "I want a hair band to hold back my hair like a lady's."

"Ah." Billy looked up at Grace.

"I know what she's talking about," Grace said. "And they're cheap."

"Yeah, I'm not worried about the money," he said with a short laugh. But he was. Already this little girl was costing him more than he'd ever imagined. Still, he didn't want to refuse her the regular kid stuff. If she wanted a hair band, then she would have it.

"First things first—tights," he said, and

Grace headed off down an aisle. "Do you know where you're going?"

"We'll figure it out." She shot him a grin. "You look seriously daunted by this, Billy. It's not so bad."

"It's the sizes, mostly," he admitted.

"Oh." The smile dropped from her lips. "Because of the size charts and all that... Look, even if there weren't other challenges, those charts are a boggle if you don't know what you're looking for. Right now she's four, so she'll be size four. Unless she were big or small for her age, but she's a pretty average four-year-old from my experience."

"Oh." Billy nodded. "That's not so bad."

"Not really," she agreed.

"So, what's with you championing my mother all of a sudden?" he asked as they headed down another aisle.

"I saw her today at Dark Roast," she replied. "We had a visit."

"Great." He eyed her for a moment, unsure if this was a good thing or not. "What did she say?"

"She misses you," Grace replied. "She's your mother!"

"Yeah, well, not everyone has a cute and

balanced relationship with their mom like you do," he replied.

Grace didn't answer that, but she stopped in front of a display of little square, clear-wrapped packages.

"What color, Poppy?" Grace asked.

Billy watched as they decided on two pairs—one pink and one white.

"She did her best, though," Grace said as they started walking again. "And she said you never came back to visit. At all."

"Did you?" he countered.

"Of course," she said. "I came for Christmas, my dad's birthday, Mother's Day... It was only a couple of hours' drive."

"I was going to come see Mom once," Billy said. "I called up to see if it would be a good time. You kind of expect your mother to be flexible, you know?"

"And she wasn't?" Grace asked.

"She had a big date," he replied.

"With Gerald," Grace said.

"Does it even matter which guy?" Billy shook his head. "There was always some guy she was enthralled with."

"So you reschedule!" Grace said.

"Like I said, it's not the same as your parents, Grace." He nodded toward some mittens and gloves. "Probably need more than one pair of mitts, right?"

"Probably," she agreed, but she eyed him sympathetically for a moment. "Gerald has stuck around, you know."

"So everyone knows about him?" Billy asked.

"He's newer to town—he bought the fish and chip place, so we kind of know who he is. He seems really decent, and he took a shine to your mom pretty fast. She was more cautious. I've only chatted with her a few times, but she seems to be in love."

In love. Wasn't she always? And the little boy who'd loved her with his whole heart had never been enough to keep her home.

"Do you know how many school performances my mom came to?" he asked, stopping close enough for Poppy to be able to reach the mittens.

"I know...she wasn't really hands-on when it came to school."

"She wasn't always working, either," Billy said. "A lot of times, she had a date with some guy from the bar, and she'd send me to my concert with the neighbor who had a kid in my grade—a girl I couldn't stand because she teased me constantly. So they'd take me to and from, and Mom would go out with whichever guy was more important than me that month. It was the same with soccer practice. She sent me with the coach, who lived on our street. I don't think she ever saw me play one game."

Grace put a hand on his arm. "I'm not saying she was right, Billy."

"Then what are you saying?" he demanded.

"I don't know…" She shrugged weakly. "I just… I guess I felt sorry for her. She feels really out of the loop when it comes to you and Poppy."

"Well, I'm pretty out of the loop for most of her stuff, too," he replied, and he could hear the bitterness in his own tone. Except part of that was his own fault. He didn't want to hear about her boyfriends, and he'd stayed away because of them. This Gerald guy…sure, he might be half decent. Frankly it wasn't about whether the guy was a waste of skin; it was about his mother's tendency to fall headlong in love with every last one of them. And Billy was tired of standing by and watching it all like a slow-motion train wreck.

Poppy chose a pair of mittens—fluffy and

warm looking—and Billy looked at the price. Seriously? That's what tiny pink mitts were going for?

"Uh—what about these ones?" he said, picking up another pair with a better price.

"I like the fuzzy ones," she said plaintively.

"Yeah, well, maybe next time, kiddo. If you want a head band…"

Poppy sighed. "Okay."

Billy pushed the cart forward again, and he saw the older woman, this time with her back to them, sorting through a sale rack.

"It's not that I don't love my mom," he said, turning to Grace and lowering his voice. "I do. I used to worry about her like crazy, and it drove me nuts."

"I remember," Grace replied softly.

"I'll get together with Mom more often," he conceded. "I'm just trying to figure out how to be a good dad, but I haven't got a whole lot of role models there. I know that I won't make the same mistakes my mom did. I'm going to put Poppy first, and I'm not going to be chasing after women."

"You never exactly were a skirt chaser," Grace said with a low laugh.

"I know, but I'm serious. Poppy's coming

first. Every time. I'm going to be at every school play, every recital, every soccer game… Whatever her jam is, I'll be there." He looked down at his daughter, his heart welling up with a love he'd never known was possible. "I'm a dad. Women can wait. I put everything I had into Tracy, and that was no guarantee, was it? But if I put everything I have into raising my daughter, I don't think that's a decision I'll ever regret."

He looked over and saw Grace watching him with soulful eyes. Why did she look sad?

"Excuse me," a voice came from behind him, and he stopped and turned to find the older woman next to him. Her gaze swept over the three of them, pausing a little longer on Poppy.

"Hi," he said.

"For the fuzzy mittens," she said hurriedly, and pushed a crisp bill in his direction.

"No, I—" he started.

But she dropped the bill into his cart and hurried away. He stood there, feeling like more of a loser than ever. Poppy picked up the money with a grin, and Billy plucked it out of her hands.

"That was nice of her," Grace said.

But it wasn't. He'd seen the way that

woman had been watching him. This was pity, not respect.

"Can I get the fuzzy mittens?" Poppy asked hopefully.

"No," he said curtly, and steered the cart toward the checkout. "And we're putting that money in the charity box."

He didn't need pity. If that woman wanted to give money to someone who needed it, he could help her out with that. But he wasn't anyone's charitable project. He glanced over at Grace, and she was watching him with a cautious expression.

"What?" he snapped.

"Nothing." She smiled faintly. "But you can't do this alone, Billy."

"I'll figure it out," he said. She wasn't sticking around town anyway.

CHAPTER EIGHT

MONDAY WAS UNEVENTFUL, which was good news for a preschool teacher. Grace managed to get her hands on some teaching tools she thought would help Billy, though, and she'd sorted through them during lunch, when another teacher was outside, supervising. These were specifically designed for dyslexic students, but Grace was still filled with misgiving. These were meant for little kids, not grown men, and she wasn't sure how Billy would react to that. The woman in Walmart yesterday had meant well—or at least that was how it had seemed to Grace—and he'd been offended by her attempt to help. So how was this going to go over?

When Billy arrived, he was holding a box of donuts in front of him, almost like a shield. Poppy saw him, brightened and skipped toward him.

"Hey, kiddo," Billy said, scooping Poppy

up in a one-armed hug, the donuts held out to the side. "How was your day?"

"What's that?" Poppy asked, looking at the box and ignoring his question. "Can I have one?"

Billy chuckled and shot Grace a grin. "Figured we could all use a little extra blood sugar."

"That works for me," Grace said, and when he opened the box, he scooped out her favorite—a Boston cream—and handed it over. "Thank you."

Poppy lost herself in a jelly donut, sugar powdering her mouth and chin, and Billy came over to sit on the corner of Grace's desk.

"You remembered my Boston cream fetish," she said, taking a bite of the pastry.

"Of course." He shot her a quizzical look. "I'm not the one who went silent, am I?"

Grace felt her cheeks heat. "Relationships change, Billy."

"All too many do," he agreed. "But the good ones should grow, not disappear on you."

"The good ones?"

"We were good together," Billy said softly.

"We were only friends," she countered.

"And that friendship meant a whole lot to me," he said. "Maybe that was one-sided, but…" He took a bite of his donut, and Grace was left without an answer.

It had been one-sided for them both in different ways. She'd been in love with him, and that was one-sided. He wanted a best friend who was everything to him that his lover couldn't cover, and that was one-sided, too.

They finished their treat in silence. When Grace had wiped her fingers on a tissue from her desk, she sucked in a breath. "Should we get started?"

"Yeah, okay." Billy licked his lips and glanced down at the manila envelope that Grace picked up. "I'm not making any promises, though."

"I am," she countered. "Stop talking yourself out of this before we even start. I can teach you to read, Billy. Just trust me."

"Can I help, too?" Poppy asked hopefully.

"Well, let me show your dad a few things first," Grace said. "You remember how you didn't like it when Sarah S. was watching you tie your shoes? It's the same kind of thing. Sometimes it's harder when someone is watching."

"Oh." Poppy nodded. "Okay."

"I have a word search for you to do, Poppy," Grace said. "It's a super hard one. There are words that even go backward. And diagonally."

"Oh?" Poppy's eyes lit up.

"And there are really long words, too."

"Oh!" Poppy was invested, and Grace picked up the word search and brought it over to a little table. When Grace returned, she found Billy looking inside the envelope, his expression grim.

"This is kid stuff," he said.

"I know. I'm sorry," she said. "But it's what I have access to. So...forgive the kid approach, but this works."

Billy eyed her silently, and Grace sucked in a breath.

"Now, with dyslexia, it's harder to learn sight words—the words we don't have to sound out but just know what they are. That's what helps us to read faster. So I'm going to start with some common sight words, and we'll look at them really closely so that you can see how they work—how they're put together."

She pulled out a card with the word *look* written in large letters. The *o*'s had little googly eyes inside them.

"Do you know this word?" she asked.

Billy was silent, but his knee started to jiggle, and she could see the crimson rising in his cheeks. He hated this—she could feel it. But if she could give him a win, he might decide it was worth it, after all.

"I don't need eyeballs on things to amuse me," he said.

"That's not for amusement," she replied with a shake of her head. "We tell kids that this makes it fun, but that's not really why we do it. Some brains work well in one 'language,' shall we call it. With sight. Image. Squiggles on a page. But other brains use more than one language at once. They need color, texture, context… They aren't satisfied with one way of viewing things. It can make regular reading hard, but if we use more than one 'language' to teach these basics, then these more complicated brains lock on to it."

"Like googly eyes," he said.

"Let's look at one letter at a time," she said, touching his wrist. His jiggling leg stilled, and she smiled over at him. "Give me a chance, Billy."

Over the next few minutes, Grace introduced Billy to the word *look*. She pointed out the shape of the letters, the double *o*'s and the way the word itself looked like a curious face. She covered the card and brought it back again, asking him to repeat the word aloud. Then she moved on to the next word—this one spelled out with a sandpaper line that he could follow with his fingers. After a while, he'd memorized the cards and knew which word was which.

"Now, I'm going to write one of these words on this paper," Grace said. "And I want you to tell me which one it is."

She wrote the word *look* in big, bold letters with a marker.

"That's *look*," Billy said.

Grace shot him a grin and nodded. "Yeah, it is."

"Big deal. It's the one with the two *o*'s. The googly eyes. That's not reading."

"Yes, it is!" she said. "Billy, that's what we all do—we see a word we know because of whatever association we have with it. We aren't sounding out every word we read. We recognize them. Just like you did now."

Billy frowned. "Give me another one."

Grace wrote another word on the page.

"At," he said. "From the sandpaper."

She wrote another one.

"The." He shook his head. "It doesn't make

sense when you look at it, but the shape is like a chair…and…" Billy's breath was coming faster now. "Give me another one—"

Grace wrote the last word on the page.

"Bed. It's shaped like a bed. Like the drawing."

Grace put a finger under each word as he read the sentence back to her.

"Look at the bed." Billy stared at Grace, shocked.

"You just read a sentence," she said quietly, and she felt tears mist her eyes. "Twenty minutes in, and you just read your first sentence."

Poppy had slipped out of her seat at the table, and she was watching her father with an expression of awe.

"Wait—" Billy swallowed "—but I'm not going to remember that."

"That's where the practice comes in," Grace said. "And we work with large letters right now to make it easier. They don't jumble up so much when they're big and well-spaced. Do you see?"

"Grace…you are really something," Billy breathed, and he raised his gaze to meet hers.

"I'm a teacher," she said with a weak shrug. "This is what we do."

"Yeah, well, I've had teachers before, but…" He licked his lips.

"Daddy?" Poppy had sidled up next to her dad and looked down at the page in front of him.

"Hey, sweetie," Billy said, sliding an arm around her.

"Good job." Poppy gave him a big smile. "You deserve a sticker."

"Hold on," Grace said, pulling out a simple book. It had been photocopied and laminated at a school office, and Grace handed it to Billy.

He opened the first page, and he stared down at the page for a long moment. Did it work? Or had those letters all jumbled up again? For a moment, her heart sank. It was okay. They'd keep practicing. The point was that he could learn this, with a slightly different technique. And she felt a rush of pride at what he'd accomplished today. She'd known how intimidated he was at the prospect of even trying…

"That might be too much for today," she conceded, reaching for the book, but then Billy put his finger down on the page.

"Look…at…the…bed," he read, his voice

low and deep. He looked to the next page. "Look…at…the…" He frowned.

"Table," Poppy said quietly.

"Table," Billy repeated. He turned the page slowly, almost reverently. "Look…at…the…"

"Truck." Poppy slipped onto her father's knee. She was tiny, propped up there, drumming her indoor shoes against his cowboy boot.

"Truck. Yeah. That's *truck*?" He looked over at Poppy. "The picture looks more like a cube van to me."

"It says *truck*," she confirmed, and father and daughter exchanged a solemn look before Billy turned back to the book.

"Look…at…the…" He stopped again.

"House." Poppy looked more confident now, too, and she pointed out the letters. "*H-o-u-s-e*. House."

"House." Billy nodded. "I've got to learn those words." He looked up at Grace hopefully. "Will you… I mean, can I…"

"We'll learn them," Grace said, trying to push back a wave of emotion. "We've only just started. If I had more time…" She swallowed hard against the tightening in her throat, and she saw the flicker of sadness in Billy's eyes, too.

"There are literacy programs here in town," she suggested.

"Not yet," he said gruffly, then looked down at his daughter, turning the little book over in his hands. "Not much of a story, is it, kiddo?"

"You read it right, Daddy," Poppy said with a decisive nod.

"Yeah." His voice was thick, and he cleared his throat. "Mostly."

"I'm going to finish my word search, okay?"

"Yeah, sure," he said, and Poppy squirmed off her father's lap and headed back to the table. Then he slowly shook his head.

"What?" Grace murmured.

"I just read a book, Grace." He met her gaze, and she saw tears moistening those dark eyes. "Granted, it was pretty small, and Poppy helped some, but I never thought I'd do that..."

"I had no doubt," Grace replied.

"Are you just that good of a teacher?" His lips turned up in a half smile.

Grace might pride herself on her teaching skills, but it wasn't that. She knew this cowboy—his determination, his heart, his willingness to do anything it took to get a job done right. And now he was funneling all that into being a dad, and he was determined to be the best dad Poppy could possibly ask for. He didn't want to let that child down.

"I just know...you," she said quietly.

She'd always seen the man he was—capable, resilient, intelligent. And she was proud of him—prouder than she'd ever been. She wanted to slide closer to him, slip her hand into his, squeeze that muscular arm of his the way she used to do...

But she wouldn't.

She reached for a second manila envelope.

"Let's make the most of the time we've got. You ready for another few words?"

THAT EVENING, BILLY glanced into Poppy's bedroom and saw that she was asleep, spread-eagle across her bed. She'd kicked off her quilt, and her pajama bottoms pushed up to her knees. She was so little—just this tiny girl with a personality twice as big as she was. He'd never understood what parents meant when they said that watching their children sleep filled them with love. It hadn't made a whole lot of sense until now, when he had a little girl of his own. She was a live wire all day, and when she finally crashed, she looked…smaller, younger, more vulnerable. He crept into her room and pulled the quilt over her again. These January nights got cold fast.

Billy tiptoed back out of her bedroom, leaving the door open a crack. Poppy hated a shut door, so this way she could see light from the living room if she woke up.

He was still a little buzzed from his lesson with Grace that afternoon. They'd gone through another envelope of words, and he'd reviewed the first words again, going over them intently. He couldn't afford to forget this…to lose it. Grace had given him a gift that seemed almost magical, and now that he'd gotten a taste, he wasn't willing to let up. He'd study every free second, if that was what it took, but he was learning to read!

Billy glanced at his watch. His mom had called a few minutes ago, saying she wanted to stop by. It was past Poppy's bedtime, but maybe that was for the best. He had stuff to talk over with his mother.

At a knock at the door, Billy headed over to open it. His mother stood on the porch, wearing a brown faux-leather coat, a pink scarf wrapped around her neck and a bulging shopping bag clutched in one hand.

"Hi, sweetie," Heather said, stamping her boots on the mat, then stepping inside. "Wow. Cold night!"

"Yeah, it sure is," he agreed, and he waited while she put down the bag and took off her outerwear.

"So where's my granddaughter?" she asked, looking around.

"In bed. Asleep."

"Oh. Right." She smiled sheepishly. "It's been a while since I had a four-year-old. You forget."

"Did I even have a bedtime?" he asked.

"Sort of." She winced. "You fell asleep on the couch to *Jeopardy!*, and I carried you to bed. Until you got too big to carry. It worked for us. I got to snuggle you on the couch."

Billy could vaguely remember that—the cozy feeling of *Jeopardy!* music, the smell of his mother's perfume, and the feeling of her cool fingers running over his forehead as his eyes got heavier and heavier... To this day, *Jeopardy!* made him sleepy.

Heather bent down and picked up the shopping bag. She handed it over to him with a smile. "For Poppy."

Billy peered inside.

"I got her a few different sizes—kids grow

faster than you'd think," his mother said.
"One day the clothes fit, and the next you've
got an inch of wrist showing. So I picked up
some pants, some shirts, a couple of packs
of underwear and socks. Oh, and this is my
favorite..." Heather pulled out a long-sleeved
shirt with gold lettering. "Cute, right?"

Billy looked at it, and his stomach sank.
Obviously he couldn't read it. The letters
seemed to clump together, and even if they
didn't... All he could see was something that
looked like a biker tattoo pattern in the center of it all. He had no idea what it said, or
why his mother would have bought something with a biker tattoo for his daughter.
He forced a smile.

"Yeah, cute," he said.

"I thought so." She dropped it back into
the bag. "If you need anything, son, just tell
me. I've got a granddaughter to spoil now,
and I intend to make good on that!"

"I'd rather you didn't," he replied.

"Well, not literally spoil..." Heather's
smile faltered. "I just meant..." She didn't
finish.

"Come on in, Mom," he said. "You want
a Coke or something?"

"Sure."

She followed him inside and Billy fetched the soda and a tall glass, then handed them both to his mother. She pulled out a chair at the kitchen table and sank into it. She didn't open the can of Coke, though.

"What did I ever do that was so terrible?" she asked after a moment, looking up at him with tears in her eyes.

"Mom—"

"I did my best!" she interrupted. "I loved you. Don't you remember that part? We used to go to the mall together and make up stories about the people we saw. And I'd buy you a small ice cream cone, and you'd try to make it last as long as possible."

"Yeah, I remember that." Billy's heart clenched. "You promised to take me every week, but what about the times that you had some guy who asked you out?"

"Sweetie, we have to be flexible," she said.

"That's what you always told me," he said. "I had to be flexible—not whatever guy you were dating."

"That isn't true!" she snapped.

"Look, Mom, I don't want to fight about it," Billy said. "It's not worth it."

"Well, apparently it's serious enough for

you to hold my granddaughter away from me," she retorted.

"We were just at your place!" he shot back.

His mother sighed and popped open the can of cola. She poured it into her glass with a practiced hand, barely any foam fizzing up.

"Then let's not fight," she said, putting the empty can down on the tabletop. "How was your day?"

Billy looked at his mom from across the table—her familiar face, the lines around her eyes that got more pronounced every year. She looked vulnerable, too, and he didn't want to hurt her. He was mad at the ways she'd let him down during his childhood, but that anger was rooted in how much he loved her. She'd been his imperfect, beautiful world.

"Good," he said after a beat of silence. "I started learning how to read."

"Har, har," his mother said with a wry smile. "Come on, son. I'm serious. I can tell you about my day, if you want—"

"I am serious," he replied, cutting her off. "Grace got some reading tools together to help me start."

"Learning to read what?" his mother asked

with a shake of her head. "Computer code, or something?"

"English. Words. Books."

Heather stared at him, and he watched her lips twitch as she was about to speak, but then stopped. She frowned slightly, then met his gaze in confusion.

"What?" she said.

"I never learned."

"Yes, you did! You took the first grade with everyone else!" she shot back.

"I never learned, Mom," he repeated. "I'm dyslexic, Grace says. When I look at words on a page, they all just jumble together, and I can't make sense of them."

His mother reached for a cereal box on the counter, and put it down in front of him. "Read that."

"Mom, stop it." He pushed the box aside. "I'm not making this up. I never did well in school."

"Neither did I," she snapped. "Not everyone is an intellectual."

"I was pushed along with everyone else, but I didn't know how to read," Billy said. "It was easier to be the rebel and pretend I didn't care than to tell anyone the truth. I'd have been laughed out of school."

"But…" His mother shook her head. "How did I not know this?"

"You were busy, and I didn't want to let you down," he said. "A guy doesn't announce this kind of thing. At least I didn't."

"Why wouldn't you *tell* me?" she asked, her voice choked. "I could have…*helped*!"

The same thing Grace had said. But these two women in his life seriously underestimated the blow to his ego that such an admission would be. Billy reached across the table and put a hand over hers. "I don't know."

"I was on your side." She turned her hand over and held his tightly. "I would have figured something out for you—"

"You were busy, Mom."

"I would have *made* time." She looked into his face pleadingly. "How did you not know that?"

"When there wasn't time for the mall?" he asked with a weak shrug. "Or for my school concerts? Or soccer games? Or for a regular bedtime? Or for breakfast together? I mean, when was there going to be time?"

"I was on my own." She pulled her hand back. "I was a single mother. I didn't have anyone else to lean on, or vent to, or have an adult conversation with. You can love your child with your whole heart and still have a desperate need for other things!"

"I guess I'll find that out," he said, leaning back in his chair.

"No, you won't," she said with a shake of her head. "Not like I did. You're not entirely alone. You have *me*."

She did have a point, but he'd have to be clear with her how things worked. She had a way of taking over, whether her way was better or not. His mom had gotten everything she had in life with that big personality of hers.

"Yeah." He nodded. "I do. But just for the record, I'm the dad. I make the rules. You're the grandma—you tell Poppy to obey the rules. Okay?"

"I might have some good insights into little girls," she said.

"I make the rules," he repeated.

"Fine." She put her hands up. "You're the big boss. Got it."

She was mildly offended, but he knew better than to let something this big go without some clear boundaries. They were both silent for a moment, and then his mother got up, brought the bag over to the table, and pulled out the shirt with the gold lettering.

"Could you read that?" she asked softly.

"No," he admitted.

"It says…" Her voice tightened with emotion. "It says, 'Back off… I have a crazy grandma and I'm not afraid to use her.'"

Billy started to laugh, and it was like all that tension in the room finally broke. And the more he laughed, the funnier that stupid T-shirt became. His mother watched him for a moment, then started to chuckle along with him.

"It's got a point," Billy said, wiping his eyes. "You're nuts, Mom. Let's just use it for good!"

Heather rolled her eyes. "I might be a crazy mom," she said. "But I'm yours. And don't you forget it, okay?"

"I won't." He nodded. "Thanks—for all of this." He lifted another couple of shirts out of the bag, then looked back to his mother. "I was wondering what kind of grandmother you'd be."

"Inked and crazy," she replied with a grin. "Best way to be."

Yeah…and Poppy's dad would be reliable and devoted. His daughter would be okay.

CHAPTER NINE

ON JANUARY SEVENTEENTH, Grace Beverly turned thirty.

She woke up that morning, feeling older. Funny—she'd never felt a progression for any other birthday. Her father used to joke with her growing up, "So, how does fourteen feel? Older? Wiser?" Of course she never had. But this birthday was an event—even more so than her twenty-first birthday had. Her twenties were officially behind her. Thirty felt like a nice, solid age—very adult and responsible. Back when she was ten, her aunt Theresa had turned thirty, and she could still remember the party they'd thrown for her. Thirty seemed almost elderly back then, but now she realized how young it was. Thirty... It wasn't quite the bastion of wisdom that she'd imagined as a kid, but it had a feel all of its own.

"Happy birthday, Gracie," her mother said,

giving her a squeeze as she came into the kitchen.

"Thanks, Mom," Grace said with a grin. She was wearing a new suit ensemble in a winter-plum color. The jacket was nipped in at the waist, accentuating her curves, and the slacks fit perfectly. Today felt like a good day to dress up a little bit.

"This is for you." Connie passed her a card, and Grace opened it to find a sweet message about parents loving their daughter, with cash enclosed.

"Aw, just what I wanted," Grace said with a chuckle. "Thank you. You guys are the best."

"Buy something pretty," she said. "Are you sure you don't want to come with us to the fund-raiser tonight?"

Grace's father, Dr. Len Beverly, came into the kitchen, looking down at his phone. He stopped to kiss Connie on the cheek, then shot his daughter a distracted smile.

"I hate these fund-raisers," he said. "I'm MCing, though."

Even worse. Her dad wasn't the most entertaining man in the world, but he had a few biology jokes that seemed to go over well in medical circles.

"No, you guys go have fun," Grace said with a shake of her head.

"You sure?" Her mother winced. "It's your birthday."

"Positive. I'm a grown woman who can shop for her own birthday gift to her heart's content," Grace said with a wry smile. "And I'm serious. A quiet night in to reflect on how long I'm getting in the tooth will be good for me."

Her mother laughed. "If you knew how young thirty was from where I'm standing!"

"Happy birthday, Gracie," her father said, and he gave her a squeeze, then turned back to his phone. "I need new jokes. There's no way around it."

And he did, but Grace was going to let him figure that one out on his own. Besides, he was a well-loved physician. People forgave him his corny one-liners.

Grace headed off to work—with her travel mug filled with coffee—determined to embrace her thirties. A new decade was a good thing, in her estimation. A fresh start. They said that each decade had a theme of its own, and her twenties had been dominated by a powerful but unrequited crush. That was all it had been, and if she had seen a friend hung up on some guy who wasn't going to be interested in her, ever, she'd think that decade had been a waste. Romantically, at least. Well, she wasn't making that mistake in her thirties. She wanted to live her life differently, more courageously. No more pining and wishing.

In Eagle's Rest Elementary School, every classroom had a Birthday Button. Every child got their turn when their birthday came, and Grace, as their fearless leader, did too. So she wore the Birthday Button with pride, had the "Happy Birthday" song sung for her over the loudspeaker by the office staff, and when the day was over, and the kids ran out to get their snowsuits on so they could go home, Grace couldn't help but feel that it was a good birthday—not like others she'd enjoyed with friends or family, but still a good start to her decade.

Billy arrived for his lesson just as he had the day before. Grace had some math for Poppy to work on this time—adding up rows of numbers, which Poppy seemed to be very good at.

Billy leaned against her desk once more, watching as she got Poppy started on her project. She glanced back at him a couple of times and hated that her stomach still flipped a little when she looked at him. He was tall and muscular, holding himself with that ease of a man comfortable in his own skin. And why shouldn't he be? Those dark eyes, the shadow of whiskers across his chin, the strong hands, the jeans that fit him just right...

She pulled her attention back to Poppy. Admiring Billy wasn't going to start this decade off right, either.

"Today is Miss Beverly's birthday," Poppy said.

"I know," Billy said.

"How?" Poppy asked, looking around Grace to see her father properly.

"I remembered." His voice was low. She glanced over at him again, catching that dark gaze of his as it enveloped her. That felt too good...and not at all like old times. She used to dream of him looking at her like that...

"I also have the Birthday Button," Grace pointed out, tapping the pin on her suit jacket. Now wasn't the time to wonder about that gaze of his.

"So, any big plans tonight?" Billy asked after a beat of silence.

"A quiet evening to myself," she said. "My parents are out at a fund-raiser. It'll be nice."

"Alone?" he said, frowning.

"Delightfully alone," she countered.

"Nope, you're coming out with me and Poppy," Billy said.

"I *have* plans," she shot back with a low laugh. "Didn't I point that out?"

"Sitting home alone is a not a plan."

"Sure it is," she replied. "Maybe I like some time to myself. I'm good company."

"You *are* good company," he replied. "But that's not a birthday plan. Me and Poppy know how to do a birthday."

"We do?" Poppy asked, looking up from her page of numbers.

"Are you saying we *don't*?" Billy replied in mock surprise. "I got us a sled, remember?"

"We're going sledding!" Poppy said with a bright smile.

"And we won't throw a fit, right?" he added.

"No fits," Poppy agreed. "I'll be good."

Billy laughed softly and looked questioningly at Grace. "What do you say, Gracie? Let us take you out for your birthday. We'll have you back home dreadfully early."

Grace smiled ruefully. Yeah, he seemed to be figuring out how this worked with a small child in the mix. Billy lounged against her desk with an almost rebellious air. She eyed him for a moment.

"Using a kid to get your way isn't fair," she teased.

"I'm not using my kid, I'm using a sled," he countered. "Remember how we used to go sledding together?"

She'd almost forgotten… The slick path for the sled to follow down the junior high school hill, the laughing, the tumbling out. He used to help her up, and he'd stop to brush the snow off her hat. It had been a sweet gesture, and something he had never done for other girls.

"Fine—I'll go out with you for my birthday. But I expect you to do as you say and get me home dreadfully early."

"I'm a man of my word."

"Only after we go through another lesson," she added, holding up a manila envelope.

"Right," he said, and that cocky smile of his faltered. Billy's gaze met hers, and all the posturing evaporated. This was just Billy—the bare, honest man she knew so heartbreakingly well.

"You still want to learn this, don't you?" she asked, hesitating.

"Please." And in that one word, she heard his whole heart.

BILLY SAT IN the same chair he'd occupied yesterday and waited while Grace rummaged about in a desk drawer. Her hair fell down in a chocolate cascade, and her purple suit looked much more serious than the other outfits he'd seen.

When he'd been missing his friend, he'd imagined her in a pair of jeans and a sports jersey, her hair pulled up in a messy bun. He'd imagined her making those indulgent waffles at eleven at night, with her homework from her college classes piled up on the floor in front of her. He'd imagined her laughing at their shared jokes and imitating celebrities. What was it about being overtired that made her so goofy and loveable?

But this Grace—the serious, impeccably dressed woman who presided over this classroom—was in a different league. And he was the same old Billy who couldn't read, and who did his best work on horseback.

"Here we go," Grace said, coming back to the table with another manila envelope.

"Now, I think we should review yesterday's work first, because these are supposed to be sight words that you'll eventually be able to read without having to think too hard about them, so a lot of repetition is key."

Grace pulled out the chair next to him and sank down. She wore some sort of perfume—or was that shampoo?—that smelled fruity and soft. He leaned toward her ever so slightly. She didn't seem to notice, and she tucked her hair behind her ear, revealing a tiny, dangling silver earring in the shape of a crayon.

Billy smiled, then reached over and touched her ear, slipping his finger behind the soft lobe so he could get a better view of the glittery bauble. Grace froze.

"It's cute," Billy murmured. He didn't move his hand.

Grace, still facing forward, licked her lips and smoothed her hand over his, tugging his fingers away from her skin.

"Where did you get them?" Billy asked quietly.

Grace glanced toward him, and her earlier breezy confidence was gone. She shrugged weakly. "A friend found them on vacation and thought of me."

"Nice…"

Her blue gaze met his for a moment, and pink bloomed in her cheeks. Her lips parted, and for a moment, an image rose in his mind of leaning closer and catching those lips with his.

"Don't do that," she whispered.

"Do what?" he asked, still unable to take his eyes off of her.

"Touch me like that. It's…" She dropped her gaze to the envelope again and started to open it.

"It's what?" he murmured. There was something about her—so vulnerable yet so removed from him—that entranced him. Grace from years ago had been all buddy. This Grace was all woman, and when he looked at her, he saw the details like those dangling earrings, the soft whiteness of her neck, the lustrous gloss of her dark brown waves…

"It's distracting," she said, pulling out a card.

He was definitely distracted—she had him there. He dropped his hand, and as she sorted out some new cards, that tantalizing scent still tugged at him.

"I'm done!" Poppy said from across the

room, and she danced toward them with a paper fluttering in her hands.

Billy suppressed a sigh and leaned back. That couple of inches seemed to matter with his daughter's approach. Grace's blush deepened. He couldn't help but smile to himself—he'd made some impression on her, at least. He found himself wanting to make her see the man in him…except that was going to be difficult now that he'd betrayed his biggest failing. What educated woman could respect a guy who couldn't read?

"Is it right?" Poppy asked, thrusting her page into Grace's face.

Grace laughed softly and took the page, looking it over. "Well done, Poppy! Wow! Okay, I have something else I want you to try…"

Grace got his daughter resettled with another sheet and some explanation. Grace bent over to talk to Poppy, and Billy let his gaze move over her curvy figure.

Grace had always been a bigger girl, and while he'd never minded it, she'd never been his romantic type, either. But now he was starting to see what he'd been missing out on all those years—what had been hidden away under layers of turtlenecks and sweatshirts.

Grace was still a bigger girl, but he was noticing just how beautiful that was. He liked the softness of her arms and hands… He'd always found Grace touchable, and he'd enjoyed giving her bear hugs or nudging her when he joked. But *touchable* seemed to take on new meaning as he looked at her from across the room. All he could think of doing right now was sliding his hands around her waist and pulling her close.

Billy dropped his gaze. What was he doing? An image of his mother primping to get ready for a date slid into his mind.

He was here for Poppy—getting Poppy some extra challenge for her growing mind, and learning a few things of his own so he could read to his daughter. This was about Poppy's needs, not his newfound attraction to his old friend!

Just how much would Poppy have to resent him for later on? He could hear her telling friends, "There was this teacher who was giving me some extra help, and my dad started dating her…"

Not exactly the kind of father he wanted to be. He wanted to be there for Poppy, not use his daughter as a way to get close to her teacher. That was…wrong.

Grace rose from her crouch, touched Poppy on the top of her head and then headed back across the room to Billy. He felt ashamed.

"You ready to get started?" Grace asked.

"Yes. Let's start." He heard the chill in his own tone, and he didn't intend it, but he didn't want to let himself get sidetracked with his feelings for her, either.

Grace seemed to notice his change in tone, because she froze for a moment, then smiled a slightly more professional smile than earlier. She slid back into the chair next to him and opened the envelope. "This one is review. So, let's start with this word…"

For the next hour, Grace went over word cards with Billy and got up to check on Poppy's progress. They were both learning— Poppy on a much higher level than him, but still… He'd managed to remember most of yesterday's words, but once those words went on paper in a random order, he couldn't make them out again.

"I don't know…" he muttered in frustration as Grace wrote out a word on a lined piece of paper. "I can't see it. Why was it easier yesterday?"

"It's just practice, Billy," she said softly. "You'll get there."

She put a hand on his arm, but he didn't want to be comforted. He pulled his arm back, and she flinched.

"I just…" he started. "We don't have much time."

"Putting pressure on yourself isn't going to help matters," Grace replied.

"Maybe not," he agreed. "But it's the truth."

"We've been at this for a while," she said. "Let's take a break. You won't get past this wall when you're tired and frustrated."

Billy sighed. He didn't want to take a break—he wanted that feeling of success back! He wanted to read words on a page and have them make sense. He wanted to read more than he had yesterday and break past this blur of jumbled letters he'd lived with his entire life! Why couldn't this be easier?

"One more time," he said, turning back to the cards.

"Billy—"

"Once more," he said with a sigh. "Please. Let me try, at least."

Poppy came over to his table, her own page in her hand. She leaned against Billy's arm, watching him as he moved his finger over the letters in the word.

"Daddy?" Poppy whispered.

"Yeah, kiddo?"

"An odd number plus an odd number is always an even number. I've tried it and tried it and tried it. It's just how it works."

Billy stopped and looked over at her. Those big blue eyes regarded him earnestly.

"Yeah?" he said.

"Yeah." She nodded. "It's true."

He glanced over at Grace and saw her eyebrows raised in surprise. "That's true, Poppy," she said. "What made you realize that?"

"I was just thinking about it," she replied.

So his daughter could pick up on some mathematical insights just by thinking, and he was struggling to recognize a simple word on a page. It hardly seemed fair. It wasn't that he wanted his daughter to have the same challenges he did, but the gulf between them was almost insulting.

Billy rubbed his hands over his eyes and leaned back in the chair.

"You know what, Gracie?" he said. "I think you're right. Let's take that break."

"Billy—" she started, but he scraped back the chair and stood up, and she fell silent.

"Daddy?" Poppy looked up at him, worry creasing that small brow.

"I think it's time for dinner, kiddo," he said, forcing a smile. "Burgers and sundaes for Miss Beverly's birthday. What do you say?"

Poppy was easily convinced and skipped toward the door. Billy looked over at Grace and shrugged.

"Tough day," he said. "Let's celebrate you for a bit, instead."

For as long as it lasted, anyway. Here was hoping Poppy didn't have a repeat of their last night out. It was Grace's birthday. This shouldn't be about his failures, anyway. There were things he was good at—like roping cattle and helping Grace Beverly relax. He might not be much in the intellectual department, but he could be a solid friend for as long as Grace would let him.

And he'd be a good dad—whether he could read to his daughter or not.

CHAPTER TEN

THEY STOPPED AT a fast-food place, and when they'd all finished eating, Poppy seemed perfectly happy to add up lists of numbers on the back of her placemat. Grace watched in fascination. She'd started by using one of the crayons that came in a little paper cup, but the crayon wrote too big, Poppy said, so Grace dug a pen out of her purse.

"And then if there are two even numbers and one odd number all added up, the answer is odd," Poppy went on. "And then if there are four even numbers and two odd numbers, the answer is even…"

Grace looked over at Billy and they exchanged a smile.

"I wouldn't be surprised to see her figuring out the physics of sledding," Grace said.

"What's physics?" Poppy asked, looking up.

"Physics is a whole other kettle of fish," Billy said. "What you should be asking about is that sled in the back of the truck. Ready to give it a try?"

Eagle's Rest Junior High was located at the top of a hill. There was still daylight, even though the shadows were getting long and the air temperature had begun to drop. Grace stood back as he rummaged around in the back of his truck, emerging with a red plastic sled. It was new, with the stickers still on it.

Poppy danced around in excitement, and they trudged together through the unbroken mantle of snow up the hill. Funny—it looked smaller now that she was an adult. Back then it had seemed like a mountain.

But everything back then was bigger and more impressive. They'd been so young, and their hearts so much easier to fill. It took more to fill her heart now, more to impress her and satisfy her. A handsome man wasn't enough, nor a close friendship. Flirtation, soaring feelings…they might be fun, but they were a waste of time. No, her heart required more now—steadiness, consistency, depth.

But seeing that hill through Poppy's wide eyes brought back all the drama from years ago, and as Poppy stared down the hill, she stilled, clasping her mittened hands together in front of her.

"Here, Poppy," Billy said, dropping the sled onto the soft, snowy ground with a plop. "Sit here." He scooped her up under the arms and sat her on the sled. "You ready?"

"Yes!" Poppy breathed.

"Hold on tight, okay?" Billy said, and he gave her a gentle push.

The snow being fresh, she didn't go too fast down the hill, and they could hear her delighted laughter as she made her way down. Grace looked over at Billy and caught the glimmer of paternal pride in his eye.

"A first sled ride," Grace said with a grin. "That's something!"

He laughed. Poppy had just reached the bottom of the hill, and she tumbled off the sled.

"Okay, Poppy, come back up!" Billy called. "But around the side—that's right. You need to build up a slippery path down the hill so you go faster next time!"

Poppy started up the hill, eyes shining and snow coating her mittens and hat. The sun had started to sink behind the mountains, and a shadow began enveloping the hills below. There was still enough light to sled by, and the school's exterior lights popped on. Poppy went up and down a few more times on her own, tramping up the side of the hill and going down her track, which got faster and faster every time. Billy went down with her a couple of times, too, and after he got back to the top, Poppy squealed for more.

"Come on, Daddy!" she pleaded.

"No, no…you do this one," Billy said, and he got her settled on her sled once more, then gave her a push. Down she went, laughter trailing behind her, along with her rippling scarf.

"I should have bought a bigger sled. Or two of them," he said, grinning at Grace.

"Yeah, I might keep up with four-year-olds, but I'm not quite as bendy as I used to be," she laughed.

"I missed you, Gracie," Billy said, his voice lowering. "I missed…this. Just doing stuff together. No pressure."

"I know."

"Was it Tracy? Because she had a real mean streak. Did she make it clear…?"

Grace tugged her scarf a little closer to her neck.

"No, the problem was me," Grace replied.

"Look, Billy, I'm not sure any good can come of talking about this."

"Well…maybe I need to know," Billy replied.

"It's…" She felt her cheeks heat, and down the hill, Poppy tumbled off her sled and tramped a few circles in the snow at the bottom.

"Did I do something?" Billy asked. "I mean, I know that Tracy and I started up pretty quickly. I thought you understood. I figured… I don't know. I just thought you'd be happy for me. You were the one who introduced us, after all."

"Thrilled," she said dryly.

"What?" he demanded. "I don't get it! We were friends. We were supposed to be happy for each other when good things happened. That wasn't supposed to end our friendship!"

"It was all cozy and fun for you!" she snapped. "You had everything you wanted. The friend to hang out with, the support when you needed it, the women falling over themselves to be with you because they thought you were so cute—"

"Except for you," he said with a teasing smile. "You always knew you were too good for me."

Grace sucked in a breath, then fell silent. Her face felt flushed, and she turned her gaze to the bottom of the hill, where Poppy stood up from making a snow angel. She waved up at them, and Grace waved back, forcing a smile. Poppy started up the hill toward them, her sled in tow.

"What was I missing?" he pressed. "Because I was there for you, too. I picked you up after work when I was off, and we'd go to the movies. I didn't let more than a day go by without us talking. I was the one who knew your birthday, your favorite ice cream, the songs that made you feel sad, the stuff you hated about our town, the dreams you had for the future... I was a good friend!"

"Exactly," she said softly. "You were a great friend."

Billy was silent, his expression softening.

"A fantastic buddy," she went on. "And I was just as stupid as those other women who were groveling after you, maybe more. I had a good thing with you, but I wanted more..."

"You..." The word came out in a breath, and he stared at her, dark eyes moving over her face, inch by inch, as if looking for a chink in her armor. A smile flickered as if he thought she were joking, but then it dropped away.

"Was there a guy I didn't know about...?" he started.

Tracy had said what she wanted plainly, and Grace had always held back... Maybe it was time to stop that.

"I wanted more *with you*." The words were so quiet, that she almost wished he wouldn't hear them. But he froze, and she couldn't read his expression anymore.

"It's nothing," she went on hurriedly. "Obviously I don't feel that way anymore, but back then... I harbored a bit of a crush."

"You wanted—"

"Billy, it was a long time ago," she said firmly. "But that's what happened. It wasn't you. It wasn't Tracy. I just...needed space. So I took it."

Grace forced herself to meet his gaze. He looked mildly confused, a little surprised.

"I didn't know," he said softly.

"I know. That wasn't your fault. There comes a point in every woman's life when she realizes that her hopes and dreams aren't going to come find her like the prince with Sleeping Beauty. She's got to go out there and make the life she longs for. When you left, I finally did that. I *am* doing that. So don't worry—I'm good. I'm fine. I'm happy, even. This actually has less to do with you than you'd think. This is about what I want out of life."

Poppy arrived at the top of the hill, breathing hard. Her hat was askew, and the cold wind had reddened the tip of her nose.

"Miss Beverly, you want to come down with me?" she asked, eyes bright.

That seemed like an excellent escape. Grace had just said more than she'd ever planned to, but Billy looked like he wanted to talk more.

"All right," Grace said. "But I haven't done this in a long time, so you've got to go easy on me, okay?"

She knocked the snow out of the sled, then lowered herself onto it, behind Poppy.

"Daddy, push us!" Poppy hollered.

Grace felt Billy's strong hands on her shoulders, and he bent down so his face was next to hers. She could smell the musky scent of his aftershave, and she kept her face forward. She'd told him those feelings were in the past, and she was going to act like it.

"I still want to talk," Billy murmured next to her ear, low and deep. If only his voice didn't make her stomach flutter like that. Then he gave her a push, and they were off.

BILLY'S MIND WAS swimming as he watched Grace and Poppy swoop down the hill. Grace's laughter mingled with his daughter's, and it filtered back up to him at the top of the hill. She wanted more with him? As in...romance?

He'd never once suspected that Grace felt anything but friendship for him...or had he just been oblivious? Maybe he'd been a selfish jerk, monopolizing her time and leading her on.

But that wasn't fair. He and Grace had been close. That friendship had meant a whole lot to him, and when she'd cut him off and stopped taking his calls, it had felt like a breakup. They weren't an item, but it definitely hurt like being dumped.

Grace and Poppy were heading back up the hill again, and he sucked in a stabilizing breath of frigid air. They were here for Poppy tonight, and talking to Grace would just have to wait. Besides, he had a feeling that he was about to find out just how selfish he'd been all those years.

Soon Poppy was getting cold and tired.

He could see her eyes drooping when she blinked, and he couldn't help but smile.

"You're going to sleep well tonight," he said to her, and she looked up at him blearily.

"I'm not tired."

"Of course not." He shot Grace a grin, and she smiled ruefully in return. And that moment—the shared knowledge that Poppy was far more tired than she thought—felt good. Sharing a parenting moment with Grace made it all easier, somehow. But was that more of the same—him getting everything he needed out of their relationship, at her expense?

"So, how does thirty feel?" Billy asked as he put the truck into gear.

"For once, it feels different."

"Yeah, for me, too," he admitted. He was a few months older than she was. "Mind you, I'm a dad now, so that factors in."

"It would." At the mention of Poppy, Grace glanced over her shoulder, into the back seat. "She's nodding off."

"Are you crashing on me, kiddo?" Billy asked, adjusting the rearview mirror to look back. Poppy's head had tipped to the side in her booster seat, and her breath was coming slow and even. "I guess we tired her out."

Grace was silent, looking out the window so that he couldn't make out her expression. Billy drove for another couple of blocks, taking the familiar streets without much thought. Three years away hadn't erased muscle memory when it came to navigating Eagle's Rest's roads.

"Grace, I've been thinking about what you said," he started.

"Don't."

"No, seriously," he said. "I thought that we were on the same page. I figured you had plans well beyond me. I mean, look at me! I'm the high school dropout. You're the doctor's daughter."

"That sort of thing never stopped you before," she said, then clamped her mouth shut.

"You're a level above me," he told her. "And... I knew that. You're smart—obviously. You had your life together. You had your shiny, happy family, with your parents, your grandparents, your aunts and uncles from the city... You had a future. I had—" he looked over at her "—I had my charm. So yeah, I know the effect I had on women. I knew I could make them feel all sorts of things, but I also knew that I couldn't make any of that last."

"Don't give me pity explanations," Grace said, her tone hardening. "I don't need them. I told you, it's fine. I'm well past it."

And that stung—that she was most definitely over him.

"This isn't pity," he said quietly. "The one thing I always thought I could count on was my friendship with you. I figured I could make that one last, at the very least. I guess I was wrong."

Grace looked over at him, her earlier rigidity softening. "I've learned a lot the last three years."

"Yeah?"

"I know that I don't have the kind of looks that attract all the men in a room," she said. "But I hold my own, Billy."

"Hell, I know that," he said, shooting her a small smile. And if she thought that she hadn't been drawing his eye for years, then she was dead wrong. "Grace, you know you're gorgeous."

"I do know that," she said firmly. "I didn't always. I used to think I wasn't as pretty as the girls you were attracted to, that you'd have to see past my figure to fall for me. But that wasn't true. I can turn heads now, and all it took was some makeup and a little shopping."

"Confidence," he countered.

"That, too." She smiled ruefully. "And I like myself better now than I used to."

"Than you did when we were friends," he clarified.

"Yes."

Her answer stabbed at him.

"You want a certain type of woman," she went on. "And that's okay! I don't hold that against you. Some men like blondes, some like women with tans, some like the nerdy type, and you like the sparkling, vivacious, thin type. I don't blame you. Tracy is truly beautiful."

"Not in the ways that matter in the long-term."

"Well, obviously compatibility matters, too, but…" Grace sighed. "But you knew what you wanted and you went after it. Well, I learned to do that, too. I know what I want, and I'm going to chase it."

"So…what are you chasing?" he asked.

"My career, for one. It's a tough market for teachers right now, and having gotten a full-time job is massive. I worked really hard for that."

"And I'm happy for you," he said.

"You're mildly annoyed that I'm leaving," she countered.

"I'm..." Yeah, he was. But it wasn't about her moving on so much as his losing her again. "I'll miss you." His mind spun, trying to pull his feelings together into words. "Grace, we had something special. You weren't just some girl I used to know, and I know I meant more to you, too. Yeah, we were hard to define, but... I'm realizing now that if anyone was compatible, it was you and I."

"I disagree," she replied. "Compatibility is about more. We didn't have the spark—and that's something I want. *I'm* not settling for less than that, Billy."

Her words slipped past his defenses, and he felt their stab. He was less than *she* wanted. And why shouldn't he be? He couldn't read. He'd just been some high school dropout, hanging out with a woman destined for better things.

"I want to get married and have kids," she went on, and her voice choked. "I need spark and excitement and intimacy and fun. For me. And I'm really sorry, Billy, but that isn't going to happen with you around."

He arrived at the elementary school and signaled, turning in. Her car was the only one in the lot, and they were silent as he pulled into the spot next to it.

She was letting him down easy...sort of. Of course she wasn't interested in sticking around—she was educated and talented. He was just the loser guy she used to have a crush on. And apparently he was a block to her personal happiness.

"Yeah," he said, nodding and releasing her hand. "And you'll get that guy."

"I will." She reached for the door handle. "Good night, Billy," she said quietly, and she hopped down, slamming the door behind her.

Billy waited until she was safely in her car and she'd pulled out of the spot before he put his truck into reverse.

She'd always been better than him, and he knew he had no right to mess with her emotions. Heck, he was trying to focus on being a dad right now, so Grace was right to brush him off.

Later, after she'd left Eagle's Rest, she'd be distant—married to that great guy, most likely.

And he'd have lost her completely.

CHAPTER ELEVEN

BILLY DROVE HOME, his mind wrapping around the problem that was Grace Beverly. How selfish had he been over the years? He hadn't ever considered that before. Of all of his relationships in his life, his friendship with Grace had been the one he'd been most proud of. But he was doing it again, even now. He could feel it. He was asking more of Grace than he should...wanting something between friendship and romance—some limbo where he wouldn't have to commit to anything but didn't have to let go of her.

"Selfish is right," he muttered.

"Who's selfish?" a little voice came from the back seat.

Billy startled, then suppressed a sigh. "No one, kiddo. Go back to sleep."

"Why is Miss Beverly mad at you, Daddy?"

"She's not mad at me," he said. "It's nothing."

"I think she's mad at you…" There was a waver in Poppy's voice. "Did she stop being your friend?"

"She's my friend still. Poppy, how much of that did you hear?"

Poppy didn't answer, and he bit back any more questions. That was supposed to be a private conversation, with a child conveniently asleep in the back seat, and now his daughter had heard it all.

"Is Miss Beverly going to be mad at me, too?" Poppy whispered.

"No! No…" Billy looked into the rearview mirror again, and she could see Poppy's wide eyes and pale cheeks. "Poppy, this has nothing to do with you at all. It's just grown-up stuff."

"Is it because of me?" Poppy asked.

And he remembered the times his mother had told him the same thing… *Billy, sweetheart, this is grown-up stuff. Uncle Gil won't be coming around anymore, and it's nothing to do with you. He liked you a lot, but…* And despite the fact that it had nothing to do with him, he'd had to ride out the bumps along with his mom. Billy had never been able to comfort his mother.

"No, Poppy. I promise. Me and Miss Beverly are still friends."

This was why he was trying to avoid romantic entanglements—because it got complicated for the kids in the middle. And whatever he was doing here wasn't much better than what his mom had done.

The drive into the foothills took thirty minutes, and by the time he got to the ranch, Poppy was asleep. Thankfully. Getting her out of her car seat and into the cabin had been the easy part. Then he had to get her out of her snowsuit, out of her school clothes and into her pajamas for bed, without waking her up too much. Teeth brushing could wait for morning.

When Poppy was finally settled, he sank into the couch with a sigh. What Grace had said changed everything. He could no longer blame her for keeping her distance. That was the worst part—he'd hoped he could talk her out of whatever had offended her and set it right. But this? There was no fixing ten years or more of oblivious selfishness on his part. Her moving on, away from him, was the right choice.

Billy rubbed his hands over his face, then pushed himself back out of his seat and headed for a closet. He pulled a milk crate out from the bottom of the closet, and he thumbed past some old yearbooks and a couple of sports trophies. He stopped when he got to the thin book he was looking for.

This was the only book his mother had ever given him. It was a picture book that she'd gotten at a garage sale one day, and she'd given it to him before she went out on a date. If he recalled properly, he'd been babysat that night by a neighbor, and he'd been angry with his mom. It was just another boyfriend with a broad smile and inappropriate groping hands toward his mother. He'd hated every single one of her beaus.

That night, before she left, his mother tried to comfort him. She took a couple of minutes on the couch with him. She'd given him the book and looked so hopeful as she passed it over.

"I'll be back," she'd said earnestly. "I always come back, don't I?"

Billy had been angry, so he tossed it aside. His mother left, and before he went to bed, he grudgingly opened it.

He couldn't read it, but he'd liked the pictures—a woman with a bright smile holding a little boy's hand. They walked in a park, ate in a bright kitchen, tramped through a grocery store and hung upside down on a railing, side by side. The illustrations were glossy and bright, and he'd found that little book comforting in spite of himself. Whenever she left after that, he'd make up his own stories to go along with it…long conversations between mother and son when there was no boyfriend hanging around that he was supposed to call "Uncle."

He flipped a page—the letters and words jumbling together as they always did. He put a finger underneath the first word, going over letter after letter, locking them in his mind. *L. O. O. K.* He froze, the letters suddenly reminding him of the card with the googly eyes on it. He knew this word!

He moved, able to decipher a few of the smaller words. "Look at the…" was as far as he got, but his heart was hammering in his chest. He'd read three words on his own, standing here beside a closet. He hadn't been prompted. He didn't have any cards lying on a table in front of him.

And the fact that three little words could make him so stupidly happy brought a lump to his throat.

His mom had tried… She'd loved him,

despite her mistakes. And she'd given him this picture book to show him she cared. He couldn't read it. Yet. That was the part that filled him with hope.

Yet.

He still had a few more days with Grace, and he couldn't lose them. He couldn't let these confusing, muddled, unreturned feelings get in the way of him learning to read at long last.

He wouldn't ask more of her. She could leave Eagle's Rest and go build that life she wanted, free and clear of the likes of him. She wasn't offering a continuation of the boundary-challenged friendship that meant so much to him. And he couldn't blame her. But before she went, he'd make the most of the one thing she was offering—her teaching skills.

He desperately wanted to read.

GRACE WOUND A towel around her hair and regarded her foggy reflection.

"You and your big mouth, Grace," she muttered. She'd said too much. She'd told herself that she didn't owe Billy any explanations—and she'd been right.

Her feelings for him had been embarrassing back then, and they were embarrassing now. The least she could do was cling to the fact that she was no longer so pathetically deluded. Billy owed her nothing. He'd find another woman to love, and he'd forget all about this fiasco.

The truth was, Billy had occupied a place in her heart that no man had touched since. She'd dated a couple of guys in Denver—nice men, solid, relationship-worthy—but no matter how hard she tried to put Billy into the past, she couldn't turn off those feelings. Not completely.

Maybe this time with Billy would help her to do that—file him away into Lesson from the Past and move on in her own life. Maybe to a boyfriend, a future husband, a family of her own.

Grace ambled out of the bathroom and toward her old bedroom. Her parents were still out at the fund-raiser, and the house was quiet. She picked up a jar of face cream from the top of her dresser and dotted some around her face. She smoothed it over her skin slowly. It was time for some of her dreams to get more realistic, and it would help a whole lot if Billy lost his ability to melt her heart with one of his boyish grins.

She smoothed the last of the cream into her face just as her cell phone rang, and she wiped her hands down her bathrobe before picking it up. She glanced at the number first and sighed.

"Billy?" she said, picking up.

"Hey." His voice was low and warm. "Bad time?"

It was good to hear his voice again, even after only a couple of hours. She was back into the mire of their complicated relationship. Where she knew what was good for her and still couldn't seem to cut herself free of the man.

"No, it's fine," she said. "I have the house to myself still."

"So… Poppy wasn't as asleep as we thought," he said.

"What?" Grace winced, her mind flying back over the conversation in the truck. "How much did she hear?"

"Not sure. Enough." He sighed. "She was pretty upset. I'll have to talk to her about it in the morning."

"Upset, why?" Grace asked.

"She thinks you aren't my friend anymore, and that if you and I have a falling out, you won't like her anymore, either."

"Shoot…" Grace shut her eyes, filled with regret. "I'm her teacher. This is probably really confusing for her."

"Yeah."

"What did you tell her?" Grace asked.

"That we are friends, and that we're fine," he said. "Aren't we?"

"Yeah…of course."

"Thing is, Grace. I know I've wanted to keep our friendship…complicated, for lack of a better word. But tonight I saw why we can't. We need those reasonable boundaries, or it complicates things for Poppy, too."

Grace sank onto the side of her bed. "True."

This close friendship wasn't going to be healthy for Poppy, either. This wasn't about just the two of them anymore, and Grace should have appreciated that fact a whole lot sooner than now.

"So… I'll cut it out," he said quietly. "I won't ask more of you."

"Thank you…"

"So, how are you going to end your birthday?" he asked, changing the subject.

"I don't know…" She glanced back at the paperback she'd been planning on reading before bed. "With a wild party. You know me."

"Ha. I'll bet."

Grace smiled at his dry response. "What's it to you?"

"I don't know. A nice round number like thirty deserves a little more fanfare, don't you think?"

"I had fanfare. We went sledding…and traumatized your daughter with our mutual dysfunction."

"We did," he said with a low laugh. "But we didn't sing 'Happy Birthday.'"

Grace chuckled. "And yet I survived."

"You want me to sing it now?" he asked, a note of teasing entering his voice.

"Not particularly." She chuckled. "So, you called to harass me during my last few birthday hours?"

"Harass? Is that what you call my singing voice?" he laughed. "Fine… I'll be reasonable and leave you to your own plans."

"Thank you."

"Look, I don't want to be the selfish guy who holds you back. You make my life so much better. Beyond your birthday, I mean. You have your own plans, and I won't make that hard on you."

"I appreciate that," she said. "And what I said before—" Her breath caught. "It was a long time ago, Billy, so things don't have to be weird between us."

"I know," he replied. "That's probably for the best, because while I was pretty much blind to your feminine wiles back in the day, I have to say, I see them now."

Grace felt heat rise in her cheeks. "Billy—"

"I'm not saying that to flirt," he countered. "I'm saying... Look, we're both healthy adults, and there was a time when you were attracted to me. You've since come to your senses. Well, now I'm the one who's realizing what I can't have..."

"And it's precisely because you can't have it," she chided. "If I were available, you wouldn't be."

"You think so?" He chuckled. "I don't. You're different, Gracie."

"You keep saying that." She caught her reflection in the mirror over her old dresser. Her towel was piled on top of her head, her cheeks pink and her eyes glistening. What was it about Billy that always did this to her?

"It's true. You're all grown-up."

"I was all grown-up before," she pointed out. "I'm the same woman, with a little more makeup and a bigger clothing budget."

"I know I've been overstepping," he said. "So I'll try and stop that."

"Okay," she agreed. "It'll make saying goodbye easier anyway, right?"

"Yeah…" He was silent for a beat.

"I need to get some rest before school tomorrow," Grace said. "I have twenty-three four-year-olds to keep up with."

"Yeah, of course," he said quickly.

"Do I need to talk to Poppy about what happened tonight?" she asked.

"No, I'll do it in the morning," he replied. "I'm her dad—it should be me."

"I'll see you tomorrow, after school, then," she said.

"Tomorrow. Good night, Gracie." His voice was deep and warm, and she leaned her ear against the phone, wishing with all her heart she could ignore logic just this once. Then he hung up, and she was left staring at herself in that mirror.

She was thirty now. And no matter how much she wished it could be otherwise, she needed to leave this man in the past. There was a little girl who needed her father to herself for a while.

CHAPTER TWELVE

THE NEXT MORNING, Grace watched for signs that Poppy was upset, but all seemed fine. The little girl came over to say hi, and Grace gave her a hug.

"Good morning, sweetie," Grace said quietly. "How are you?"

"Good," Poppy whispered.

"I'm glad. We're going to have a good day!"

It was the teacher thing to say—but that was who she was to Poppy, her teacher. She couldn't get herself mixed up in Poppy's life on a personal level. This was why professional boundaries existed, wasn't it? To protect the kids.

The day wore on, and soon it was almost time for music class, when Mr. Shaw would lead the class in a line to the music room and Grace would have forty-five minutes to herself before that line of preschoolers came trailing back into the classroom again.

She would use the time to think, get herself re-centered.

"All right, friends," she said, raising her voice over the noise of chatter. "It's time to clean up so that we're ready for music class. Let's put everything away. Puppets in the box. Crayons in the buckets. Paper in the recycling bin."

The kids already knew the routine, but transition times took some prompting from her, so she went around the room, redirecting children back to the task at hand. Poppy stood at a window, staring outside. She had a forlorn expression, and Grace watched her for a moment. Poppy wasn't okay...and Grace might need to talk about last night with her after all.

But would that be wrong? Billy had said he'd take care of it, and if she went against a parent's wishes... She watched Poppy for a moment longer before turning back to a little boy who was methodically breaking crayons in half.

"Nigel, we don't break crayons," Grace said. "Do we?"

Nigel stopped, looking down at the crayon pieces on the table. "I do."

Grace fixed him with a no-nonsense stare,

and he put the crayon in his hand back into the bucket.

A child's shriek sliced through the air, and Grace looked up to see Poppy flying across the room. She shoved a chair out of her way, and as Grace jumped up, Poppy disappeared out the classroom door. Grace dashed after her, but when she got to the door, the hallway was empty, the outside door swinging shut.

Grace's heart pounded. She didn't have time to call the office—she needed to get Poppy back into the school. So she jogged to the next classroom door, and poked her head inside.

"Trinity, could you watch my class? I've got a runner."

And without waiting for a reply, she ran to the outside door and pushed out into the biting winter wind.

Poppy was running across the playground, her indoor shoes slipping and sliding as she sank ankle-deep into the dry snow.

"Poppy!" Grace shouted.

There was a woman walking along the sidewalk that passed by the playground, and Poppy was struggling toward her. Snow clung to her pink pants, and the biting wind ruffled through her hair and her thin shirt.

"Mommy!" Poppy screamed.

Grace started out after her, rushing through the snow. The leather of her shoes would be ruined—there was no way around that—and the wind was searing cold, whipping through her sweater. Grace could see her own breath billowing out in front of her as she ran after Poppy, closing the distance between them.

"Mommy!" Poppy wailed once more, and she stumbled, then sank to her knees in the snow.

The woman on the sidewalk looked toward them, surprise on her face, just as Grace caught up with Poppy, and Grace bent down next to her, sliding an arm around her thin, trembling shoulders.

"Poppy?" Grace said softly.

The woman stared at them and Grace gave her an apologetic smile before she moved on again.

"That's not her..." Poppy whispered.

"I know, sweetie," Grace said, scooping Poppy up and rising back to her feet.

"That's not Mommy..." Poppy said. Then she sucked in a ragged breath and started to cry. Hot tears soaked into Grace's sweater, and she hugged Poppy a little bit closer.

Poppy thought she'd seen her mother out here, and she'd run after her like her life had depended on it. How often had Poppy searched for that familiar face? This little girl still couldn't quite wrap her heart around the fact that her mother had walked away.

Tracy had walked away, too. And Grace had told her father last night that she couldn't stay in his life... From Poppy's perspective, how did all this feel? Did she blame herself?

As Grace turned back toward the school, she did her best to shield Poppy from the wind. She ducked her head down and plunged forward, her toes already getting numb from the snow that had slithered into her shoes. The outside door opened, and she saw Evan Shaw, the young music teacher, standing there. He held the door open for her as she came back inside, then released it.

"Everything okay?" Evan asked. "What happened?"

"She took off," Grace said. "I caught her, though."

"Yeah, good... I'll take the rest of the class to the music room, then—"

"And I'll get to the bottom of what happened here. Thanks, Mr. Shaw," she said with a smile. Then she turned to her colleague who she'd interrupted to watch her class. "Thanks, Mrs. Ryan. I've got her."

As her colleague arranged the children in their line, Grace kicked off her wet shoes and lowered Poppy to the ground. She attempted to put her down, at least, but Poppy had her arms wrapped around Grace's neck, and she wasn't letting go.

The children stared as they walked past— Poppy having done the unthinkable when she made a run for it. She hoped none of the others got any ideas there.

"Poppy," Grace said quietly.

Poppy still trembled with sobs, and Grace scooped up her wet shoes with one hand and then carried Poppy back into the now-empty classroom. She shut the door, then went over to her desk and sank into the chair. Poppy curled up in a ball on Grace's lap and finally released her neck.

"What happened, sweetie?" Grace asked quietly.

"I thought that was Mommy."

"You can't just run off," Grace said. "You scared me!"

"But I thought it was Mommy."

"I know, I know…"

Grace closed her eyes and rested her cheek

on Poppy's head. Grace couldn't fix this one. She couldn't bring Carol-Ann back, or fill the hole in this little heart. She couldn't be the mom Poppy so desperately needed, but oh, how she wished she could. Poppy needed a mother who would stand by her, make her feel loved, and safe, and special.

"Will my mommy come back?" Poppy whispered.

"I don't know, sweetie..."

"I want my mommy." The tears started again, and Grace understood all that Poppy was grieving. How could a child be expected to accept that her mom was just...gone?

Grace rocked Poppy back and forth. She longed to say that Poppy could count on her... that she'd be here always. But that would be wrong. Grace wasn't a mother figure for Poppy; she was a teacher, and there were professional boundaries for a reason. Refilling Poppy's broken heart wasn't Grace's job— it was Billy's. Billy was the one who would have to make up for Carol-Ann's absence, and Grace had to step back and let him.

"Poppy," she said softly. "One day your mom will see you again, I'm sure. I don't know when, but she won't just show up at school, or surprise you in a grocery store or something. When she comes, she'll talk to your dad about it, and he'll let you know what to expect. Okay?"

At least Grace hoped she was telling the truth, because this little girl couldn't go through every day of her life with a pent-up breath, waiting to see if her mother emerged from the shadows. That was cruelty.

The door opened just then, and one of the receptionists poked her head inside. "Miss Beverly, a message for you." She hesitated. "Everything okay?"

"Yeah, Poppy just needed a hug. She tried to make a break for it, so I'll have to talk to her father." She'd also have to write up an incident report.

The receptionist came into the classroom and handed Grace a pink slip of paper. "Speaking of which," the receptionist said.

Grace looked down at the message slip. *Phone call from Billy Austin, father of Poppy Austin. He is running late. Please call him on his cell phone at your earliest convenience. He says you have the number.*

Grace sighed. The timing was terrible. Today, of all days, Poppy needed her father to show up right on time. She nodded a farewell to the receptionist, then looked down at Poppy. "It's from your dad. He says he's running late."

"Can I see?" Poppy asked.

Grace showed her the note, and Poppy wiped a hand across her watery eyes, then nodded.

"I'm going to call him now, okay?" Grace said. "Do you think you could sit on a chair next to me?"

Grace pulled her cell phone out of her bag in the side drawer of her desk and noticed there had been a couple of missed called from Billy's cell in the last hour. She tapped one instance to call him back.

"Gracie?" Billy said, picking up. "Did you just get my message now?"

"Just got it," she said.

"Yeah, so I've got a cow with a broken leg. I'm almost done here, but I can't just leave. I was hoping you might be willing to do me a favor…"

"And wait for you?" Grace said.

"No, it would be too long and she'll be hungry… Could you bring her to my place? I mean, if you wouldn't mind. I'll make you dinner—try and make up for the massive inconvenience. What do you say?"

"Just a second," Grace said, and she pulled

a picture book from her desk, then bent down to Poppy's level. "Why don't you read this one, Poppy? I think you'll like it."

Poppy took the book wordlessly and opened it. Grace walked a few paces away and lowered her voice.

"I can bring her home," Grace agreed, then lowered her voice further. "She thought she saw her mom out the window today, Billy."

"What?" Billy paused. "What happened?"

"She ran for it—she took off and I had to catch her. She almost made it to the fence outside without a coat or boots or anything. She thought it was Carol-Ann."

"Ah, hell…"

"Yeah." Grace didn't know what else to say. "I thought you should know."

"Thanks." He was silent for a moment. "This is awful timing—"

"I'll drive her home," she reassured him. It was the least she could do after the worry she'd caused the little girl last night.

Some days, being a teacher felt amazing and like she had her fingerprints on the future. But sitting here with the tiny girl staring toward the window and the empty playground outside, it didn't feel like she was half enough.

"You'll have to call the office and tell them that you're giving me permission to drive her home," Grace added, clearing her throat.

"Yeah, right." But he sounded relieved. "The spare key to the cabin is under the thermometer on the doorjamb. So you can just let yourself in when you get there. I'll hurry home. I promise."

"Okay. I can do that."

"You're one in a million, Gracie." And he didn't sound like he was joking or smoothing things over this time. He sounded deeply grateful, and a little shaken.

"I'm aware," she said. "But call the office. I can't leave after school until you do."

THAT AFTERNOON, BILLY pushed his hat back on his head as he drove up the road toward the cabin. He'd been worrying about Poppy ever since the phone call… She'd run into the snow, looking for her mom?

A mental image tore at his heart. His daughter was with Grace right now, which meant she was safe, but even his relationship with Grace was turning into a stressor for Poppy. The one woman to give him a bit of comfort… Ironic.

The truck rattled over the bumpy road, the

sky turning to dusk. He pushed his hat back on his head and heaved a sigh.

He was starting to have some compassion for his mother's balancing act—trying to work enough to pay the bills and find ways for his life to go along normally. At least she'd come home! His mom hadn't been perfect, but she'd never walked out for something "better" than him, like modeling in Germany.

Billy took the turn that led up toward his little cabin. He could see Grace's car parked out front, and the interior was lit up with a homey glow. He pulled up next to her car, and he saw Poppy appear in the window, her expression somber. Her little shoulders were slumped, and she watched as he got out of the truck and headed toward the front door. Grace materialized behind her and waved.

He smiled back and met her gaze. She was here—for now, for this one tough evening—and while he knew that his relationship with Poppy's teacher only confused his daughter, he was grateful to have her here. For him.

"Daddy!" Poppy said as he came in, and looking up with big, soulful eyes. He scooped her up in a hug, holding her close for a minute, then giving her a smile.

"Hi there, kiddo," he said, and he put her back down so he could take off his coat and boots. He dropped his cowboy hat on Poppy's head. "Thanks, Grace. I appreciate this."

"Sure." Grace smiled as Poppy walked blindly with Billy's hat over her eyes. "I did a lesson with her already. And we read more of *The Secret Garden*."

"She must have liked that," Billy said. Business as usual—this was for Poppy's benefit.

Grace angled her head and they moved a little further away from Poppy. "I didn't talk to her about last night. You'd said you wanted to do it, and—"

"Yeah, no, that's what I wanted," he replied. "Thanks."

"She's scared, though. She's dealing with a lot, and if our talk last night only made things worse, I'm sorry."

"It's on me," he replied, then cleared his throat. "I'll figure it out. Isn't that what parents do? Wing it?"

"Sort of," she said.

Billy rubbed a hand over his hair. Grace was wearing a soft gray sweater with a loose cowl-neck. It was paired with some slacks that were almost the same color.

"Thanks for being here," he murmured.

"I wouldn't do this for just anyone," she said with a faint smile, and he believed her.

"Are you hungry?" he asked. "I've got steaks in the fridge."

"I'm hungry!" Poppy declared, pulling the hat off her head and leaving her hair rumpled.

"Good. So am I," Billy said, forcing joviality that he didn't quite feel.

He headed into the kitchen, gratified when Grace followed him. He hauled open the fridge and reached for the cellophane-wrapped steaks, then glanced over at her.

"If I make your steak just the way you like it, will you peel these?" he asked and he caught her eye, waiting for her to relax just a bit. He nodded toward a bag of potatoes.

Grace's cheeks pinked slightly and she reached for the potatoes.

"So you make a decent steak now, do you?" she said, and he caught the teasing glint in her eyes.

"You're not the only one who's matured the last few years." He shot her a grin. "I cook. I'm not bad."

Grace stood next to him at the counter and

she started to peel. It felt good to have her with him.

"Grace, do you ever think of taking a teaching position here in Eagle's Rest?" he asked.

"There aren't any," she replied. "I snapped up the maternity leave, but teaching spots aren't that plentiful."

"So Denver is the place for you," he concluded.

"Afraid so." She dropped a peeled potato into a pot and grabbed another one.

"Yeah, I get it. Decent-paying jobs aren't so plentiful for the guy who can't read, either."

"What happened in Denver?"

He'd been humiliated in Denver, and while he didn't exactly want to make himself look more pathetic in her eyes, he wasn't going to lie, either.

"I got a few different jobs. But for training, they always give you a book. A lot of good that does me, right? I started off trying for mechanic positions. I mean, I can fix pretty much anything, right? But they want you to follow a certain set of steps—all written down in a book. And I couldn't memorize it. And then there were these forms you had to fill out… It just didn't work. So I got hired and fired about a week into training. Tracy was furious." He could still remember the look on her face as she did the mental math there, trying to figure out why he couldn't make things work in Denver. "That's when I had to tell her the truth."

"And?"

"She…just seemed surprised, I guess." Billy sighed. "So then I applied for work at a factory. She had to help me fill out all the forms. That was humiliating. But I was doing okay there—I just hated the work. I mean—boring as anything, and no respect. My direct supervisor looked like a fifteen-year-old, and he'd holler at me for no reason at all. Just a small man trying to feel big. But when I mentioned anything about it at home, Tracy said that I'd better be grateful for what I could get. And I guess she had a point…"

"Not really," Grace retorted. "Everyone deserves respect."

"Yeah, well…" He turned on the fry pan and poured in some oil. "My point is, I like cattle. I like horses. And around here, I have a reputation for being good at that kind of work, so I get respect, too, and not just the basic human respect that should be passed out to everyone. I'm respected for my ability here. So my life is here—whether I like it or not. And it looks like yours is in the city."

What could he do? He couldn't give a woman in his life the world. He was hobbled.

"Would you have listened to me before if I'd told you Tracy was bad for you?" Grace asked.

"Nope."

Grace laughed softly. "Didn't think so."

And that was the truth. He'd been blinded by Tracy's long legs and model figure. A whole lot like Carol-Ann's. But neither woman had been good for him—or for his daughter, for that matter. And neither woman could hold a candle to Grace.

He looked over at her, methodically peeling those potatoes. She was beautiful—but in a different way from other women he'd known and loved. She was physically attractive, too. There wasn't a one-size-fits-all mold for beauty, but Grace's beauty went deep, and it was forged in the same place her character had been formed. It was a heart-deep kind of loveliness that just made him want to slide closer to her.

Except whatever was between him and Grace, it wasn't sitting comfortably with either of them, and it was messing things up for Poppy. For his daughter, they'd better get into conventional territory.

This wasn't about his emotional needs anymore—it was about his daughter. And it was about Grace. Sometimes a man had to put his own heart aside for the women he cared about most.

CHAPTER THIRTEEN

POPPY LIKED STEAK, and it felt better than Billy realized to have both Grace and Poppy enjoying his cooking. Poppy perked up as they ate together, and she'd consumed half a steak—which was quite a bit. It felt good to feed her—see her get some good, wholesome food inside her. When she'd eaten all she could, he stabbed the leftover steak and dropped it onto his own plate, giving her a wink. For the first time ever, the food on his rickety kitchen table felt like a family dinner.

He was doing it—he was growing into fatherhood.

Except his little girl was carrying grief deep inside of her that he couldn't seem to fix—at least not fast enough.

"What happened today, kiddo?" Billy asked her quietly when the meal was over.

"Nothing," she murmured.

"Miss Beverly says you thought you saw your mom," he prompted.

"Yup."

"And...you tried to go after her?"

"It wasn't her, Daddy," she said, and tears welled in her eyes.

"I know, sweetie." He gathered her onto his lap and snuggled her close. "She's in Germany. That's really far away."

"How far?" she asked.

"It's a very long plane ride. And when she comes back to Colorado, we'll see her... together. I promise. Okay? I'm not going to keep you away from your mom."

"Miss Beverly says she won't surprise me," Poppy said.

"Did she ever surprise you before?" What Billy wanted to know was exactly how much consistency she'd had in her young life, but Poppy didn't seem to know how to answer that. She leaned against his shoulder and heaved out a long, sad sigh.

"Poppy, do you like living here with me?" Billy asked hesitantly. "I mean, do you feel safe here? Do feel happy?"

"You make supper," Poppy whispered. "And you pick me up from school."

"Yeah..." He kissed the top of her head. "Look, Poppy. Because I'm your dad, I can make sure that you can live with me always.

And if we do that, then I promise that you'll see your mom, too, but I'd be the one to take you home every night, and to make your dinner, and to buy your snow pants…and… I'll learn how to read you stories, too."

"Okay…" Poppy said softly.

"Yeah? Is that a deal?" he asked.

Poppy nodded. "Will you go away, Daddy?"

"Never. Not in a million years. Not in a billion years. I'm your daddy for always, and I'm not going anywhere. That's a promise you can take to the bank."

Poppy smiled at that, as he'd hoped she would, and she straightened. "Can I read stories now?"

"Sure thing."

Poppy curled up on the couch with a storybook while Billy and Grace did a sink load of dishes. The plates and cups, the crusty pan… Billy ran the cloth over a plate, then pulled it dripping from the sink.

"I'm going to make sure Poppy stays with me," he said after a moment.

"You're going to go for full custody?" she asked.

"There's enough evidence that Carol-Ann wasn't caring for her properly—I mean, leaving a kid in the car when she went drinking? Yeah, I'm pretty sure I can get her full-time."

"I think you should," Grace said, glancing back toward the couch. "She deserves better than what she had."

"She needs her mom, though," he said. "I won't cut Carol-Ann off or anything, but she's not going to be the functional mother figure that Poppy's going to need as she grows up."

"You want a wife, then," Grace said, and he looked down into Grace's warm eyes.

"No," he admitted, grabbing a dish and plunging it into the hot water. "I've had all sorts of experience with dating the wrong women, and the drama that comes with it. You know how shaken up my daughter is. She needs a stable home with a dad who's focused on her, not his girlfriend."

Grace didn't answer.

"You think I'm wrong?"

"I didn't say that," she replied.

"You're doing that whole silent thing that means you think I'm wrong," he countered, a smile playing at his lips. "I know you."

"No, I was just thinking that Poppy is going to have a happy childhood with you. She's lucky that you're her dad."

"Thanks." He shot Grace a grin. "I wish you were sticking around, though. You could be that female role model she'll need. If Poppy learned from you…turned out a bit like you… I'd be proud."

"You need the real thing, Billy," Grace said, and her expression turned sad. "I'm not that. I'm just…convenient."

"You're a spectacular woman, Grace," he said, sobering. "You're smart, kind, full of wisdom. You're a truly good person, and the fact that you're my friend doesn't make you a convenience."

"You need a wife," she said. "You might not be ready to find a woman to marry yet, but that's what you need—someone to raise Poppy with you, to love both of you. And me—I've never been your type. Right now you're scared, you're alone, you're a dad for the first time and wading through all of this… I stand by what I said. I'm convenient. You don't need me—you just think you do."

They'd have to agree to disagree on that. Grace had always been more of a necessity in his life than he'd realized. He was finally recognizing it. She'd always been so much more than a pal.

Billy glanced toward the sofa. "Is Poppy still reading?"

There were some things a guy didn't even try to talk about if his daughter was anywhere within earshot. Grace didn't answer, and Billy tiptoed over to look over the back of couch. Poppy had the book in her arms, hugged against her chest like a teddy bear, but her eyes were shut and she was snoring softly.

"Oh, man..." he murmured and glanced at his watch. It was half an hour past her bedtime, and he felt that pang of guilt.

"Come on, kiddo," he murmured. He rounded the couch, pulled the book from her arms and scooped his daughter up. "Time for bed..."

Poppy moaned in her sleep, but didn't wake up, and he carried her into her bedroom and tucked her into her bed. She rolled over and snuggled into her stuffed dog, heaving out a sleepy sigh. When he looked back, Grace stood in the doorway, watching him.

"I hate doing that," he said softly, coming to the doorway and back out into the living room.

"Why?" she asked.

He pulled the bedroom door shut, leaving only a crack, as usual.

"Because I feel guilty," he admitted. "My mom never sent me to bed. I stayed up as late as I wanted. I fell asleep on the couch because I liked the TV to keep me company, and I would go to bed when I woke up, freezing, in the middle of the night."

"Oh…" Grace met his gaze, and he felt a tickle of warmth.

How many times the last three years had he saved up thoughts and memories, wanting to tell Grace about them? How many times had he unloaded it all in his mind, imagining how he'd explain…how he'd joke…how he'd feel better for having had her to talk to. And now he did have her—for a few days longer, at least.

"Thing is, my mom kept me up with her because she missed me," he went on, his heart giving a squeeze. "And I guess I can understand that now."

"Isn't that a good thing?" Grace whispered.

"I'm more like her than I want to be."

"You're a good father, Billy," Grace said firmly. He met her gaze for a moment. She meant it—he could see that in her clear blue eyes, and he was grateful for that, even if he wasn't sure he entirely believed her.

"I'm going to be," he said after a beat of silence.

Grace slipped her hand into the crook of his arm—an old, familiar gesture—and he sighed, sliding a hand over her soft fingers. It felt good to lean into her again, to touch her.

"You aren't a convenience, Grace," he murmured.

"Billy—"

"I'm serious," he said. "I might not have realized how much you meant when I had you around, but that doesn't make you a convenience. It just makes me an idiot."

Grace chuckled. "Okay…"

"I missed you, Gracie. Really, really missed you." The words caught in his throat.

Grace looked up at him and tears misted her eyes. "Me, too."

"Did you really have to cut me off?"

"I think so," she said, shaking her head helplessly. "I'd lived in this stupid hope that you'd suddenly be attracted to me for years. And I felt like an idiot, because then when I was in Denver, I met guys who *were* attracted to me right off the bat. Instead of looking in on romance, I was someone's ideal." Grace dropped her gaze. "I figured out what it meant to be desired, and I liked it."

Well, he couldn't help but see what those other guys had seen in her. She was definitely beautiful—full lips, sparkling eyes, skin like milk.

"You are beautiful," he murmured.

"You don't have to—"

"Hey." He brushed a tendril of hair away from her face and stepped closer, the cool air evaporating into warmth between them. "You know me. I don't say stuff I don't mean."

If he only had a few more days with her, he had to say it all, open up. He wouldn't forgive himself if he held it back. He'd only go over it again and again on sleepless nights, wishing he'd found the courage to tell her how much she meant to him. And she *was* beautiful. He couldn't let those Denver guys be the only ones who had told her.

She blinked, looking up at him with widened eyes. "Thanks," she said feebly.

Suddenly the moment struck him as funny, and he chuckled. "You're not good at this."

"At what?"

"Flirting."

"Well, you shouldn't be flirting," she countered.

She looked so serious that it sparked a bit of defiance inside of him. He *should* have been crossing these lines years ago, truth be told. He should have seen what was going on with her. He should have recognized what she meant to him all this time... So maybe he wanted to flirt with her right now. It might be all he had.

"You're still terrible at it," he said with a soft laugh. "Do you have more skills in Denver, or something?"

Grace's cheeks colored again, and he was gratified when she laughed. "Yes, I do."

"Maybe you were just awkward," he teased. "Like now. I think I like it. It suits you."

"I'm not the awkward one," she retorted. "You're the one trying to flirt with someone you know too well."

"So that's my problem here?" He stepped closer still and closed the gap between them, sliding a hand down her soft arm until he reached her waist. "I know you too well."

He didn't, though. He knew her as a friend, but not as more. Not as a woman who could melt under his touch. He'd missed out on a whole lot.

"Yes…" Her voice came out in a breath.

Her gaze flickered up to his and he looked down into those ocean-blue eyes. Her lips parted and she sucked in a breath but didn't say anything. He could see her heart beating in the soft flesh of her neck.

This was dangerous territory, and he knew he should stop. Friendship and flirting were one thing, but he was quickly moving in a new direction—one he had no right to with Grace.

"I have to work tomorrow," she said.

"Yep. Me, too." He waited for her to move away from him, but she didn't. He could still see the quiver of her pulse. Billy slid his hand around her waist. He wasn't meaning to keep her from leaving, exactly; he just wanted to see what she felt like in his arms before she rightfully pulled away.

"Not fair…" She licked her lips, then ever so gently rested her fingertips on his arms. She knew what he was doing, and her tentative move toward him sped his heart up into a hammering rhythm. His skin warmed at her touch, and his gaze dropped down to her mouth again.

"Not going?" he murmured.

"Soon…" she whispered.

"What if I kissed you right now?" He tugged her a little closer.

"Why?" she whispered, wide-eyed.

"Because it's all I seem to be thinking about right now," he admitted.

This was where she could push him away, tell him off, give him a smack. Her options were endless, and he'd never hold it against her.

"You had all the time in the world before—" she said, but he didn't let her finish. Billy dipped his head down and closed that space between them. He paused before his mouth touched hers, feeling the tickle of her breath against his face, waiting for her to flinch, pull back, show some kind of dislike. But she didn't, and when her eyes fluttered shut, he closed the last whisper of space between them, covering her lips with his.

Billy felt a flood of relief as his lips touched hers. She softened under his touch and leaned into him, fitting perfectly against his chest. She smelled like flowers, and kissing her felt so right. He'd missed her, but as his lips moved over hers, he knew it had been more than that…

He pulled back, shutting his eyes and resting his forehead against hers as he tried to find his rational thought again. She straightened away from him, and he opened his eyes, releasing her.

"Oh…" she breathed, her fingers coming up to her lips.

"Yeah…" He met her gaze once more, wondering what she was feeling. He hadn't expected to kiss her like that, exactly. He'd definitely meant to kiss her, but…

"I…um…" She reached up and wiped his bottom lip. "I smudged your lip gloss."

Billy chuckled at her joke. "Yeah, looks like."

She smoothed her lips together, evening the shine of her lip gloss once more. "I have to go."

"I know." Had he overstepped? Probably. But had he upset her? That was his biggest worry. "Grace…"

He stepped closer again, looking down into her eyes, trying to decipher what she was feeling. She stepped back and dropped her gaze.

"It's late," she reminded him.

"Okay. Yeah." He nodded quickly and shot her a tentative smile. "I just wanted to point out that, mistake or not, you kissed me back, Grace."

Her cheeks colored again, and she smiled slightly. "Shut up, Billy."

He laughed at that. "I noticed."

"We can't do this," she said. "I'm the kind of woman who likes some clearly defined boundaries, and this—" she shrugged helplessly "—this isn't defined at all."

"Sorry," he murmured.

Grace sucked in a deep breath as if steeling herself, then grabbed her jacket and stepped into her boots. Billy opened the front door for her, and she paused, looking up into his face. For a moment, he thought she might change her mind and stay a little longer... For a split second, he saw such a depth of conflicting emotion roiling in her ocean-blue eyes that he felt it like a vise on his chest.

But then she stepped past him and outside, her shoulders hunching against the cold.

"Drive safe," he said, and she shot him a smile, then opened her door and got in.

He stood there in the doorway until she'd pulled out and her taillights had disappeared down the gravel drive. Only then did he shut the door.

He stood in the soft light of his living

room, his arms crossed over his broad chest as he remembered the feeling of her lips on his, his heart swelling with the realization that his feelings for her had been well past friendship for a very long time. Why was he the last to figure this stuff out?

Yeah, things had changed. She wasn't his old buddy Gracie anymore, and he knew without a doubt that he'd been wrong to kiss her. She wasn't like the other women he'd been involved with. A kiss for Gracie meant something, and he'd just proven that there was more between them than just an old friendship.

But that didn't change what he could give, which meant whatever he felt for her had better stop at a kiss.

As GRACE DROVE down the highway, she tried to calm the pounding of her heart. What had she just done?

Billy was right—she'd kissed him back. That was the kiss she'd been waiting for for years…that was the way she'd wanted him to see her all that time she'd been silently and agonizingly in love with him. And his kiss had been everything she'd imagined and more. She'd never known what Billy was like when he focused on a woman that way…and just remembering that intense gaze of his as he moved closer to her made her breath catch.

For just a moment, she'd felt like the only woman in his entire world. His touch, his breath, his kiss… She leaned against the headrest and let out a slow sigh.

"Don't fall in love with him," she said aloud.

Because that was the problem here. She'd been kissed before. She'd had a couple of relationships and breakups before she'd come to this moment. She wasn't naïve or hopeful enough to think that a kiss promised something. It was just a kiss. It had been a moment when they were completely alone, when he'd opened up a little bit, and he'd suddenly seen the woman in her.

These things happened. To other people, mostly. But still.

Grace swallowed hard. It would be easier to be all metropolitan and push it aside if it had been a little less memorable. But she'd never been kissed like that, never had a man make her melt into a puddle with nothing more than his deep voice and his touch.

But, oh, his voice… Billy's laughter and

teasing always made her smile, but that low, soft murmur just before he kissed her...that was something else altogether.

Some women could enjoy a kiss like that and walk away with minimal emotional trauma, but Grace wasn't sure that she could. She'd loved him, and she'd done her best to put him behind her in Denver. To come back, see him again and finally get that kiss she'd yearned for all these years...

"Do *not* fall for him, Grace," she told herself firmly.

Because he chose now to open his eyes and see the woman in front of him? Other women had snapped their fingers, and he'd been attracted right away. And she'd quietly waited...and gotten nothing back, until now. It was exasperating. She'd had her heart through the wringer too many times with Billy. They knew each other very well, and she knew his tendencies. Right now she was his only choice. She was the one woman under his nose, and Billy was a testosterone-filled cowboy. It was the man in him reacting to the woman in her...at long last. And in a way that was gratifying. But if this were meant to be, it would have happened a long time ago.

Grace drove the rest the way back to her parents' place. There was a light on in the kitchen. She sighed. She wasn't in the mood to chat tonight, but there might not be any way past it.

She got out, locked her car and headed across the frozen, hard-topped snow, toward the side door.

Nothing had changed for her, she reminded herself. Two adults had momentarily given in to some chemistry. That was all. It didn't mean anything.

When Grace let herself in, she found her father sitting at the kitchen table, a mug of hot chocolate in front of him. He wore a bathrobe and a pair of slippers, and he looked up when she came in with a distracted smile.

"Hi, Gracie," he said. "Out late, huh?"

"Yeah," she said, slamming the door shut and undoing her coat. "Where's Mom?"

"In bed already," her father replied. "Out like a light."

"One of those days," Grace said, and she looked over at her father's hot chocolate. "That looks good."

"Want one?" her father asked. "Here, take this mug. I haven't started it yet. I'll make myself another."

Her father slid it across the table and got back up. It was nice to be home and cared for. She sank into the kitchen chair and took a sip.

"So, how's Billy?" her father asked as he poured some steaming water into a mug.

"Um." She looked up at her dad quizzically.

"Ah, hit on it, did I?" he asked with a smile, then turned back to the task at hand. "I figured you'd be out with him."

"Yeah, he's okay," Grace replied. "He's got his hands full with his daughter, so…"

"I'll bet. I remember having a young daughter. They keep you hopping." Her father came back to the table with another hot chocolate, then picked up the can of whipped cream and gave it a shake. "Want some?"

Grace held her mug out toward her father and he put a generous coil of cream on top, and then did the same for his own.

"So, what did you buy with your birthday money?" her father asked.

"Oh, nothing yet," she replied. "The shopping here is miserable. I'm waiting for Denver."

"I thought as much. Looking forward to getting back?"

"Yeah." She didn't sound convincing, even in her own ears.

"You've got the job waiting, right?" he prompted.

"I do," she said. "And I'm looking forward to it—especially the permanent position. Dad, I've been working toward this for so long, and it feels…" She stopped.

"Don't let him ruin this for you, Gracie," her father said quietly.

"He's not," she said.

"You sure?" her father pressed. "You've got a good life, sweetheart. You've worked for it, and I'm so proud of you. But you've got to enjoy it, too."

"It's hard seeing him again," she admitted.

"I always said he'd drag you down if you settled for him," her father said quietly. "He's nice. I'll give you that. And he's well-meaning. But he's not aimed at the same target you are."

She sighed. "He wants to pick up our friendship again."

Billy possibly wanted more than that…but it was hard to tell.

"And what do you want?" her father asked.

"I want…" She paused, considering. "I

want to keep my balance. I want to enjoy everything I've worked for."

"Good goals," her father said, taking a sip.

"And I want to get married and have kids," she said after a beat of silence. "Is that desperate, Dad?"

"Nah." Her father sucked in a deep breath. "You have to be ready for something to jump at the opportunity when it presents itself. Being ready for that kind of thing normally means feeling a little bit lonely. It's normal."

Except Grace had dated a couple of very marriageable men in Denver. Kind, respectable, honest, devoted. And she hadn't been able to commit.

"Is Billy wanting more from you, then?" her father asked, and she heard the hesitation in his tone.

"I don't think so," she replied honestly. "He had the better part of a decade to try for that, and he never did. I'm just...here."

"You don't have to rescue everyone, Gracie," her father said quietly.

"I know," she replied.

The problem was, the only man she wanted to rescue was Billy. The others she managed to waltz past without too much trouble.

"Dad, I think I'll take this hot chocolate upstairs with me," she said, rising to her feet.

"All right," her father said. "Good night, sweetheart. Love you."

"Love you, too, Dad."

She picked up her mug and headed toward the stairs. She glanced back once and found her father staring moodily at the tabletop.

Her father wanted more for her than a relationship with Billy Austin, but this wasn't about her father, either. She wanted to move on with her life and get to that sweet spot she'd been working toward. She'd have a full-time position with the Denver school board, a career she cared about, and maybe she'd finally meet that great guy who could eclipse Billy in her heart. Was that possible? A man capable of being her best friend and curling her toes with a kiss?

CHAPTER FOURTEEN

THE NEXT AFTERNOON, Billy made sure he was done his shift early enough to pick Poppy up on time. Being a dad had a whole new set of pressures. Not only did he have to make enough to support his daughter, but he had to physically be there for her, be on time. He was normally a pretty punctual guy, but this wasn't about impressing a boss. This was about his daughter waiting for him in a classroom, looking out a window, wondering if her mother might walk by.

And Grace… He'd grown to regret that kiss when he'd finally gone to bed. He'd wanted it, and she'd kissed him back, but that didn't change the facts. She wasn't some woman to pass the time with; she was the best friend he'd ever had. And he'd just crossed the line.

He *was* an idiot.

Billy cruised down the highway, the sunlight sparkling off the snow that weighted down tree branches along the side of the road. The day felt more cheerful than he did. He was tired—he hadn't slept well. He'd been too busy beating himself up.

An image of Grace's lips, the way her eyes had sparkled just before her lids had fluttered shut...

He pulled his mind away from those thoughts. What had he been doing last night? He felt a wave of guilt. He'd had a lot to hold against his own mom, and he wasn't off to a great start with Poppy. He had four years of absence to make up for still.

The heat was pumping into the cab of his truck, and he turned it down, then cracked a window, breathing in a welcome breath of frigid air from outside.

He'd kissed Grace, and it was tangling up his emotions. Now he was looking forward to seeing her again, and it would be awkward. Instead of enjoying her as the friend she'd always been, he was going to be facing the woman he's crossed the line with. He remembered a talk in a youth group one year when he was a teenager trying to date a church girl, and they'd said that it was best to behave before marriage so there were no regrets. The girl had taken that seriously, which was probably for the best. Billy hadn't been the kind of kid she could count on as future-husband material. And now, he could see the wisdom in that preachy lecture, as irritating as it had been at the time. This had only been a kiss, but it still changed things. It still left him with regrets.

He owed Grace an explanation…and an apology, at the very least.

Billy's phone rang, and he eased his foot off the gas, slowing down a little as he punched the speaker button to pick up the call.

"Yeah," he said.

"Billy?"

He knew the voice, and he cleared his throat.

"Tracy," he said, trying to sound more confident than he felt right now. "What's up?"

"I just wanted to say hi," Tracy said.

He fought down a wave of anger. What could she possibly want from him now? He'd left her with everything. He wasn't the kind of guy to quibble over furniture. She'd humiliated him in front of his daughter, and now she wanted to talk? "Don't do this to me, Tracy," he said with a sigh. "You dumped me. We're over. No calling to say hi."

"Sorry." She sounded regretful. "I wasn't feeling well today, so I stayed home from work, and I...missed you. The apartment isn't the same without you, and..."

"Ah." Billy sighed. "There's bound to be a bit of that, I guess."

He missed what he'd thought he'd had with Tracy—in the beginning. He'd thought they'd been in love.

"Do you miss me?" she asked, and he could hear the hope in her voice that had always been so hard to resist. Except right now he was still remembering how Grace had felt in his arms, and how desperately he wanted to pull her into his embrace again.

But his breakup with Tracy wasn't that long ago, and he'd be lying if he said he'd simply banished the last three years from his mind. He wasn't a monster.

"A bit," he admitted.

"We were good together, Billy—"

"Don't remember us better than we were," he countered. "We were fighting a lot toward the end."

"We were..." He could hear her suck in a deep breath.

"Breakups make you forget that stuff," he added. "I drove you nuts."

"But maybe with some good talks, we could get to the bottom of that. Long-term relationships take a lot of work, and I'm willing to put it in. We could go to a relationship counsellor, or—"

"No." He clenched the steering wheel tighter. "Some things end for good reason. I'm not coming back to talk it to death in some therapist's office. We weren't even married."

"Maybe just some time alone, then. A vacation. I'd pay for it—I got a bonus. We always talked about lounging on a beach, didn't we?"

"I'm a dad, Tracy," he said. "That doesn't go away."

And he wasn't about to have his way paid by his heartbroken ex, either.

"True, but if we had some time for just the two of us... Maybe your mom could watch her for a week—"

"Tracy!" His voice was angrier than he'd meant it to be. "I'm not leaving my daughter behind while I go on some vacation. Sorry. She's been through enough and she needs me."

"Maybe I need you, too," Tracy said quietly.

Billy sighed, willing his grip on that steering wheel to relax.

"How is Poppy?" she asked after a moment of silence.

"She's dealing with a lot. I'm not sure you even have a right to ask about her."

"I know," Tracy said. "I should never have said what I did in front of her."

What the hell, Billy? I put up with a lot from you, and now you dump a kid on me? I'm supposed to be the stepmother now? I didn't sign on for this! Yeah, Billy remembered that clear as day.

"True. That was petty on your part. And cruel. Her mother had just abandoned her with a dad she'd never met, and you treated her like the worst punishment a woman could imagine."

"I get now how awful it was," Tracy said, her voice quivering. "I do. And I'm sorry. I know that's not worth much. I wasn't thinking. Sometimes people mess up."

"Yeah." He couldn't curb the bitterness in his tone.

"I want to make up for it," Tracy added.

"I don't see how."

"I could...talk to her," Tracy offered. "I

could tell her that I'm sorry. That I was wrong to say those things, and that I didn't mean them. I mean, I'd say it in child-friendly terms, but I could explain that my reaction was about me, and not about her. It might help…"

Would it? He wasn't sure if his anger about this was on behalf of his daughter or himself. He and Tracy were most definitely over, but if there was a way to take her words back, to take away their power so Poppy didn't carry them with her…

He passed the town's limits and took the first left onto Callaway Drive, which circled toward the elementary school.

"Look, that isn't me trying to get you back," Tracy added. "If we're over, then we're over. I'll miss you—" her voice shook "—and I'll never forgive myself for breaking up with you…but this is about a little girl I don't want to hurt. If talking to her might help make things better for her, I'll be glad to do it."

"I…um…I really do appreciate it," he said, his voice growing thick.

"Think about it," Tracy said.

"Yeah, I will. I've got to go. I'm almost at my daughter's school."

"Okay. Call me. Anytime. I mean it."

"Sure. See you."

Billy wouldn't call her "anytime." Tracy had said some things she never should have said when she was angry, but they also revealed a whole lot that she'd been hiding. She saw Billy as a charity case, a guy she put up with who owed her a whole lot to make up for all those inconveniences that came with him. First his illiteracy, and then his daughter. If Tracy thought she could do better, then she was welcome to. His daughter was not an inconvenience to be tolerated. She was the best thing Billy had ever done.

But if Tracy were willing to talk to Poppy about some of that stuff…without any expectations…should he turn her down?

He knew who he wanted to talk to about this—Grace. She'd always been the one who understood him better than anyone. She had a depth to her that he'd counted on for a very long time. She'd know what to do—and she was the one woman he knew would give him an answer based on what was best, not what she wanted from him. That kind of integrity was priceless.

That was part of the friendship he didn't want to throw away with something as stupid as a kiss.

"HEY," BILLY SAID as he came into the classroom.

The other children had all gone, and Grace put a sheet of paper down on Poppy's table. It was some simple graphing, and she had a feeling Poppy was going to love x and y coordinates. Grace looked down at Poppy, because it was easier than looking up at Billy.

"Daddy, I'm going to do calculus now!" Poppy announced.

"Not quite calculus," Grace said, laughing softly. "But graphs. And that's a step toward calculus."

"It's almost calculus," Poppy said.

Billy came into the room and his presence seemed to fill it up. He smelled like musk and the outdoors. He had his cowboy hat under one arm, and as he eyed her, her cheeks warmed. She looked away, trying to compose herself.

"So, it's awkward now?" Billy asked, his voice low. He crossed the room to look down at Poppy's page.

"Sort of," Grace said. "Let me get Poppy started."

For the next few minutes, Grace explained graphing to the little girl and showed her how it all worked. Grace tried to ignore Billy's gaze as she finished her explanation.

"There," Grace said, joining him where he sat. She didn't know what to say, exactly. Last night he'd kissed her and she'd kissed him back. And she'd replayed that kiss over and over in her mind all night and for her entire workday. And now she was going to teach him to read—and not talk about it?

How did the day after a heart-stoppingly emotional kiss go, anyway? Especially when it couldn't possibly go any further?

"So, we're not okay, then?" Billy asked quietly.

"I'm embarrassed," she admitted.

"Don't be," he replied, his voice a low rumble. "Things happen."

"Things happen," she repeated, unconvinced. "That's it?"

Grace had never been kissed like that before. Maybe Billy went around kissing women like that on a regular basis, but she'd never experienced that kind of longing. What did that say about her last relationships?

"Sometimes that's all we have, isn't it?" he said, and she saw a flash of sadness that broke through his confidence.

"Sometimes," she admitted.

"I'm sorry, all the same," he said quietly. "I...I wasn't sorry yesterday. I am now. It was all me. I was...attracted to you. I wasn't thinking about what it would do to us, to our friendship. I just followed my instincts."

"Yes," she said simply.

"And I'm sorry," he repeated.

Grace sucked in a wavering breath. "Me, too. I can't let you blame yourself. I could have stopped you. I'm not exactly an innocent."

Although with that kiss, she'd almost felt like one.

Billy smiled ruefully. "I know."

"So..." Would this fix it—erase that one mesmerizing kiss so they could move on? "Friends, then."

"Yeah." He exhaled a breath and his shoulders relaxed.

Grace met his gaze hesitantly, and he shot her one of his familiar grins and slid a hand over hers. "I don't want to mess up what's left of our friendship."

"No, me neither." For while she was in

Eagle's Rest, at least. But it would be easier once they had a couple hours of highway between them again and she could get her balance back.

"So, we're okay, then?" Billy asked.

"Yes. Of course." She forced a smile and pulled her hand back.

"Good, because I need your advice, Gracie."

"Okay." She glanced over to Poppy, whose tongue was sticking out the side of her mouth as she worked on her page.

"I got a call from Tracy."

Grace froze, and all of a sudden, she slid back into the past, when she was the pal and he'd come to her for advice with whatever girl he happened to be dating…

"Okay," she said slowly.

"She feels bad about how things ended," he said with a weak shrug. "But that's not the problem. She wants to talk to Poppy."

"About what, exactly?" Grace asked.

"She said some things when we broke up—in front of Poppy. She's concerned that Poppy might carry those words with her, and she wants… I don't know…to try and fix it."

"What did she say?" Grace asked.

"How awful it was to discover that there was a child in the mix. That sort of thing."

"Yeah, that would stick with a kid," Grace said bitterly. She looked across the room to where Poppy was hunched over her page. "And?"

"And...what do I do?" Billy asked, focusing that dark gaze on her. As easy as that, they were focused on his life again, his problems, his ex.

"As in, do you allow Tracy to try and fix things," Grace concluded.

"Yeah. Exactly. I mean, Tracy isn't the devil. She can be very selfish, but I wasn't the ideal partner either. I mean, I tried, but... Anyway, our relationship wasn't at the point where it could support a child..."

She listened as Billy rambled on. She knew the drill. They'd been here before, countless times. Women came back into his life if he let them. He was tall, muscular, sweet... And they always came back for another try—to see if they could mold him into their ideal man.

Grace had wanted to cut free of Billy because of moments like this—where she had to sit here and listen to his complicated feelings for another woman, and try to give him some unbiased advice that wouldn't reveal what she really felt.

She'd ended their friendship because it hurt too much, and here she was, right back in the same position, and after that kiss. After knowing what it felt like to be held in those strong arms, to have those lips on hers... After that kiss, they were back to where they used to be, where Billy got exactly what he needed, and she pretended it didn't hurt.

Her chest felt tight. She couldn't stay here—do this again.

She stood up, faster than she'd intended, and as she did, Billy stopped talking.

"Grace?"

"No. I'm not doing this." Her voice shook ever so slightly, but she couldn't help herself.

Billy didn't answer, staring up at her in surprise.

"Last night you were kissing me," she said, keeping her voice low. "And today we're back to you unloading your relationship problems onto me. And I'm not doing this!"

"I'm not trying—"

"Billy, I'm done here."

Grace could feel the tears of frustration rising inside of her. He'd likely get back together with Tracy, and probably break up again, too, but it was all the same routine, wasn't it? Grace, standing by as she hid her true feelings, as whatever undeserving woman flitted in and out of Billy's heart.

"I'm done," Grace repeated. "I need a break. If you'd like to bring those worksheets home with you, Poppy can probably figure them out from the instructions."

Grace went over to her desk and pulled out her purse. Then she grabbed her coat from the back of her chair and tried to put it on, but one arm caught in the sleeve and she struggled a moment to get her jacket on properly. So much for a graceful exit. Billy stood there, watching her in silence, his expression betrayed and confused.

She cared that she was hurting him—but she shouldn't. She was tired of being the one to hide her pain, pretending that this relationship didn't hurt. Not this time.

"Grace, did I offend you?" Billy asked, his voice echoing through the classroom, and this time Poppy looked up, too.

"I'm tired," she said decisively. "I need a rest. Poppy, you can finish those sheets at home, okay? Or here, if you two want to use the classroom for a few more minutes, but I have to go."

"You have to go?" Poppy echoed uncertainly.

Another scene in front of the poor girl.

"Yes, I'm not feeling very well, sweetie," Grace said, softening her tone. "So I'm going to go home and get some rest. I'm sorry."

"That's okay," Poppy said. "You should use a cold cloth on your head."

"Okay." Grace smiled, swallowing back the emotion that swelled inside her. "That's good advice. I'll see you tomorrow, Poppy."

Her hands were trembling, and Grace balled her fingers up into fists to control it. The tears were close to the surface as she strode out of the classroom and down the hallway, her heels clicking loudly on the terrazzo flooring. She didn't turn around to see if either Billy or Poppy were watching her go.

If she'd ever questioned cutting Billy off, she'd just been reminded of why it was so necessary. He had nothing but romantic options, and she wasn't willing to be his rock-steady pal.

CHAPTER FIFTEEN

THAT EVENING BILLY did the dishes after supper. He was frustrated because he knew it was his fault that he'd ticked off Grace. He'd been the one to kiss her last night, even if she hadn't exactly dissuaded him. He was the one to cross that line when he knew he couldn't offer more than before, either. This was on him. And now Poppy was the one to pay for it. Each time Poppy asked him why Miss Beverly was mad at him, he didn't know what to say. Even Poppy hadn't been fooled by her claim of illness.

Billy sighed. From the bathtub, he could hear Poppy chattering to herself as she played with some bath toys and she squeaked across the tub bottom.

Poppy would have had a full lesson if Billy had avoided any kind of romantic entanglements. Because he couldn't lie to himself anymore and claim this wasn't romantic. It might be doomed, but whatever he was feeling for Grace had passed friendship a long time ago. He was just too stubborn to admit it. This was precisely why he should have kept to his earlier vow. Romance complicated everything, and he wouldn't complicate his daughter's childhood.

What he needed was to talk to her—without a kid in tow. This was for Poppy's sake, as well as his own. He knew better than to let a woman stew. Grace was mad, and he needed to fix this now.

When he'd washed the last dish, he let out the water and dried his hands on a towel. Then he pulled his cell phone out of his pocket and dialed his mom's number. It rang twice before a man's voice picked up.

"Hello?"

"Uh...hi," Billy said. "I'm looking for Heather. Do I have the right number?"

"Yep, sure do," came the reply. "Hold on." Then in a muffled tone, he heard the man say, "For you." His mother came on the line then.

"Hello?" she said.

"Hi, it's Billy."

"Billy!" He could hear the smile in her voice. Then to the side, "It's my son." Then back to him again, "Hi, sweetie. How are you?"

"I'm…um…who's that?"

"Gerald. I told you about him. We're just watching some TV together, but don't worry. I can talk."

He winced. He wasn't sure he should even ask. Obviously she had a date. "I was actually hoping you might be up to…babysitting."

"I'd be happy to," she said, her voice softening. "Really happy to."

"Tonight," he added. "Without Gerald."

"Gerald is a good man, son. You're going to have to accept that eventually."

"Yeah, yeah. I will. It's on the list. Just not right now. I need someone to watch Poppy for an hour or two tonight, and I was hoping you might be open to that."

There was a pause. "Fine. Okay. I'm sure he'll understand." A pause. "Yep, he says he understands. See? Easy peasy. He's sweet that way."

Gerald was actually sounding like a half-decent guy, after all, but Billy didn't have time to get into that right now. "Good. Thanks. She's got a bedtime, by the way. Seven thirty."

"Yes…yes!" His mother's voice sounded

flustered. "I can come now, if that helps. I'll read her some stories and tuck her in properly. That's a promise."

"And no tales from the bar," he added.

"No bar tales. Got it."

"Great. Thanks." He cleared his throat. "I appreciate it, Mom."

"No, I appreciate it, son. I'll see you soon."

Billy hung up and stood in the stillness for a moment, listening to the splashes and rambling one-sided conversation from the bathroom. He'd have to get the balance here, somehow—work, school pickups, other obligations... The hardest part was going to be getting used to doing all this alone. He'd have to figure it out—especially the loneliness part. His mom had been right. He loved his child with all his heart, but he still longed for some romance. He'd just have to do better than his mom had.

Heather arrived thirty minutes later, and Poppy was rather pleased to have her grandmother to herself for the evening.

"We'll play toys!" Poppy declared.

"I promised your dad that I'd get you to bed," his mother said, then turned to Billy. "Out, out! We're fine. Don't worry about a thing."

BILLY KNEW THE way to Grace's parents' place. He used to go with her to Sunday dinner there from time to time, and he'd squirm somewhat uncomfortably as her father stared him down. He'd been a threat back then—but not anymore, he was sure. Grace knew the worst now, and she'd already made her feelings clear.

When he got to the door, Grace opened it before he could knock.

"Hey," he said, somewhat surprised. "You saw me drive up, I guess."

"Yeah." She crossed her arms under her breasts and eyed him warily. "What do you want, Billy?"

"To talk to you," he said.

There was a beat of silence, and he looked over her shoulder, into the empty kitchen. At least there wasn't an audience.

"Grace, I don't know how I ticked you off today, but I managed to…and I wanted to talk about it."

"What if I don't want to?" she countered, raising her gaze to meet his. Anger glittered there.

"I don't know," he admitted, suddenly uncertain. "I was just hoping… Look, it's cold out here. Let me in, or come out to my truck. Whatever I did, I'm sure you can fill me in."

She reached around to grab a coat, then stepped into her boots.

"Fine," she said. "In the truck."

Billy didn't see anyone else in the warmly lit kitchen, but he was grateful for her choice. He didn't feel like facing her parents. They walked together toward his truck, and he glanced over at her, trying to gauge her anger.

"So...what did I do?" he asked as he pulled open the passenger-side door, but Grace didn't move toward it.

"We can skip this," she said.

"No, we can't," he replied. "I want to know what I did, not pretend it never happened and watch you sail off to Denver in a few days."

"Maybe I don't want to talk about it!" Tears glistened in her eyes.

"Gracie..." He softened his voice. "What did I do?"

"You..." She shook her head. "Nothing. You didn't do anything."

"Okay...that isn't ringing true." He slammed the truck door shut, since she wasn't getting in. "So why did you take off like that?"

"It was more of the same," she said with a shrug. She pulled her coat closer around her. "Your old buddy Grace, listening to you go on about some other woman."

"You don't want anything more with me, though," he said, frowning.

"No, I don't."

"So what's the problem?"

"I don't want more with *you*—I want more, period!" she shot back. "I'm not going back to that...to the miserable attempts to make a man see me."

"Grace, I think I've proven that I definitely see you," he said. "What do you think is happening with me and Tracy, anyway?"

"Getting back together, obviously," she replied. "Some back-and-forth, a few reproaches and then the inevitable. And you'll thank me for my advice, as you always did, and then move on with Tracy Ellison."

"No," he said simply.

"No, what?" she demanded.

"You're wrong. I'm not getting back together with Tracy," he said. "I know what kind of woman she is, and that's no mother for my daughter. I wasn't asking for your advice on my relationship with Tracy! Good Lord, Grace! I don't need *relationship* advice. That one is incredibly clear—she and I are over. I was asking you for parenting advice."

Grace was silent, but the icy reserve started to crack. She licked her lips and dropped her gaze. He didn't say anything else, just stood there watching her. She raised her eyes again and he saw tears in them.

"Oh…" she said at long last.

"If you want to be friends—" he started.

"I don't," she whispered, and the words cut through his heart.

"Then what do you want to be?" he demanded.

"Nothing at all."

"And you think that's possible?" he demanded. "You think we can just be nothing to each other?"

She didn't answer him, and her silence was infuriating. She was mad at him. Well, maybe he was mad at her, too! After nearly a decade of close friendship, she wanted to be "nothing at all"!

"After all you've been to me," he said, his voice catching. "After all I've been to you—and don't you dare say I was nothing!"

"You weren't nothing, you idiot." Her voice shook. "You were everything!"

Her words echoed through his heart, and he felt his own eyes mist.

"Grace…" He stepped closer, and there was only a whisper of winter air between them. She looked up at him, tears sparkling in her eyes, but this time she didn't back up. She met his gaze, and those pink lips parted ever so slightly. He dipped his head down and caught her lips with his. It was a short kiss, and when he pulled back, he looked down into her glittering blue gaze.

"You were everything to me, too," he murmured.

"No, I wasn't."

He let his hands drop. "I'm realizing it now," he countered.

"Then you're only wishing I'd been everything, because back then I was all buddy. And there is a whole lot more space to fill than that."

A cold breeze picked up, ruffling her hair and making them both hunch their shoulders against the cold. He had a few better ideas of how to fight off the chill—none of them appropriate for the moment. She pushed her hair out of her face, and a blush crept into her cheeks.

"I'm sorry I was so blind back then," he said.

"It is what it is." She heaved a sigh, looking away. "And that has to be the last time we do that."

Billy looked at her for a long moment. He didn't want to swear off holding her in his arms or kissing her like that. Whatever this was, nothing had ever felt quite so right before.

Not a relationship—that wouldn't work. But maybe something in between?

He was an idiot. That couldn't work, either.

"Okay," he admitted quietly. "Now get in the truck, would you? It's cold and we'll cause a scandal for your neighbors."

GRACE STOOD BACK while Billy opened the truck door, and she hopped up into the warm interior. He came around the driver's side and got in, too, turning the key in the ignition to get the heat pumping into the cab once more.

Kissing him had been furthest from her intentions…but they seemed to keep falling into it. She shivered in spite of the warmth.

"I'm not sorry for that kiss," he said. "And I won't apologize for it later, either."

"You don't have to be sorry," she said, looking over at him at last. He was watching her, his dark eyes swimming with unnamable emotions. "I'm just as much to blame. But we still have to stop it."

"Yeah..." He sighed. "Easier said than done, I think."

"Even so." She met his gaze pleadingly. "Billy, whatever this is can't last. It would be a passionate fling, and then..." She stopped.

"Heartbreak," he said softly.

She leaned her head back against the headrest. "I can't endure any more heartbreak..."

"I don't want to be the one who hurts you," he murmured.

What was wrong with him—always saying just the right thing?

"Billy, we've got to be more careful," she said. "No more evenings out together, or you coming over, or..."

"Give me a reading lesson tomorrow," he requested, and she looked over at him quizzically. "You're still my teacher. For a few days, at least."

"Billy—"

"At the library," he conceded. "Poppy would love more chances to learn, too. It's just... I'm not ready to say goodbye."

Grace sighed, considering. She wasn't, either.

"Okay," she said softly. "At the library."

Billy's gaze locked on hers once more, and she read that intensity in his gaze. She put her hand on the door handle.

"You want to stay a few minutes?" he asked.

"No."

She didn't dare meet his gaze again, because she did want to stay. She just didn't dare. She pushed open the door and hopped out. Only then did she lift her gaze to meet his once more.

"Two o'clock," she said. "At the tables in the front."

"Fair enough." His warm gaze moved over her face once more. "See you then, Gracie."

Grace stepped back and slammed the door shut, then turned back toward the house. He was tempting—he always had been—but she had to get her head together. She knew every reason why Billy was bad for her, but when faced with his pleading expression, the hardest thing in the world was to walk away.

She glanced back—Billy hadn't pulled away from the curb yet, and he waited until she got to the door before he started to drive.

Grace pulled open the side door and

stepped in as his truck's engine rumbled off down the street.

Why couldn't keeping these boundaries be easier? She knew what she wanted. She knew what was good for her. But for some reason, she still found herself in Billy Austin's arms.

CHAPTER SIXTEEN

ON SATURDAY MORNING, Grace slept late and was determined to get some time to herself to sort her emotions out. It didn't work. Not only was she reliving that kiss by his truck, but she was kicking herself for it.

She knew better! She knew Billy. For crying out loud, she'd seen him go through girlfriend after girlfriend, and she knew his ways. This—whatever it was—would be a passing memory for him while he moved on to some other woman. But Grace was made of different stuff, and she wouldn't be able to just sweep it away like a wild weekend in Vegas. Her heart had been entwined with this man for years now, and whatever she was doing with him right now would only make getting over him that much harder.

She dragged herself out of bed and got dressed in a pair of jeans and a Raiders sweatshirt that she'd left at her parents' place years ago. She'd promised to meet Billy at the library today, which was better than cozying up with him at his little cabin. And she was working her last day at the school on Monday. Mrs. Powell was taking over her class again on Wednesday morning, and Grace would be on her way back to the city, to her apartment, to her life free of Billy.

Grace pulled her hair back into a ponytail and stared at her makeup-free face in the mirror. She looked the same as she ever had here in Eagle's Rest. A little angrier, maybe, and a little less willing to waste her time.

She smoothed on some face cream and applied lip gloss. Here at home with her parents, she didn't have anyone to impress, and a loose sweater, paired with some blue jeans, felt just about perfect. She headed down the stairs to the kitchen and flicked on the kettle.

The side door opened and her father came inside.

"Morning, sunshine," her father said. "Your car won't start."

"How do you know?" she asked with a frown. She grabbed a mug down from the cupboard.

"I was going to move it to get my car out," he replied. "I've tried boosting it, and that didn't work. So I'm tapped out. I'm a doctor, not a mechanic."

"True." Grace shot her father a grin.

"If your car is going to give you trouble, it's just as well it does it while you're here at home," her father said.

Grace had to agree. Still, it was a frustration.

"I suppose I'll call a tow truck," she said. "And I have to cancel with Billy."

"Cancel what?" her father asked.

"I was going to give him and his daughter a lesson at the library this afternoon," she said.

"You've been seeing a lot of him," her father commented.

"Yeah, well...you know the situation," she replied.

"Just don't let him take advantage," her father said. "You're a giving person, and you tend to care more than you're obliged to."

"I'm in control, Dad," she said, giving him her most teacherly smile. "Completely."

A lie, but one she was determined to make true, so maybe it wasn't so bad. She pulled her cell phone out of her back pocket, and her father ambled out of the kitchen, leaving her in relative privacy.

Grace wanted to call Billy, and that was the problem. She missed him, and she'd seen him last night! This was worse than it used to be. Before, she'd only imagined what his arms around her would feel like, and now she knew. Not only was she attracted to him, but he was equally attracted to her—and it still wouldn't work!

She dialed Billy's phone number and waited. It rang three times, and then he picked up.

"Yeah?"

"Hi, Billy, it's Grace."

"Hey, Gracie." His voice warmed.

"I have to cancel on you," she said. "I'm sorry, but I'm having car trouble, and I won't make it to the library today, so…"

"What kind of car trouble?" He didn't seem in the same hurry she was.

"It won't start," she said. "So I'm calling a tow, and I'll have it taken care of. But tell Poppy I'm sorry. I know she'll be disappointed."

"What happens when you turn the key?" Billy asked. He sounded more interested in the mechanical problem than the fact that she was canceling on him.

"I don't know. Dad's the one who discovered it," she replied.

"Because if it kind of clicks when you turn the key, it might be the starter. I've got a spare one around here somewhere. But if it kind of grinds, over and over again, that's something different again. I could probably—"

"No," she said. "I'm not hinting that I need help. I'm fine."

"Who's hinting?" he teased. "You do need help. Unless you can fix your own car, you're in a bind."

"I can call a tow truck!" She was feeling exasperated now. "This is what people do!"

"And how long will the garage take to get to your car? It's the weekend," he replied.

Grace sighed. He did have a point. And she was planning on leaving town on Wednesday. It would be frustrating to have to put that off for a few more days because her car was still in the shop.

"I'll take the grudging silence for agreement," he said. "I'm your friend, Grace. Friends help each other out."

"Look, after yesterday—" she started.

"Your parents will be around, I presume," he interrupted. "Very effective chaperones,

I'm sure. And there's Poppy, of course. Besides, I promise I'll keep my hands to myself." She could hear the smile in his voice, and in her mind she could see that flirtatious grin of his.

"Fine," she said. "I do need a hand."

"Glad to help." His voice was warm again. "We'll be there in an hour."

He hung up before she could wisely change her mind. She looked down at her clothes. She wouldn't change—that was a conscious choice. She'd keep her hair back in a ponytail, wear her comfy sweater and she wouldn't put on anymore makeup, either. Maybe it would be good to give him a jolt—remind him of the woman she was underneath all the primping she now enjoyed. He'd never been attracted to her when she looked like this, and it might do her good to have the desire in his eyes fade.

An hour later, Billy arrived as promised, and he and Poppy came up to the side door. Grace had told her parents of Billy's offer to help, and while her mother had been glad to hear it, her father had been mildly annoyed. Now her mother sat in the kitchen with an egg white omelet in front of her, and when

Grace opened the door, Connie waved at their new arrivals.

"Hey," Billy said, his dark eyes meeting Grace's for a beat, then slid down to her clothes. He was noticing it, she thought, but his expression didn't betray anything. He waved over her shoulder at her mother. "Morning, Mrs. Beverly."

"Good morning," Connie replied. "Hi, Poppy, I haven't gotten to meet you yet."

Poppy came inside and leaned against Grace's leg, and she felt a wave of love for the little girl. It was sweet that she'd lean into her teacher for reassurance, and Grace would miss her dearly. She smoothed a reassuring hand over Poppy's shiny blond hair.

"That's my mom," Grace said. "You can call her Mrs. Beverly, if you want."

"Hi," Poppy said.

"I hear you like numbers," Connie said. "That true?"

Poppy nodded.

"Good, because I'm an accountant. Or I was one until I retired. That's someone who works with lots and lots of numbers."

"Oh, yeah?" Poppy's eye lit up.

"You want to see a spreadsheet?" Connie asked with a sparkle in her eye. "I can show you debits and credits and all sorts of fun stuff."

"Yeah!" Poppy didn't even ask for permission, and Connie grinned up at Grace.

"Finally, a child who sees the joy in numbers," Connie said with a chuckle. Then she turned back to Poppy. "Have you had lunch yet? I'm pretty sure I have chocolate milk."

Grace glanced up at Billy. "Ready to see the car?"

"Yep." He caught her eye and smiled—that slow, melting smile she'd always associated with him—and he turned toward the door. "Let's get 'er fixed."

Grace glanced back at her mother, who was already rooting through the fridge for Poppy's chocolate milk. Then she grabbed her coat, stepped into her boots and followed Billy out the door. This felt more like old times—Grace dressed down and Billy heart-stoppingly gorgeous. She followed him over to her car and handed him the keys.

"You look like you used to," he said, closing his warm hand over her fingers. "I think I recognize that Raiders sweatshirt."

Grace smiled. "Sometimes a girl likes to be comfortable."

"I gave it to you," he said.

Grace stopped, remembering. "Yeah, you did, didn't you?"

"When you got drenched by my broken tap that one time. You borrowed it to get home and never gave it back," he added. "So you stole it, more accurately."

"It was comfortable," she said in defense. Billy had been a part of everything...every part of home. There was no way to weed him out of all of her memories—she simply had to accept his presence there. Her future, however, *had* to be different.

Billy pulled open the car door and slid into the driver's seat while Grace stood there, waiting. Always waiting... It had been the story of her life back then, and while it had hurt, she'd gotten used to that ache in her heart.

Yes, this felt a whole lot more familiar.

BILLY TURNED THE key and listened to the grind of the engine. So not the starter, after all. He could see Grace outside, her expression grim. She looked more like the old Grace today—the sweatshirt, the jeans, the hair pulled back into a no-nonsense ponytail. Even the lack of makeup made her look more like she used to—more approachable, maybe. Still beautiful, though. Still alluring. He could see the soft pink in her cheeks, the sparkle in those blue eyes, the fringe of dark lashes that didn't need a hint of makeup. He still wanted to find a way to get her back into his arms today...except that he'd promised he wouldn't.

Why was it that he could see all the logical reasons they'd never work, but get him within six feet of her lately, and he couldn't seem to remember any of them?

Billy got back out and smiled reassuringly at her as he popped the hood. He missed the days when Grace was only a short drive away, when he could hang out with her whenever they were both free and when he topped her list of priorities. He'd squandered it—that was for sure. And he couldn't understand how he'd missed out on her understated allure. Makeup or not, new clothes or not, she was stunning. And somehow he'd never associated that with what they could have had between them. He'd always gone for women with problems as big as his were, women more on his level. Women like Grace Beverly, with the educated parents, top grades and a world of possibilities unfurling in front of them, were not destined for the likes of him.

"Come on," Billy said, shooting her a grin. "You missed this."

Grace shook her head, those clear blue eyes meeting his easily enough. "Not really."

"Hanging out, me fixing your car..." He smiled hesitantly. Had she really been so unhappy all that time?

"It's different now, isn't it?" Grace said.

"What?" Billy asked. "Us? Hanging out?"

"The sweatshirt. The ponytail. This helps with our little problem—going back to what I was."

Suddenly the lightbulb went on and he saw what she meant—except she was dead wrong.

"*That* helps?" he asked incredulously. "Not exactly. I promised you I'd keep my hands to myself, and I'm trying to make good on that. Besides—" he glanced over her shoulder "—I think I see your father in the window."

Grace looked behind her, then raised an eyebrow at him.

"Now, your dad in the window? *That* helps me keep my hands to myself."

Grace glared at him. "You can admit it, Billy."

He knew what she was getting at—that

her new clothes had made her suddenly seem more attractive, and she was trying to remind him of days gone by when he'd missed out on her beauty. But he wasn't going to give her that satisfaction. Besides, it wasn't true that his feelings for her were based on her clothing and a little lipstick.

"I'm a man," he said quietly, fixing her with a stare.

"I know. And you have a type of woman you're drawn to. I get it. My point is that this is what I am. I can dress it up. I can put on a little makeup, but under that primping is *this*. In the morning, when I wake up—"

"Shut up, Grace!" he said with an exasperated sigh. "I'm going to try and explain this real quick before your dad comes out. I'm male. I'm visual. I like what I see, and you're right—I like those new outfits. Here's how my brain works. I kissed you before, and I haven't stopped at least thinking about doing it again."

"I wouldn't get ahead of yourself," she replied with a short laugh.

"Trust me, I'm not," he replied. He wasn't joking right now. "I'm not trying to toy with you. I'm just saying… I'm more interested in the woman than the fashion statement. So lipstick, new clothes—sure, I can appreciate that. But it's not *about* that. I missed you like crazy for three years, and it was never about some clothes…"

She blushed. "Maybe, but right now I'm someone you can flirt with safely."

"I wouldn't call you safe," he said, his voice dropping. "Safe flirting is with a woman who I don't care if I ever see again. You—I *care*. And yeah, you're a big risk for me, but I want you in my life. Somehow. And we agreed that we'd cool this off. For good reason. So I'm doing that. I don't want to mess up my last chance of keeping my best friend."

Holding himself back from pulling her into his arms—it was taking a whole lot more willpower than she was giving him credit for. He was holding himself back because he cared about her…and his daughter. He wasn't going to be the guy who toyed with his best friend, his daughter's beloved teacher. Maybe he was growing, too.

Tears misted Grace's eyes. "I don't want to lose my best friend, either, Billy."

Billy couldn't help the smile that came to his face. "Am I allowed to hug you like old times?"

"Nope. But you can fix my car." She met his gaze, and he saw the playful smile he'd missed so much.

"Yeah, yeah, that was a given," he chuckled.

It took all of the self-control he could muster to keep himself from closing that distance between them. There had been a time that hanging out had been the norm, but it wasn't enough anymore. Now he wouldn't ever feel satisfied without her in his arms, covering her lips with his and letting the world fade away around them...

But what was satisfaction? He'd have to make do without it. She had for a whole lot of years, and now it was his turn. He turned back to the open hood of the car and leaned over the engine.

"I'll give you another reading lesson when we're done," Grace added.

"Thanks."

He needed Grace in his life one way or another. It wasn't about her teaching him to read, or even tutoring his daughter—he needed *her*. She was the one who plugged up the hole in his heart and made him feel like he could face the world.

He'd finish fixing her car this afternoon,

and in a few days, she'd go back to Denver, and at least he'd be able to call her. Maybe she'd come back to visit her parents and he and Poppy could take her out to dinner. Even that didn't feel like enough, but it was better than facing life without her in it entirely.

He'd take what he could get.

CHAPTER SEVENTEEN

MONDAY WAS GRACE'S last day of teaching, and as she looked over her class of energetic preschoolers, her heart filled with love. They were sweet kids—each one a unique compilation of passions, feelings and challenges they were working through. In twelve weeks, she'd seen one child stop wetting his pants every day, and another child learn how to share. A little girl had stopped eating glue sticks. Then there was little Nathan, who started breaking crayons every chance he got... But that was life with teaching. And in the last two weeks, Poppy had arrived and blossomed as she soaked up every bit of knowledge Grace could send her way.

A few weeks could change so much in the life of a little kid...and in a woman, too. A few weeks was enough time to get attached.

"All right, friends," Grace said, raising her voice above the hubbub of chattering children. "It's time to clean up and get ready to go!"

Poppy wasn't in the classroom right now. She was having a special chat with Mr. Shaw, who wanted to see if Poppy had musical aptitude, as well. Grace had done everything she could to prepare the school for Poppy's brilliance. A school counselor and several teachers, including Mr. Shaw, were determined to give Poppy all the encouragement and challenge she needed.

Billy wasn't going to be on his own with his daughter's education, and perhaps that was the best gift Grace could leave him with—a cooperative and enthusiastic educational team.

"So let's clean up the crayons and stick them in the crayon buckets!" Grace sang out. "And remember, you get Mrs. Powell back tomorrow, so make sure you tell her how much you missed her while she was gone!"

"Is her baby out of her tummy now?" a little boy asked.

"Yes, he is," Grace said. "So now she can come back and teach all of you. Isn't that great?"

"Will she bring the baby to school?" a little girl asked.

"I doubt it," Grace chuckled. "But she'll have missed all of you a whole lot. I know that, because I'm going to miss all of you, too."

That seemed to satisfy the inquiring minds, and Grace turned her attention to the flurry of end-of-day cleanup. Before she knew it, the parents were picking up the children who didn't catch a bus. One by one they left, until Grace was alone in the classroom. This was it...her time at Eagle's Rest Elementary had come to an end.

She turned in a full circle, taking in the room. Funny how she could get so attached to a space in so short a time. The sand table, the work spaces, the little pots of play dough and the corkboard where she'd displayed all the most recent artwork from those little fingers...

"Grace?"

She knew his voice immediately. She turned to see Billy in the doorway. He stood tall, and she felt a rush of tenderness at the sight of him. She'd miss this man more than he probably knew.

Billy came into the classroom and glanced around the room.

"Hey," she said.

"Hey." His voice was low and warm. "Where's Poppy?"

"She's in the music room with Mr. Shaw."

"What are they up to?"

"I set her up with an appointment so that he could assess her musical ability."

"Why would that matter?" Billy asked, frowning slightly.

"It might be a great creative outlet. You never know."

"Ah." Billy nodded, then broke off the eye contact. "Getting ready for when you're not here, you mean."

"Yes." Her throat tightened. It was an emotional day all around, but with Billy, everything went deeper.

"I really wish you were staying."

"Mrs. Powell isn't about to give up her position," Grace said with a forced smile. "And she's a good teacher. At least I've heard really good things about her. I'm making sure that there is strong educational support here at the school for Poppy to move forward with—"

"Yeah, but what I'm feeling for you isn't just about teaching, Gracie," he replied, and he pulled off his cowboy hat and rubbed a hand through his hair. Those dark eyes searched out hers again.

There was nothing she could do about it. Her life was in Denver; this had just been a trip home, a short maternity-leave position. And yet it had become something much deeper and more painful to leave behind.

"Poppy's down the hall," she said after a moment. "We should go get her."

"Sure..." Billy turned toward the door, and she could see the tension in his shoulders.

The hallway was empty, except for some stray boots—there seemed to be at least one every day, and for the life of her, she couldn't figure out how. She bent and picked it up on their way to see Poppy. She'd drop it off at Lost and Found.

Grace could hear a piano playing—something complicated and cheery. Then there was silence, and then a repetition of the same piece, much simpler—one note at a time.

"I felt better knowing Poppy had you in her corner," Billy said. "I'll just do my best to keep up with her. If I can."

"You can call me—" she started.

"Can I? Really?" Billy met her gaze with a dry look. "You'll pick up?"

She felt the heat in her cheeks. Could she really promise to be here for him, through thick and thin? She was trying to start fresh—find a family of her own. She couldn't be the woman in his life, no matter how much she wanted to be.

Grace opened the door to the music room, and the piano notes grew louder, tugging them into the room. Billy held open the door for her, and Grace went in first.

There was an upright piano against one wall, and Mr. Shaw sat on the piano bench, with Poppy next to him. He played something ornate, said something quietly to the girl and then she reached out with one hand, and that simple tune came back.

"You see here..." Mr. Shaw was saying, pointing at a piece of music. "Every note is just a dot on the lines. See? The more notes we play at once, the more dots on the lines. It's just a matter of learning the language."

"Hi." Billy's voice reverberated through the room, and Mr. Shaw and Poppy both turned.

"Hi, Daddy," Poppy said with a smile, hopping down from the bench. "Did you hear me?"

"Yeah, that was pretty good, kiddo," Billy said.

"Your daughter has quite an aptitude for music," Mr. Shaw said. "We spent—" he looked at his watch "—forty minutes together, and we covered some musical concepts, and I tested her ability to repeat what she's heard. She's able to hear the main tune in a musical piece and reproduce it. That's… frankly quite amazing. Has she had any musical training so far?"

"Uh…no." Billy looked over at Grace again, and she could see the helplessness in his dark eyes. Everyone else was excited about his daughter's abilities, but for Billy… He seemed overwhelmed. Poppy went back to the piano and picked up the music, scrutinizing the page.

"She's quite an exceptional girl," Mr. Shaw went on. "Have you considered music lessons for her? She'd benefit from them. I know she's excelling academically, but with this kind of ability…"

Mr. Shaw chattered on enthusiastically, and Grace glanced around the room. Billy looked stunned, more than anything, and when Poppy came bouncing back with the music sheets in her hand, Billy slowly looked down at her.

"Daddy, can you read this?" Poppy asked.

Billy didn't even touch the pages.

"Nah," he said with a small, pained smile.

"I'll keep you updated on her progress," the teacher went on with a smile. "If you want any assistance getting her set up with music lessons outside of school, just let me know."

After the appropriate goodbyes, the teacher turned back to straightening up the music room, and Grace, Billy and Poppy headed into the hall. Billy chewed on the side of his cheek.

"You okay?" Grace asked softly.

"Something else she excels at," he said woodenly.

"That's a good thing, right?" Grace could see all the complicated emotions swimming in his eyes.

He looked down at his daughter. "Go get your snow pants, your coat and your bag, and all that, okay?" he said.

"Okay!" Poppy danced off down the hall, and Grace slipped her hand into his. A friendly gesture, she told herself—but she knew that it was more than that. It was supposed to comfort Billy, but it sent a wave of warmth through her, too.

"Just one more thing she's great at that I can't help her with," Billy said, his voice low. He squeezed her hand in his iron grip. "One more thing that requires someone else to teach her. She's four..."

"I want to learn how to read music!" Poppy

called back at them as she dropped to the ground to wrestle with her snow pants. "And I want to learn how to make the songs on the piano like Mr. Shaw does. With all his fingers. That's what I want to do."

"She needs you, Billy," Grace said quietly. "Don't forget that."

"I can't even read English, let alone music," he said bitterly.

"She needs you just as much as you need her," Grace said past the lump rising in her throat.

He might not realize it now, but he would eventually. And maybe this would make their goodbye a little easier. Grace wouldn't be leaving him on his own, because he'd have his little girl. He might feel overwhelmed, and he might want the comfort that Grace could bring, but when it came down to his deepest needs, Poppy was there. He *needed* his daughter.

Billy would find his balance, and when he did, he wouldn't need Grace.

THAT EVENING, THE woman from child-welfare services came by for their little home visit. It wasn't bad. She asked them some questions, listened to Poppy chatter, looked around the cabin, poking into cupboards, making notes on her tablet and giving him a nod of approval when she saw the full fruit bowl on the counter.

She'd left her number and said she'd come again in another three months, but Billy wasn't worried. He seemed to have passed with flying colors, and when she shook his hand before she left, she said, "Mr. Austin, your home is warm, comfortable and well-stocked with good food. Your daughter is happy, and she seems to be well-bonded with you in this short time. I'm pleased with what I see."

Later that evening, Billy sat on the couch, his head resting against the cushion, and his eyes shut. Grace swam through his mind—her glittering blue eyes, the sound of her voice, the confident way she had with Poppy that made him feel so entirely reassured with the world. His success with child-welfare services had a whole lot to do with Grace's help, and he knew it.

He couldn't help how much Grace meant to him. She was in his thoughts when he woke up, and when he fell asleep. He wondered what she'd think about his ideas, and he wondered if she'd laugh at something he found funny. He thought of that soft skin and her round curves, all highlighted by her new, confident way of dressing that drew his eye more than any other woman had.

With Grace at the school, he didn't worry about Poppy. But without her, he would be facing down teachers and principals, all with his invisible handicap. He could hear their advice now: just look this up online, just get a book on whatever subject, here were some articles he might want to read...

And he'd have to pretend that was all an option. Or fess up that he was functionally illiterate. They'd think he was stupid, lose a bit of respect.

"Daddy, read me a story."

Billy opened his eyes to find his daughter standing in front him, her blue eyes fixed on him earnestly.

"You don't like how I read stories," he said. "I do it wrong, remember?"

"I think you could do it right," she countered. "And I'll help."

So grown-up, and yet so small. Billy lifted his head and saw that Poppy had a book clasped in front of her—a red cover that he recognized. He paused, looking at that familiar, slightly tattered book in her hands.

"Where did you find that?" he asked.

"In the closet."

"I don't know that book," he admitted with a sigh. "I don't know the words, kiddo."

"But you could try, Daddy," she pleaded, crawling up onto the couch, next to him. She thrust the book into his hands.

"Why don't you read it to me?" he suggested hopefully. Maybe at long last, he'd hear the story his mother had never read him.

"No, I want you to read it," she insisted.

"Do you know where this book is from?" he asked her.

"No."

"Your grandma gave it to me when I was little." A flash of that night when she was going out on yet another date came back to him. His heartbreak. That book. His mother's soft kiss on his forehead...

"Did she read it to you?" Poppy asked.

"No, she never did," he admitted. "But I used to like the pictures. I made up the story that went with them in my head."

"So let's read it!" Poppy said. "I can help with the words you don't know yet. I'm good at that."

"Yeah," he agreed quietly. "You are."

His little girl was good at all the stuff he'd

failed at. His stomach twisted with misgiving. It was one thing to try to read those cards, or the words Grace wrote on the foolscap, but Poppy was the audience he dreaded. He was her dad—he was supposed to be the one in control, the one with the answers, not the one stumbling over letters that kept swimming in front of his eyes.

Poppy held the book up. "You're supposed to use your finger, Daddy, remember?"

He sighed. She wasn't going to give up on this, so he put his finger under the first word.

"It's…um…" He licked his lips, trying to focus on the first letter. But the word was a long one, and it kept slipping away from him.

"Seventeen," Poppy whispered.

"Seventeen." He moved his finger along. "W…wah…yah. Way. Ways."

"Seventeen Ways…" Poppy murmured.

"I L… Lo… Love… You." He knew the last word by sight, once he got his finger under it and made the letters stop swimming around.

"Seventeen Ways I Love You," Poppy said, and she opened the book.

"Poppy, I'm not a good enough reader to do this yet," he said.

"But you are doing it, Daddy," she replied stubbornly.

"Not very well."

"Well enough," she replied simply. "Come on, Daddy. Let's read it."

Billy looked over at her. "Sweetie, I'm good at lots of things."

"I know," said Poppy.

"And I'm a big strong cowboy who's going to keep you safe always."

"Uh-huh."

"But I'm not good at reading."

"That's why we'll do it together!" Poppy snuggled in closer, tipping her head onto his chest. "Put your finger under the word, Daddy…"

She wasn't giving up, it seemed, so he rubbed a finger over his eye, then exhaled a deep breath. He'd try…

Every time he struggled with a word he didn't know, Poppy would supply it in her matter-of-fact little voice, and he'd plunge on to the next one. When he was in danger of forgetting all the words he'd managed, she'd read it back to him.

There are seventeen reasons I love you.
First of all, I love you because you are

my child. You belong to me, and I belong to you. That's the best kind of belonging. That's number one.

I love you because you turn my whole world upside down. Everything looks different now that I have you. I didn't know I was lonely before you came along. I didn't know I was missing out on any fun! But then I had you, and my whole world went head over heels, and the world looks better this way.

That's number two.

I love you because walks in the park are an adventure when I walk in the park with you…

The book never did get to number seventeen, because the little boy falls asleep, and the mother kisses his forehead and says she'll tell him more tomorrow…

Was this how his mother had felt about him…that her world went upside down in the most wonderful of ways just because of his existence? She might not have been the perfect mother, but perhaps he'd underestimated her love for him. Funny how a child of his own changed his capacity to understand love.

Maybe it was time to forgive his mom for

her failings, and to embrace her for all the stuff she was doing right. He'd mess up a whole lot, he was sure. He already felt like he was jogging behind his little girl, and she was only four years old. Here was hoping she'd forgive him one day for being less than the hero she deserved.

Poppy sat quietly, and Billy ruffled the top of her hair.

"Okay, bedtime," he said gruffly.

Poppy didn't move, and when he looked down at her, he saw tears shining in her eyes. He slid his arm around her.

"Hey...you okay?" he asked softly.

"Why did Mommy go away?" Poppy whispered, her lips trembling.

"For a job."

"Why didn't Mommy take me with her?" A tear trickled down her cheek.

Why hadn't her mother loved her like the mother in the book loved her child? That was what Poppy wanted to know, and he didn't have the answer. Why hadn't she called? Why didn't she worry about her daughter more? How was life bearable without her child?

And yet, if Carol-Ann had been a more functional mother, Billy might never have known about his little girl at all… The irony was bitter.

"I don't know that, Poppy," he said quietly. "But I do know that your mother loves you enough that she made sure you'd be safe and loved by bringing you to me. And you are very, very loved. You're my girl, and I can promise you that I'll never leave you behind, or go away, or anything like that. From now until forever, it's you and me."

"You and me…" she whispered.

Billy gathered her up in his arms. "That's a promise."

For a couple of minutes, he held her close. He had his big, strong arms and a stubborn streak that just might work out in his daughter's favor. Nothing was going to get between him and his kid.

"Now bedtime, okay?" he said, giving her one last squeeze.

"I'm not tired," Poppy said.

"Well, I am." He hoisted her to her feet.

He needed time to think—to process. He needed to rid his mind of the constant battle to hold those letters in place. Besides, it was seven thirty, and his daughter had a bedtime.

There was a glass of water, a trip to the bathroom, a lost stuffed animal and finally a good-night kiss that Poppy insisted never happened, so one more was needed. But at last, she was tucked in.

Bedtime was getting to be more of a battle lately, and he wondered if his mother had just been too tired after her shifts to fight with him. She'd mostly worked waitressing positions, which kept her on her feet and running around. He could only imagine trying to convince a ten-year-old Poppy to go to bed after a long day of calf-pulling... He'd get his taste of all the hard stuff, too. There was no avoiding it.

Except for those boyfriends—the constant flood of men that came through their home. There was no getting around that. Billy might end up falling into his mother's shortcuts on some things, just to keep his sanity, but he wouldn't be like her in his romantic life. Poppy might not have a dad who could read much of anything, but she would have a father fully focused on the raising of her. What he could offer would be hers, as imperfect as it might be.

He sat on the couch, dozing to the jangly tune of *Jeopardy!*, and just after eight, there was a knock on the door. Billy roused himself. If this was about work, they'd just have to manage without him, because he couldn't leave his daughter alone.

He pulled open the door, ready to tell them he couldn't come, then started. It wasn't the ranch manager with a request; it was the one person he'd been missing most, with those sparkling blue eyes and the skin like milk…

"Hi," Grace said, holding up a cloth shopping bag, her smile tentative. "I come bearing books."

CHAPTER EIGHTEEN

GRACE STOOD ON the step, the frigid winter wind coiling around her and making her shiver. She held the book bag in front of her like a shield, and she had a sudden rush of misgiving as she looked into Billy's surprised face.

I shouldn't have come.

Leaving Eagle's Rest this time was supposed to be an ordinary goodbye. Even with her parents, she wouldn't be agonizing over the right words, the right farewell. Those goodbyes weren't going to be permanent. She'd said she would stay friends with Billy, but she'd realized tonight that she couldn't... and their last words hadn't been a proper goodbye.

"Hi." Billy stepped back. "I didn't know you were coming over. Come in."

"I came across these books at the school—they were going to send them to Goodwill, and I thought of Poppy." She stepped inside, the warmth of the cabin enveloping her, and Billy closed the door behind her. He paused, standing close to her as he pushed the door shut. She tipped her head back, looking up into those chiseled features.

"I hope you don't mind," she added.

"No, no—it's great." Billy smiled slightly, then took a step back. "I wasn't sure I'd see you before you left."

"I didn't think I'd see you, either, but... the books."

"You came here for the books." He crossed his arms and looked at her for a beat. "You sure?"

"They were an excellent excuse." She met his gaze then, and a smile tickled the corners of his lips. There he was—her old friend— and a rush of warmth flooded through her. What she wouldn't sacrifice for another evening of forgetting just how temporary all of this was.

"Excuse or not, I'm glad you came," he said. "Come on in. Poppy's asleep already."

Billy waited while she took off her outerwear. Then she followed him into the small living room. A fire was burning in the woodstove, pumping heat into the room. The kitchen looked like it had been cleaned up after supper, and there was a pizza box perched on top of the garbage can. It was cozy, and Grace felt a pang of nostalgia already for this little cabin she'd only been inside a handful of times.

"I'm not actually leaving town until Wednesday morning," she said, edging toward the woodstove. "But I probably won't see you after this."

Billy crossed the room and stood with her in front of the stove. His arm rested against hers, and she had to resist the urge to lean into his muscular shoulder. She stole a glance up at him, scrutinizing his profile. His chin was scruffy, and there was something older about the set to his jaw.

"Why don't you want to see me again before you go?" he asked, his voice a low rumble.

"Because it will only make things harder," she said, looking back at him.

"And yet you're here." He turned and met her eyes. "You sure you can stay away?"

"Quit teasing," she said, turning back to the woodstove again.

"I'm not teasing," he retorted. "I'm serious. I think what we have together is bigger than your neatly organized plans for how you're going to cut off your feelings!"

Grace shook her head. "Whatever I felt for you—"

"You still feel," he finished for her.

"You're just being mean now," she said, shooting him an annoyed look.

"I'm being honest," he clapped back. "You still feel it. I'm not just your buddy from your single years. I'm more than that. And you know it."

"And what does it matter?" She spun to face him. "What does that do for us? This—whatever this is between us—is complicated and messy."

"It's a fact!" Billy shook his head. "There's a handful of really special relationships in life, and what we have is one of them. This counts...for something! And it deserves more than to be pushed under the rug because it isn't convenient!"

"That's easy for you to say," she replied. "You have your friend you can call from time to time, a dinner date when I come back to see my parents... It's all fine for you right now! But what about when you meet a woman you want to marry?"

Billy shook his head. "I don't have one. I'm focusing on my parenting."

"But you will. Don't be so stubborn," she said with a sigh. "Women throw themselves at you. It's only a matter of time before one sticks. You'll find some nice woman who will love you and Poppy both, and she'll hate me."

"If she's so nice—"

"Billy, just listen for once!" she snapped. "She'll hate me because I'm not just some pal from the old days. I'm more than that. And if she has half a brain in her skull, she'll see that plain as day, and she'll want me as far from you as possible. Women are territorial."

"We'll deal with that when it comes," he replied.

She smiled bitterly and then turned back to the stove. "And what about me?"

"What about you?" His voice had gotten louder. "You mean, what about some guy who gets jealous of me?"

If only that were her primary concern! That would be a rather pleasant worry...the man in love with her who was jealous of the guy who'd always been a little too close to her.

"No, I mean what happens to me when you

fall in love with some woman, and I'm left with a broken heart all over again?" Tears welled in her eyes and she shook her head in frustration with herself. She didn't want to cry. She wanted a straight path, something easier. But with Billy, she kept getting tied into knots.

"You're the one who wants to cut ties." Billy's voice was thick with emotion. "That's not me!"

"Because there is only so much my heart can take!" She rubbed her hands over her face. "Billy, I can't stay halfway in love with you and move forward in my life, too."

It was so much easier for him! He could have pretty much any woman he wanted, and he wanted to hold on to her as a friend...who he kissed from time to time? Who he cuddled up to when he got lonely?

"Halfway in love..." His voice softened, and she wasn't sure if she heard teasing there or not. Whatever. It was true.

Grace looked up at him miserably. "This isn't fair, Billy."

"So, I'm the selfish jerk who isn't considering what my friendship does to you," he concluded. "That's it?"

"This is way past friendship."

"Yeah, it is." He stepped closer, and she was forced to tip her chin up to look him in the face. He slid his hand into her hair, then trailed his fingers down over her cheek until his thumb rested on her bottom lip. "This is past buddies. Past going to movies together, and hanging out. This has sprinted way past all of that. Now when I look at you, I'm trying to figure out how to get you to kiss me again…"

He rubbed his thumb against her lip, then slid his hand behind her neck again, deep into her hair. She shut her eyes for a moment, feeling that rhythmic movement of his fingers against her neck.

"This is my point," she whispered, her voice trembling. "Whatever this is…it can't last!"

"I agree," he said woodenly, and he stared down into her face with agony in those dark eyes. "But I don't want to say goodbye. Is that so terrible?"

Tears sprung to her eyes. "Billy—" she started, but he hushed her by leaning down, his lips a whisper away from hers.

"No," he breathed, then his lips covered hers. His mouth was warm and urgent, and he wrapped his other arm around her waist, pulling her firmly against him. The warmth from the fire mingled with the heat that built between them, and when he finally pulled back and broke off the kiss, Grace was breathless.

"You're halfway in love with me," he said softly. "Well, I'm all the way in love with you. So where does that leave us?"

BILLY HADN'T MEANT to say it…and as he stared down into Grace's shocked face, he wished he could take the words back. Although it wouldn't stop them from being true. She'd hidden her feelings for him for years, and he would have been wise to do the same now. But looking down the barrel of a lifetime without Grace had shaken it all together for him.

"You…" she whispered. "You love me?"

Billy nodded. "I know you don't feel that way for me anymore…"

"I've always loved you," she said softly. "That never stopped."

"Not halfway?" he asked, his voice choked.

She leaned in and caught his lips with hers, her kiss tender and sad. And when she pulled back, she wiped a tear from her cheek.

"But I can't do this, Billy! It's me—I can't."

"Because I'm not good enough," he said. "I can't read, I'm not a provider and—"

"Oh, Billy, you're enough," she countered, and her words coiled around him temptingly. How he longed to show her just how much man he was...

"It's not that," she went on. "It's..." She sucked in a deep breath, and for the first time, she seemed to still, to center herself. "Despite whatever we're feeling now, I'm not your type."

"My type..." He shook his head.

"You know what I mean. You had so many chances to be with me, but when you had a choice between the friend who loved you and some cute blonde you hardly knew..."

He'd chosen the other woman. Again and again. Stupidly and blindly. He hadn't seen the romantic possibility between them back then, but he sure did now. How he could have missed her simmering sensuality, he didn't know.

"I was an idiot," he said. "I know it now."

"I was never enough!" she countered. "If I had been, you'd have seen it long ago—you'd have chased after *me*. And if I wasn't enough back then, why would I be enough now?"

"You could have said something," he said, his words catching in his throat. "You could have told me that I wasn't giving you what you needed—what you deserved. You could have *told* me how you felt."

"I didn't know how," she said softly. "I'm not like those other women who just put it out there...and maybe that's for the best. You'll thank me for this later, when your life settles down and you find a woman you're more naturally attracted to—"

"Stop that!" he said, anger rising inside of him. "You are not putting this one on me and saying it's because I'm not attracted to you enough! If you hadn't noticed, I've had a real problem keeping my hands off you! You're beautiful. You're smart. You're perfection. I love your curves, your hips, your eyes, your lips...your brain...your heart...all of you! I don't need you to change anything. I'm not looking for a different woman!" His gaze fell on that little red storybook on the floor, and the words evaporated from his tongue. In the bedroom, his daughter was sleeping, and his future would be tied up in his life as a dad.

"Then what are you looking for?" she demanded.

"I'm just trying not to mess up my daughter too much. Besides, I can't ask you to give up your life in Denver."

Billy knew what he could give, and right now it didn't look like much compared to the life she'd already lined up for herself. He had a little girl to raise who needed to be able to trust her dad to put her first.

"You're doing great with Poppy…" Grace whispered.

"I can't do to her what my mom did to me," he said. "You wanted me to reconnect with my mom, and that was good advice. The thing is, it doesn't take a bad person to mess up as a parent. Mom meant well. I just… I have to succeed as a dad. I can't be stupid, or selfish, trying to sort out a romance when my daughter needs me. I can't be that guy."

They stared at each other sadly, and Billy reached forward, tucking a curl of hair behind her ear. How he longed to pull her into his arms and just forget about reality.

"But I love you," he added feebly. "Staying friends is going to be torture—for both of us. I know that."

Loving her, and not being able to kiss her, or hold her… Loving her and having to pretend that she was nothing more than a pal… Loving her and having to watch her fall in love with some other guy who would be so much more deserving of her, while he stood by and watched her look up at that other guy with those glittering blue eyes…

"It would be," she said, her voice quivering.

"That's a torment I'd be willing to endure just to keep you in my life, but I won't ask you to do the same," he said, swallowing hard.

"I have to get over you…" she whispered. "It's been too many years of loving you and coming up empty. I have to move on…"

"I get it," he breathed.

Grace looked up into his face, her eyes filling with tears. "Goodbye, Billy."

He hated the finality of those words.

Billy wrapped his arms around her and held her close. He shut his eyes, inhaling the soft scent of her perfume. Then he released her.

"If you ever change your mind and want to call…" he said huskily.

She didn't answer. She wouldn't call. She went to the door and pulled on her boots and slid into her coat once more. When he closed the distance between them, she shook her head, her chin quivering.

"No, Billy," she breathed. "Just let me go…"

So he watched her walk out of his cabin. Then he stood in the frigid air of his open doorway, and he watched her get into her car and drive away.

When he finally closed the door and locked it, he went over to the couch and sank into its depths, picking up that little red storybook and hugging it against his chest the way his daughter had.

The tears stayed locked just under the surface, making his heart ache with the weight of them. He was a dad, and no one said that being a good father wouldn't hurt.

This time, being a good father meant giving up the love of his life…the one woman he longed to be with, but who didn't trust him with her heart in return. She was wrong about that, of course. If he didn't have anything else holding him back, he'd never even blink in the direction of another woman again, if he had Grace Beverly to come home to.

His little girl would never know what he'd given up for her. He'd never tell her. And she'd have a proper, loving, supportive childhood at long last.

But he'd never stop loving Gracie. He'd just have to get used to the weight of this sadness and learn how to carry it with him. They both would.

CHAPTER NINETEEN

BILLY DROVE POPPY to school the next morning, and he met her new teacher. Mrs. Powell was a sweet woman with a big smile and jangly jewelry, and she'd been all caught up on Poppy's situation. All would be well... academically. Still, this classroom didn't feel the same without Grace in it.

"You gonna be okay?" he asked Poppy, bending down to kiss the top of her head.

"Yep," Poppy said. "But I miss Miss Beverly."

"Yeah..." he said gruffly. So did he. "Okay. You be good. No biting or kicking."

"Ha, ha, Daddy," Poppy said, and he tried to shoot his daughter a regular grin, but he wasn't sure he managed it.

"Let's all go inside now, friends!" Mrs. Powell said. "Boots off! Coats off! Let's go!"

Friends. That's what Grace had called the kids. He'd assumed it was her thing, but maybe it was a school thing, instead. The things that seemed personally hers...maybe they hadn't been. Not all of them.

As he headed out of the school, he felt a wave of sadness. Today he had the morning off. He glanced at his watch. Raising Poppy on his own was going to require a whole village of people who loved her, too. That was what the child welfare agent had said during her visit last night, at least. And maybe a visit with his mom, without a little girl watching them with that confused look on her face, would be a good thing.

So Billy drove to his mother's house. As he parked, the front door opened and an older man stepped outside. He wore a pair of steel-toed boots that Billy could recognize from a distance, and he had a lunch box in one hand, a thermos in the other, and a hard hat tucked under one arm. He turned back, dipped his head down and kissed Heather. Billy pushed open his door, and as he got out, Gerald saw him for the first time.

"Morning!" Billy said.

"Morning." Gerald headed across the crunching snow, dropping his hat on his head and switching his load to free up his right hand. "I'm Gerald Heeler—your mom's friend."

"Yeah, she mentioned you." Billy shook his hand. "Pleasure."

He glanced back to where his mother stood on the step. She was fully dressed, an apron around her waist, June Cleaver–style, and she waved.

"I just want you to know, Bill, that I'm real fond of your mom. She's a good lady. And I'm going to do right by her," Gerald said.

"Well, she's always made up her own mind about stuff," Billy said with a wry smile. "I hope I didn't offend you when I didn't want you to come along for babysitting my daughter."

"I've got three daughters of my own," Gerald replied. "All grown-up now, of course. But I get it. You're a dad, and you've got to make sure your little girl stays safe. So no insult here. You're doing a good job. You'll take your time and get to know me."

"Thanks." Billy eyed the older man for a moment. Maybe his mother had finally chosen a good one.

"Well, I've got to get to work. I come by early sometimes, and your mom makes me breakfast. Just in case this looks...untoward."

"Have a good day," Billy said with a small smile. "I'm sure I'll see you around."

Gerald headed for a beat-up Chevy that was parked behind his mother's car, and true enough, his mom's car windows looked frosted over, and Gerald's truck was completely thawed. Not that it should matter, but the honesty was a nice touch.

"Hurry up!" his mother called from the door. "I'm freezing!"

Billy picked up his pace and met his mother on the step.

"Hey, Mom," he said.

"Come on in, sweetie," Heather said, stepping back. "This is a nice surprise."

"You got time?" he asked.

"Don't have to work till one," she replied and shut the door behind him. "Poppy's at school?"

"Yeah," he said, unzipping his jacket. "And I've got the morning off, so I thought I'd come see you."

"I'm glad." His mother smiled at him. "So, what did you think of Gerald?"

"Nice," Billy said, glancing toward the front window. Gerald's truck had already left, though. "He seems like a decent fellow."

"He really is, you know?" she said, leading the way toward the kitchen. "He's a good man, and for whatever reason, he's in love with me!"

"Is it mutual?" It was a dumb question. He could see that it was by the way she talked about him.

"Yes, it's mutual," she said. "But we're taking it slow. I don't exactly have a great track record, so… But speaking of taking it slow, is Gracie still in town?" Heather stopped at the fridge and opened it. "You hungry?"

"She's…um…leaving for Denver tomorrow," he said.

"Oh, sweetie…" Heather turned toward him, letting the fridge fall shut again.

"Mom, it's not a big deal," he lied. "We're friends, and her life is in Denver. That's it."

"You've been in love with her for years," Heather countered.

"Nah—"

"Well, you didn't see it, but I sure did," she retorted. "And that girl is in love with you, too."

"I know." He rubbed his hands over his face.

"So what's the problem?" his mother demanded. "You're both healthy, single, decent human beings, in love with each other—"

"I'm a father!" he blurted out. "That's the problem!"

"Single parents get married all the time," she said, but the easy tone had left her voice. She crossed her arms protectively over her chest and eyed him for a beat.

"I know…" He shook his head. He hadn't come here to fight with his mom. It was his life to live, and these were his choices to make. "Mom, it's nothing. It just won't work out between us. That's all."

"Come. Sit." Heather led the way to the kitchen table and pulled out a chair.

Billy followed his mother's lead and pulled out the chair opposite hers. He picked up a ketchup bottle that was still on the table, then put it back down again.

"Spill, sweetie," she said earnestly.

"Mom, this isn't worth it," he countered. "I don't want to hurt your feelings—"

"Son, I'm a grown woman. I raised you! I throw men your size out of the bar on a regular basis. Now, tell me what's the problem."

Billy sucked in a deep breath. "It was hard growing up," he said quietly. "Really hard. I know that it was no cakewalk for you, either, so I'm not trying to judge you or anything…"

"You are, but go on," she said with a small smile.

Billy sighed. "I always felt like your boyfriends were more important than I was. You worked hard at your day job, and then you dated. A lot. And I got left in the dust."

"I always made sure you had food on the table, new clothes to wear…" Her voice trembled slightly. "You have no idea how close it came to having the electricity shut off on us!"

"I know, Mom," he said. "You worked hard. It's more than that, though. I needed more. I slipped through the cracks at school, and I felt like the same thing happened at home."

"Because I dated?"

"I'm sure it's not quite so cut-and-dried," he conceded. "But you wanted to know why I can't start up with Gracie. Well, from my side of it, it's because I need to be here for Poppy. I need to make sure she gets all the attention she needs. She's been through hell and back, and somehow she's still got a smile on her face. Well, I've got to protect that smile."

"By not dating," his mother said.

"By focusing on her!" he retorted. "Mom, last night I read a book with Poppy for the first time, and she had to tell me what most of the words were. I'm functionally illiterate. No one caught that."

"I tried, son!" she said, tears in her eyes. "I did my very best, and you think that because I had romantic needs that I failed you?"

"Yes!" he exploded. "How many guys did you introduce me to? How many nights did you go out, leaving me with the neighbor to look in on me? Mom, you made a choice—and I wasn't your priority!"

"You damn well were!" she said, her voice rising. "Do you know why those men didn't stick? Because of you! Because I saw something in them that made me think twice! Yes, I was lonely. Yes, I needed love and comfort, and forgive me for *not* putting that kind of burden onto my child! There are women who do, you know. They treat their sons like husbands in some twisted, emotional way, and I wouldn't do that to you…"

"I didn't realize that," he said quietly.

"My first boyfriend when I was a teenager—his mom was divorced," she said with a sigh. "She leaned on him for everything. All he wanted was to be a regular kid, with a girlfriend and a band…and his mom needed him for everything, from emotional support to being her date to her work functions. She replaced the man in her life with her son. And it wasn't good for either of them. When I had you, I swore I'd never do that. If I needed romance, I was going to look for it—and I was going to find emotional support from men my own age!"

Billy sighed. It looked like they were all reacting to something, didn't it? Something didn't work, and everyone grimaced and veered left, looking for a better path.

"I'm glad you didn't do that, Mom," he said with a low laugh.

"Thank you," she said with a sad smile.

"And I'm not going to do that to Poppy, for the record."

"I know that," Heather said quietly. "Here's the thing, kiddo. I was looking for the kind of man who could love you just as much as I loved you. I wanted a man who'd stand by us, respect us both and be a good role model to you as you grew up. I didn't find him, but that's what I was looking for. And now I've found a good guy, son." She wiped her eyes and went on. "He's everything I was looking back then, and more. He's kind. He doesn't want to get between me and my son, either. He understands when I need to take

care of my other relationships on my own…
He's adoring, but not smothering. He's handsome…and…" She winced. "He asked me to marry him."

"Oh…" Billy let out a long breath. "Yeah?"

"This morning." She smiled hesitantly.

"Congratulations, Mom," he said, his throat thickening with emotion. "Wow. He seems like a good guy."

His mother…getting married. It was what she'd wanted all this time, and he was happy for her. But he was also a little heartbroken, and he couldn't explain why.

"Son, I was wrong to put so much of my energy into finding some romance," she said quietly. "I'm sorry… To think I wasted all those years with men unworthy of being your stepdad. And I find him now!"

"Hey…it's the past," Billy said, reaching out to squeeze his mother's hand.

"I just wish I'd found him when I was young like you," she said softly. "The right one…that match is worth the time you put into it. I do believe that. And the right woman won't take you away from Poppy—she'll love that girl just as much as you do."

Except Billy had found the woman to both fill his heart and Poppy's. He'd found her years ago and never realized what a gift she was in his life. And Grace didn't trust him to love her like she deserved to be loved... because he'd been a blind idiot before.

"YOU PROMISED ME one day together," Connie said, leaning against the doorframe of her daughter's bedroom.

Grace wiped a tear from her cheek and turned away from the open suitcase on her bed. "Mom, I need to get home..."

Her heart ached in her chest. She'd cried for the best part of the morning. She'd told herself she wouldn't grieve for this man twice, and yet here she was doing just that. Loving him was a miserable mistake that she kept slipping into, even when she knew better.

"You *are* home!" her mother countered.

"You know what I mean." Grace tossed another folded shirt into the suitcase. "I need to get away from here—"

"From Billy, you mean." Connie came into her room and sank onto the edge of the bed. "You're running from your feelings."

"I'm not." Grace sighed. "Fine. I am. And I have every right to. Now he loves me, and it still won't work!"

"He loves you? Did he say that?" Connie flipped the suitcase shut and caught Grace's hand. "Sit down and talk to me!"

Grace sniffled into a tissue, then sank onto the bed, next to her mother. "It won't work."

"But…"

"He told me last night. We talked about it. We're in love with each other, but he's focused on being a good dad right now, and me… I don't trust him."

"To be faithful?" her mother asked, frowning.

"Right now I seem like a good thing because he's overwhelmed as a new dad. I'm Poppy's teacher, and I can support him in getting her settled. But I don't want to be that—the friend who slides into his life because he needs a mother for his child. I need to be more than that—the one who fills his heart because of who I am, not what I can offer him."

"You've changed, though," her mother said quietly.

"Yeah?" Grace asked sarcastically. She looked at herself in the mirror above her dresser. Just her face was visible—eyes puffy, hair pulled back in a ponytail. "I look the same as I always did…"

Sad, she realized. She'd spent a lot of years being sad, and hoping for more but never getting it.

"No, dear, you're different," Connie said matter-of-factly. "You've deepened, matured. You changed the way you dress, the way you do your hair, the way you face the world."

"And I wake up makeup-free!" she retorted. "How can you say that clothes make any difference in who I am?"

"Because they show how you see yourself!" Connie retorted. "Three years ago, you saw a fat girl in that mirror. You tried to hide in your clothes, and you loved a man who never saw you."

The words stung, and Grace winced. It was how she felt, and yet she'd still hoped for more with that handsome cowboy. Silently hoping... It had been stupid.

"I'm no thinner, Mom," she said, tears choking her voice.

"Neither am I, but you no longer dress like you're trying to hide," Connie said, leaning forward. "You dress like the beauty that you are, and frankly you demand a whole lot better treatment from the world around you! I'm so proud of you, baby, because you finally see yourself the way you are!"

Grace sighed. "The way I am…"

"Beautiful." Connie's eyes misted.

"I learned that from you," Grace said, shooting her mother a wobbly smile.

"And you're being a little hard on Billy right now."

"I don't think so," she said with a sigh. "I want what you and dad have. I want a guy who sees the beauty in me like dad does in you. I don't want to be dieting for the rest of my life. I want to be living!"

"Amen," her mother said with a small smile. "Have you asked for that?"

"Asked…" She shot her mother a confused look. "I shouldn't have to."

"Yes, you do. Here's a painful truth," her mother said, her tone firming. "We all want someone to see our value when we don't see it in ourselves. But people don't—not at first. A lot of times, we have to ask for what we want. Your dad doesn't read my mind—I tell him what makes me happy and what ticks me off. I tell him exactly what I'm worth, in so many words. Your father is a wonderful man, dear, but give me some credit, too!"

Grace laughed softly. "Sorry."

"You changed while you were in Denver, and Billy noticed because he saw the woman that you finally decided to be! He didn't notice the woman in you when you hadn't found her yet, either!"

"I was still a woman!" Grace retorted.

"A woman, yes, but not *this* woman," her mother replied. "The woman who takes pride in her appearance and works her tail off for the stuff she cares about. This isn't about weight—it never was! This woman is willing to walk away from the love of her life if she can't be sure of that love lasting. And I can't judge that... Only you can. But if you're holding yourself back because it took him ten years to see the woman you are... Well, it took you thirty years to get here, too."

Grace smiled weakly. "It's complicated, Mom."

"I know." Connie rose to her feet. "But you might want to forgive him for falling in love with such a lovely creature. You're truly breathtaking, inside and out. Take your mother's word for it."

Grace stared at her mom for a moment, then swallowed hard.

"You promised me a day together," her mother added. "And I'm not giving it up."

"Fine." Grace sighed.

"Get dressed," her mother said. "We're

going to look nice. Together. Mother and daughter."

"All right, all right," Grace said, and her mother left the room, closing the door behind her.

Was it possible that her mother was right? Was it as simple as asking for what she wanted? Grace wasn't willing to bet the rest of her life on it. People had their types, and people didn't change something so fundamental about themselves. Even if she asked him to.

CHAPTER TWENTY

BILLY PUT HIS truck into Park and sucked in a stabilizing breath. His mother's words were still ringing in his ears. *The right woman won't take you away from Poppy—she'll love that girl as much as you do.*

Billy looked at the Beverly house—so nicely kept, so appealing. He'd always been mildly jealous of the way Grace had grown up, but now he realized that he'd had it better than he'd thought. At least he had a mom who loved him. She might have messed up, but she'd had a lot of hurdles.

Billy got out of his vehicle and started toward the house, but before he got there, the side door opened and Grace appeared in the doorway. She was wearing boots, a creamy sweater and no coat. She came outside a few steps into the crunchy snow and wrapped her arms around herself. His heart squeezed inside his chest at the very sight of her.

He stopped just short of pulling her into

his arms, and looked down into those clear blue eyes.

"Hey..." he said softly.

"Hi." She hitched up her shoulders against the cold. "Aren't you supposed to be working?"

"Nope." He grinned as he took off his coat and settled it around her shoulders. The brisk wind whipped through his shirt, but he wouldn't be distracted by it. "I'm supposed to be right here. I couldn't let you leave without..." His smile fell. "Gracie, you know I love you."

"I love you, too. I have for years. It isn't enough!" she said. "I'm the easy way out right now—"

"Easy?" he said with a short laugh. "You call this easy?"

"I'm here. I'm convenient."

"You're not convenient. Your life is in Denver!" he retorted. "And if you think I'm here because I need a mom for my daughter, you're way off."

"Plus, I thought you said you had to focus on Poppy," Grace said, tugging her hand free.

"I'm not dating around. If it's not you, then I'm just going to be a single dad. That's it."

He looked toward the window, where

Grace's mother stood watching them. Great. An audience. "I talked to my mom like you wanted me to, and she made me realize that the right woman makes all those problems go away. If I'm with the right woman, she'll love Poppy like I do. There won't be any competition. If I'm marrying her, then we become a family."

"Marrying?" Grace whispered.

"You're it, Grace," he said softly. "There's this kids' book my mom gave me when I was pretty young. Obviously I never read it back then, but I did read it with Poppy."

"You read her a story?" Grace said, tears springing to her eyes.

"Yeah. Well, Poppy helped me a lot, but we got through it together. But there's this part that talks about how the mom's life is completely changed when the child comes along. She sees the world differently. When Poppy came along, my life turned upside down, and it's not going to go back again. I'm a dad now. The whole world looks different. So I didn't see you before—not fully— and I can't change that. I can't take it back. But I can tell you that I'm not the same guy I was before, either. I'm...a dad."

"I don't want to be the one you choose

for rational reasons over—" she began, and he closed the distance between them, covering her lips with his. He kissed her long and deep, pulling her close against him. When he pulled back, she looked up at him blearily.

"I want you," he whispered. "I want all of you. I want a wife! I want a life partner. I want you by my side when Poppy is grown and out of the house and starting her own life. I am asking you to be Poppy's mom, but I'm also asking you to be my soul mate, my resting place, my partner in all of this. I'm asking you to come home to me, and to let me come home to you. Grace, my whole world is tipped upside down, and you're a part of that. You make me a better man."

"What about what I want?" she asked, her voice firming.

"What *do* you want?" he asked, searching her face.

"I want you to be sure of this—absolutely sure. I want a man who puts me and our child first. If things get hard between us, I want you to come home and talk to me about it. Me, no one else. I want date nights. I want thoughtful gestures…and I want you to tell me what you're feeling and going through, and not hide it from me."

"Done." A smile tickled the corners of his lips.

"And I want compliments," she said. "Daily. That's something that matters to me. My dad always tells my mom how beautiful she is, and I want that."

"I don't compliment you?" he asked with a small smile. "That's one thing I do pretty well, I think."

"I'm just putting it out there," she replied. "For the record."

"Okay, well, you're beautiful. You're smart. You've got this way of seeing the world that makes me think, and I like that. You're kind—have I told you lately how much that means to me? And, Gracie...you're perfect. Inside and out. I wouldn't change a thing. And I mean that. Not a thing."

"You're sure about me?" she asked softly.

"I've never been more sure in my life, Gracie. Does this mean...?"

"What about our jobs?" she whispered. "I have a full-time teaching position waiting for me in Denver, and you're so good at what you do here... If we're getting married, we have to figure this out!"

His heart was hammering hard in his chest, and a grin broke over his face.

"I don't care. Wherever we go, as long as we're together, we'll find a way," he said. "I'll go to Denver if that's what you want. Or if there's a way for you to stay here, we can settle down in Eagle's Rest... Just tell me that was a yes!"

Grace's eyes brimmed with tears and she nodded. "That was a yes."

Billy gathered her up in his arms and kissed her all over again. He felt a flood of relief, like his heart had finally come home.

"I love you..." he whispered.

"I love you, too!"

"We need to shop for a ring," he added with a grin. He looked up at the window again, and this time he saw Connie with tears in her eyes and her hands clutched in front of her heart. Yeah, he had her mom's support, at the very least.

"First things first," Grace said, shaking her head. "We have a little girl to let in on the secret."

"Deal. You going to let me in the house? Because I'm freezing."

Grace laughed softly. As they headed for the side door, Connie emerged with a smile on her face.

"Tell me that you finally realized you're in

love with each other," Connie said, stepping back to let them in.

"Yeah," Grace said, looking up at Billy with a teary smile. "A little more than that, actually..."

"I asked her to marry me," Billy said. "And she..."

"Said yes," Connie finished for him, and when she got a nod, she let out a whoop of delight and threw her arms around them both.

Yeah, this was coming home... Dr. Beverly might be a little harder to bring round, but with Grace at his side, Billy was willing to weather it.

He'd be her hero, the guy who stubbornly stuck by her and loved her with his whole being. He'd be the dad that Poppy needed, and he'd keep learning to read so that, one day, maybe he could even get his GED. Maybe Poppy could see the value of hard work by watching her dad get the education he'd missed out on. Most importantly, though, he was hoping that by watching Billy love Grace, Poppy would see the kind of love she'd want in her own home one day, and they'd all get the love they longed for, wrapped up together as a family.

EPILOGUE

ON A SATURDAY morning in April, Grace and Billy stood in the front of Eagle's Rest Church. Grace's breath was caught in her throat, and she fiddled with the diamond solitaire that she'd moved to her right hand in preparation for the ceremony.

She wore a strapless dress with a fitted bodice and creamy tulle. Her father had been the one to find the dress in a catalogue and had insisted that Grace meet up with him in Denver while she worked that last maternity leave so that she could try it on. It had been perfect, and after some texted photos with her mom, they bought it.

Grace had given up the full-time position in Denver when Eagle's Rest Elementary offered her a position in special education, right there in Poppy's school. It had all been too perfect, and it allowed Billy to stay at the ranch he loved and gave Grace the chance to grow her career and be there for Poppy.

Billy hadn't waited to apply for full custody of his daughter, and Carol-Ann hadn't put up much struggle. She was allowed weekly supervised visits, none of which she'd taken advantage of since she was still in Germany and didn't seem to have any immediate plans to return to the US.

And now, on a cool Saturday in April, with the first tulips just poking up in the flower beds outside of the church, Grace stood facing Billy, his dark eyes fixed on her with gentle steadiness. Their friends and family were all out there in the pews, and Grace was too nervous to even look toward them. Heather and Gerald were leaving for their own elopement next week, but of course that was a huge secret that only Billy and Grace were party to.

This was Grace's day with Billy...and Poppy. Because Poppy was not only flower girl but kept sidling closer and closer to them as the minister took them through their vows.

"Do you, Billy, take Grace to be your lawfully wedded wife, to have and to hold, for better or for worse, in sickness and in health, for as long as you both shall live?"

Grace held her breath, and Billy smiled, slow and warm. "Sure do."

She let her breath go as the minister turned to her.

"Do you, Grace, take Billy to be your lawfully wedded husband, to have and to hold, for better or for worse, in sickness and in health, for as long as you both shall live?"

"Yes," she breathed. "I do."

"Do you have the rings?" the minister asked.

Poppy stepped a little closer as Billy pulled the ring from his pocket. He slid it onto Grace's waiting left hand, and then Grace did the same for him.

"Then by the power vested in me by the state of Colorado, I now pronounce you husband and wife! You may kiss the bride."

Billy grinned and pulled her close, his lips covering hers in a tender kiss. When he leaned back, Poppy squeezed between them, beaming up at them.

"It's done!" Poppy squealed. "We're a married family!"

Grace couldn't help but laugh and bent down to press a kiss onto Poppy's glossy head. Everyone cheered, and as Grace and Billy headed down the aisle, Poppy stayed firmly in the middle. Grace didn't mind a bit. Poppy was right—this was the beginning of their family, and Grace was just as devoted to Poppy as she was to Billy.

"Gracie…" Billy's deep voice tugged her gaze up, and she caught her husband looking over at her tenderly. "I love you."

"I love you, too!" she said. And as they got to the church door, Billy leaned over his daughter's head and they shared a soft kiss.

"My God, you're beautiful," he murmured.

"Extra special beautiful," Poppy piped up, and Grace laughed.

She was well and truly married to the only man she'd ever loved so completely. She ducked her head against the shower of rice as they walked out of the church, into warm spring sunlight.

They were the Austins, and Grace could finally let her heart open completely to them. Billy and Poppy were well and truly hers.

* * * * *

*Don't miss the next book in
Patricia Johns's
Home to Eagle's Rest miniseries,
coming July 2019 from
Harlequin Heartwarming.
And check out the first book
in the miniseries:*
Her Lawman Protector

Get 4 FREE REWARDS!

We'll send you 2 FREE ~~Books~~ plus 2 FREE Mystery Gifts.

Love Inspired® books feature contemporary inspirational romances with Christian characters facing the challenges of life and love.

FREE Value Over **$20**

YES! Please send me 2 FREE Love Inspired® Romance novels and my 2 FREE mystery gifts (gifts are worth about $10 retail). After receiving them, if I don't wish to receive any more books, I can return the shipping statement marked "cancel." If I don't cancel, I will receive 6 brand-new novels every month and be billed just $5.24 for the regular-print edition or $5.74 each for the larger-print edition in the U.S., or $5.74 each for the regular-print edition or $6.24 each for the larger-print edition in Canada. That's a savings of at least 13% off the cover price. It's quite a bargain! Shipping and handling is just 50¢ per book in the U.S. and 75¢ per book in Canada.* I understand that accepting the 2 free books and gifts places me under no obligation to buy anything. I can always return a shipment and cancel at any time. The free books and gifts are mine to keep no matter what I decide.

Choose one: ☐ **Love Inspired® Romance Regular-Print** (105/305 IDN GMY4)   ☐ **Love Inspired® Romance Larger-Print** (122/322 IDN GMY4)

Name (please print)

Address   Apt. #

City   State/Province   Zip/Postal Code

Mail to the **Reader Service:**
IN U.S.A.: P.O. Box 1341, Buffalo, NY 14240-8531
IN CANADA: P.O. Box 603, Fort Erie, Ontario L2A 5X3

Want to try 2 free books from another series! Call 1-800-873-8635 or visit www.ReaderService.com.

Get 4 FREE REWARDS!

We'll send you 2 FREE Books plus 2 FREE Mystery Gifts.

Love Inspired® Suspense books feature Christian characters facing challenges to their faith... and lives.

FREE Value Over **$20**

YES! Please send me 2 FREE Love Inspired® Suspense novels and my 2 FREE mystery gifts (gifts are worth about $10 retail). After receiving them, if I don't wish to receive any more books, I can return the shipping statement marked "cancel." If I don't cancel, I will receive 4 brand-new novels every month and be billed just $5.24 each for the regular-print edition or $5.74 each for the larger-print edition in the U.S., or $5.74 each for the regular-print edition or $6.24 each for the larger-print edition in Canada. That's a savings of at least 13% off the cover price. It's quite a bargain! Shipping and handling is just 50¢ per book in the U.S. and 75¢ per book in Canada.* I understand that accepting the 2 free books and gifts places me under no obligation to buy anything. I can always return a shipment and cancel at any time. The free books and gifts are mine to keep no matter what I decide.

Choose one: ☐ **Love Inspired® Suspense**
Regular-Print
(153/353 IDN GMY5)

☐ **Love Inspired® Suspense**
Larger-Print
(107/307 IDN GMY5)

Name (please print)

Address   Apt. #

City   State/Province   Zip/Postal Code

Mail to the **Reader Service:**
IN U.S.A.: P.O. Box 1341, Buffalo, NY 14240-8531
IN CANADA: P.O. Box 603, Fort Erie, Ontario L2A 5X3

Want to try 2 free books from another series? Call 1-800-873-8635 or visit www.ReaderService.com.

---

*Terms and prices subject to change without notice. Prices do not include sales taxes, which will be charged (if applicable) based on your state or country of residence. Canadian residents will be charged applicable taxes. Offer not valid in Quebec. This offer is limited to one order per household. Books received may not be as shown. Not valid for current subscribers to Love Inspired Suspense books. All orders subject to approval. Credit or debit balances in a customer's account(s) may be offset by any other outstanding balance owed by or to the customer. Please allow 4 to 6 weeks for delivery. Offer available while quantities last.

Your Privacy—The Reader Service is committed to protecting your privacy. Our Privacy Policy is available online at www.ReaderService.com or upon request from the Reader Service. We make a portion of our mailing list available to reputable third parties that offer products we believe may interest you. If you prefer that we not exchange your name with third parties, or if you wish to clarify or modify your communication preferences, please visit us at www.ReaderService.com/consumerschoice or write to us at Reader Service Preference Service, P.O. Box 9062, Buffalo, NY 14240-9062. Include your complete name and address.

LIS19R

MUST ♥ DOGS COLLECTION

SAVE 30% AND GET A FREE GIFT!

Finding true love can be "ruff"— but not when adorable dogs help to play matchmaker in these inspiring romantic "tails."

YES! Please send me the first shipment of four books from the **Must ♥ Dogs Collection**. If I don't cancel, I will continue to receive four books a month for two additional months, and I will be billed at the same discount price of $18.20 U.S./$20.30 CAN., plus $1.99 for shipping and handling.* That's a 30% discount off the cover prices! Plus, I'll receive a FREE adorable, hand-painted dog figurine in every shipment (approx. retail value of $4.99)! I am under no obligation to purchase anything and I may cancel at any time by marking "cancel" on the shipping statement and returning the shipment. I may keep the FREE books no matter what I decide.

☐ 256 HCN 4331   ☐ 456 HCN 4331

Name (please print)

Address   Apt. #

City   State/Province   Zip/Postal Code

Mail to the **Reader Service:**
IN U.S.A.: P.O. Box 1867, Buffalo, NY. 14240-1867
IN CANADA: P.O. Box 609, Fort Erie, Ontario L2A 5X3

Get 4 FREE REWARDS!

We'll send you 2 FREE Books plus 2 FREE Mystery Gifts.

FREE
Value Over
$20

Both the **Romance** and **Suspense** collections feature compelling novels written by many of today's best-selling authors.

YES! Please send me 2 FREE novels from the Essential Romance or Essential Suspense Collection and my 2 FREE gifts (gifts are worth about $10 retail). After receiving them, if I don't wish to receive any more books, I can return the shipping statement marked "cancel." If I don't cancel, I will receive 4 brand-new novels every month and be billed just $6.74 each in the U.S. or $7.24 each in Canada. That's a savings of at least 16% off the cover price. It's quite a bargain! Shipping and handling is just 50¢ per book in the U.S. and 75¢ per book in Canada.* I understand that accepting the 2 free books and gifts places me under no obligation to buy anything. I can always return a shipment and cancel at any time. The free books and gifts are mine to keep no matter what I decide.

Choose one: ☐ **Essential Romance**
(194/394 MDN GMY7)
☐ **Essential Suspense**
(191/391 MDN GMY7)

Name (please print)

Address   Apt. #

City   State/Province   Zip/Postal Code

Mail to the **Reader Service:**
IN U.S.A.: P.O. Box 1341, Buffalo, NY 14240-8531
IN CANADA: P.O. Box 603, Fort Erie, Ontario L2A 5X3

Want to try 2 free books from another series? Call 1-800-873-8635 or visit www.ReaderService.com.

Get 4 FREE REWARDS!

We'll send you 2 FREE Books plus 2 FREE Mystery Gifts.

Harlequin® Romance Larger-Print books feature uplifting escapes that will warm your heart with the ultimate feel-good tales.

FREE Value Over **$20**

READERSERVICE.COM

Manage your account online!

- Review your order history
- Manage your payments
- Update your address

> **We've designed the
> Reader Service website
> just for you.**

Enjoy all the features!

- Discover new series available to you,
  and read excerpts from any series.
- Respond to mailings and special
  monthly offers.
- Browse the Bonus Bucks catalog and
  online-only exculsives.
- Share your feedback.

Visit us at:

ReaderService.com